HER COWBOY BILLIONAIRE BAD BOY

CHRISTMAS AT WHISKEY MOUNTAIN LODGE, A
HAMMOND BROTHERS NOVEL, BOOK 5

LIZ ISAACSON

feel-good fiction

ELANA JOHNSON

ISBN-13: 978-1-63876-170-9

CHAPTER 1

A mes Hammond pulled into the park-and-wait lot at the Denver airport, already ready to be out of the eight-passenger SUV he'd rented. He put the vehicle in park, thinking maybe he'd buy something like this for his next car. He'd always liked driving a pickup truck or his police cruiser, but maybe he should start to switch things up.

He'd been making a lot of changes in the past several months. Why not extend that to what he drove?

The temperature in Colorado would not allow him to stay outside for long, but he'd been driving for two hours, and the trip back to the farm in Ivory Peaks would take just as long. He tucked his hands in his parka pockets, his mind on the people flying in from Wyoming.

Three of his brothers and their significant others, along with baby Michael. Thus, Ames needed the eight-passenger vehicle to get them all from the airport to the farm. Gray had flown to Coral Canyon a couple of days ago, and he, Elise, Hunter and their new baby had parked at the airport, so they'd drive themselves back to the farm. Gray had promised Ames he'd pay for the SUV and bring everyone back to the airport in several days.

Ames had accepted, though he didn't need the money. He had plenty of money. "You're going to have to tell them," he muttered to himself, his breath steaming in front of him. He shivered, because it *was* cold and he didn't want to make any announcements on this Christmas Day.

He drew in a deep breath, the cold air making his lungs turn brittle. Still, he inhaled and inhaled until he felt like he would pop. Then he held all that chilly air in his lungs for a moment and finally blew it all out.

He turned around, his muscles humming with the short walk, and hurried back to the SUV. He got the vehicle started again and pressed the button for the seat heaters.

The flight should be arriving any moment, and Ames kept his eyes on the big screen with the flight numbers. He swiped on his phone and checked the text Cy had sent with the number on it. Glancing up, he found the number on the screen, and the big, bright words PICK UP NOW were flashing.

He didn't even have time to flip the SUV into drive before Cy called. The phone rang on his device for half a ring and then transferred to the Bluetooth system and came through the speakers.

"Hello?" Ames asked. "Can you hear me?" He put his phone in the cup holder and flipped the car into Drive.

"Yeah," Cy said, and his voice sounded among a ton of other noise. "We just arrived at baggage claim, so we'll probably be a few minutes." He didn't sound super happy, but Ames knew better than to ask his twin what was happening while Cy was in a crowd. He wouldn't say anyway, and he'd just end up more frustrated.

"Okay," Ames said, pressing on the brake. "How about you text me when you're almost ready? It's not very warm."

"It's twenty degrees warmer here than Coral Canyon," Cy said. "I'll text you."

"Great." The call ended, and Ames stayed in his parking spot. He needed to get excited to see everyone. Once he pulled up to the curb and saw them, the joy would come. He just hated the anticipation of it. He didn't want anyone looking at him and making a judgment, which they'd all do once he made his announcement.

He and Gray had worked really hard to get the whole family to come to Ivory Peaks for the holidays, as Coral Canyon seemed to exist inside a magical bubble of Christmas charm and holiday tinsel.

Ames had experienced it last year, and he sure had enjoyed going up the canyon to Whiskey Mountain Lodge a few months ago. While Cy worked in the shop and had others around him, Ames would make the drive and spend afternoons with Sophia. And later, if Colton or Wes could come sit with Cy, Ames would return to the cabin in the corner of the back yard and sit with Sophia.

He'd really liked her. He liked holding her hand. He liked talking to her. He liked kissing her. He simply didn't like where she lived. She didn't like where he lived. Neither of them were willing to relocate or sustain a long-distance relationship, and when Ames had finally left Coral Canyon to return to Colorado, he'd left Sophia in his rear-view mirror too.

Don't be so salty, ran through his mind, in his mother's voice. She'd told him that so many times growing up that Ames had the words imprinted on his soul.

Ames took another deep breath and decided to just go to the pick-up zone. There would be airport personnel there, making sure no one pulled up and parked, but Ames didn't care. He was feeling salty, and he'd argue with the crossing guard if he had to.

"He's not a crossing guard," Ames told himself. "Be nice." He had to be nice for the duration of the next week, and he was determined to do it.

He just wished he wasn't the only brother without a woman to spend Christmas and New Year's with. His thoughts went straight back to Sophia, but he refused to so much as look at her social media.

He'd made his decision. She'd made hers.

He eased around the corner and into the lane that led to the pick-up zone on the bottom of the Denver airport. There were five levels here, and at least it was covered so there wasn't snow piled everywhere. They'd had quite a few storms in the past week, and without Gray and Hunter to help, it was all Ames and his father could do to keep the road to the farmhouse clear and the path out to the barns and stables walkable.

Ames stopped against the curb, tapped on his phone

screen, and listened to Cy's line ringing. He kept glancing in the rear-view mirror, expecting the man wearing the orange traffic vest to notice Ames had been there longer than five seconds. But he was helping someone with their luggage, and Cy answered in the next moment.

"We're on the way out now," his brother said.

"I'm outside door twelve," Ames said.

"I see you," Cy said. "Red SUV?"

"Yep." Ames got out and let his brother hang up. He opened the back gate so the traffic guy would know Ames's people were coming. He turned, and his face split into a grin when he saw a carbon copy of himself coming toward him.

Well, Cy wore his hair longer than Ames ever had, but everything else was the same.

"Ames." Cy laughed as he abandoned his suitcase a couple of steps away and embraced Ames. They laughed together, each pounding the other on the back. Ames moved to Patsy and lifted her right up off her feet as they hugged. He'd been so angry with her this past fall, but she made Cy happier than anyone else ever had. She'd made things right between them, and she loved his brother with her whole heart.

Ames set her down and looked at her, half a dozen unspoken questions streaming between them. He'd told her she could text or call him anytime she didn't know what to do with Cy. If she needed help dealing with him.

Cy was an amazing man, but he struggled with some mental issues that Ames could feel, even from hundreds of miles away. But he'd waited for Patsy to text before he'd just barged into their relationship. And she'd only reached out to him a few times.

She nodded at him now, and Ames moved on to Wes and then Colton. Everyone loaded their luggage in the back of the SUV, and then the jostling for seats started.

"Let's put Michael in the back," Bree said. "And Patsy and I will ride back there." She looked at Wes. "That leaves Annie, Colt, and Wes for the middle. Cy can ride up front with Ames."

"It's a plan," Wes said, ducking into the SUV to get the car seat buckled in where it needed to go. Ames marveled at the change in his brothers. The past few years had brought a lot of changes to the Hammond family, and Ames sure did like seeing the little dark-haired boy on Bree's hip who looked so much like Wes.

Elise and Gray's daughter was only a couple of months old, and she was so much lighter than Michael. That came from Elise's nearly-white features, and Jane had been born bald, but she had some wisps of blonde hair coming in. Her eyes showed some evidence of Gray, because they were a dark brown that almost didn't fit among all of her pink skin.

With everyone situated in the SUV, Ames got behind the wheel and adjusted the air that was blowing. "This thing has four temperature zones," he said, feeling the extra weight in the vehicle as he eased away from the curb. "So settle in. We've got a two-hour drive."

Knobs got adjusted and conversations started, and Ames focused on getting on the freeway and away from the airport. He talked easily with Cy about how the proposal had gone. Ames had been on speaker phone, but he hadn't been there in person. Cy had said it wasn't a big deal, and he wasn't acting like it was either.

He talked about it for a while, and he seemed so happy.

"So what's going on with you?" he finally asked.

"Nothing," Ames said, and that was so true it wasn't even funny. His voice still sounded false, though.

"Sure," Cy said dryly.

"I'm telling everyone at the same time," Ames said, throwing his brother a glance.

"Are you kidding me?" Cy practically hissed. "I always get to know before everyone else."

"Well, Gray already knows," Ames said. "So that's not true this time." His fingers clenched around the wheel, because he hadn't told Cy first the way he normally would have.

"What is going on?" Cy demanded.

"Nothing," Ames said again, glaring openly at him now.

"We're all here then," Cy said. "If Gray already knows."

"Cy," Ames said, but his twin was already turning around.

"Listen up, guys," he called to everyone else in the car. "Quiet down. Shh. Ames has something to tell us."

The chatter in the back of the car stopped, so Ames's voice sounded really loud when he said, "No, I don't."

"You said you were going to tell us all at the same time," Cy said. "So tell us."

"Gray's not here," Wes said.

"Gray already knows," Cy said, glaring holes into the side of Ames's head. He folded his arms. "So tell us, Ames."

Ames looked in the rear-view mirror and found everyone looking at him and waiting. His chest pinched, and he wanted to stride away. Put some distance between himself and this situation.

But he'd put this off for long enough. It wasn't like he could keep this secret with everyone here, and he wanted them to know.

He did.

"I quit my job," he said. "Months ago. Maybe four or five."

The silence in the SUV was suddenly far too loud and unbelievably heavy. Ames shifted in his seat and glanced at Cy. "Happy now?"

"No," Cy said, the word barely audible.

"You quit your job?" Wes said. "At the police station?"

"Yes," Ames said.

"Four or five months ago?" Colton asked.

"Before I came to Coral Canyon in the fall," Ames said. "So yes."

"Why?" Cy asked. "You love being a cop."

Ames looked out his side window, because he couldn't answer that question. He hadn't been able to when Gray had asked, nor when his parents had wanted to know. His boss had been stunned, as had his partner.

Heck, most of the time, Ames would wake up in the morning in a state of pure panic, thinking he was late for work.

"I don't know," he said. "It just felt like the right thing to do."

"You went to Texas, right?" Wes asked.

"It didn't feel right," Ames said, hating the words. But he knew no one would question his decisions if he said they just felt right or didn't feel right.

"You should come to Coral Canyon," Colton said.

"No," Ames said, practically growling the word. "I'm not looking for job recommendations or life advice. Okay? I'm fine. I'm doing fine."

He focused out the windshield as it started to snow again, and he flipped on the windshield wipers.

He wasn't doing all that fine, but Gray needed help around the farm, and Ames had plenty of time to do that now. They ran at the gym together after dropping Hunter off at school, and Ames managed to fill his afternoons and evenings with...something.

Quitting his job on the Littleton force *had* felt like the right thing to do. He couldn't meet a woman as a cop, and he really just wanted to find someone he could fall in love with. They could start a family, and his life would be filled with good things again.

"What about private security?" Cy asked. "You've always wanted to do that."

Thankfully, his phone rang, and Ames kept both hands on the wheel as he glanced at the screen where the call came up.

Sophia's name appeared there, and Ames sucked in a very audible breath.

"I thought you two broke up," Patsy said from the back seat, and Cy wore a look of intense interest on his face.

"We did," Ames said, reaching to press the red icon that would end the call.

Cy's hand shot out and blocked Ames's, and Ames had half a second to growl before Cy tapped the green icon to connect the two lines.

"Hello?" he said, actually making his voice a touch deeper so he'd sound more like Ames.

"Cy," Ames said. "I'm going to kill you."

His brother just grinned at him, and then noise started coming through the line.

"Hang up," Ames said.

"Sophia?" Cy said instead, and Ames grabbed for his phone as her voice came over the speakers for everyone to hear. He jabbed at the button that would disconnect the phone from the Bluetooth, and he glared at his brother as he put the phone to his ear.

"Hey," he said, but Sophia clearly wasn't talking to him. She was talking though.

"...put the cups over there, Stockton. We'll call everyone into the kitchen once Celia finishes with that cake."

Scuffling came through the line, and Ames knew she'd dialed him on accident.

A pocket dial.

How embarrassing.

Darkness crowded into his mind and soul, and he became very aware of how quiet the SUV still was.

He'd just admitted to something crazy and humiliating.

He wasn't going to tell his brothers Sophia had called him on accident.

"Yes," he said, as if she'd asked him something. "Merry Christmas to you too."

"Thatta boy," Cy said, and when Ames looked at him, he wore such a happy smile.

Guilt pulled every muscle tight in Ames's body, but he'd committed to this charade and he'd have to see it through now.

"That's right," Ames said. "I just picked them up. We're on our way to the farm now."

Another scuffle, and then Sophia said, "Ames? Are you there?"

CHAPTER 2

S ophia Cooke pulled the phone away from her ear, and sure enough, she'd called Ames. And the call was still connected.

"Yes," he said, and she hurried to put the phone back to her ear. "I'm here."

"I guess I called you," she said, trying to figure out why her heartbeat was sprinting through her whole body. She glanced at Bailey and Stockton, who'd been helping her set up the hot bar for that afternoon's movie event.

There would be coffee, tea, and hot chocolate, and Sophia had bought some flavored syrups and creams to go with everything.

She ducked out of the kitchen—the hub of activity at the lodge—and moved down the much quieter hall toward Patsy's old office.

Julianne Wallace had taken Patsy's job, and therefore, she'd taken over the office too. She liked scented candles and lots of knickknacks, so the office wasn't the same at all anymore.

"How's your Christmas?"

"A lot of driving," he said. "What are you up to?"

"The afternoon movie is starting in a few minutes," she said. "So I was putting together the hot bar with the teenagers."

"Ah, the hot bar," he said, and his voice strummed something inside her that no one else ever had. They'd spent three amazing weeks together, but Sophia couldn't let those twenty days dictate her whole life.

Ames obviously hadn't.

He hadn't called or texted her once since he'd left Coral Canyon in September. *Of course he hasn't*, she told herself. They'd agreed that they weren't dating, and they could text if they wanted to.

She hadn't reached out to him either. She'd coached herself relentlessly to allow him to be the one to make the first move post-break-up, and he hadn't.

She blinked, realizing the conversation had stalled completely. "Sorry," she said. "I'm a little swamped."

"I'll let you go then," he said. "I've got everyone in the car with me, and I'm driving, so."

"Ames," she practically shouted.

"Yeah?"

"Can I...maybe you'll be free to...call me later?"

Heavy silence came through the line, and Sophia pressed her eyes closed as she pressed her back into the wall behind her. "Never—"

"Sure," he said at the same time. "I'll text you first to see if you're still swamped."

"Okay," she said.

"Okay."

She didn't hang up, and neither did he. Finally, the line beeped, and Sophia pulled the device away from her face to see Ames's handsome face on the screen. He wasn't smiling in the picture, because everything about Ames was so straight and proper. So laced up tight. So right at the speed limit.

In fact, she couldn't believe he'd answered the phone while he'd been driving at all. That was completely out of character for him.

A sigh passed her lips, and she was aware of what it held. Longing and bliss. The kind of sound she used to make after he'd kissed her goodnight for the final time, settled that cowboy hat on his head, and ducked out the door of the cabin.

She'd liked Ames Hammond very much. She still did, if she were being honest with herself. A hint of humiliation hummed through her though. She wasn't going to be yet another female to fall to the charms of the Hammond brothers. She'd watched all of her friends do that, each of them falling in love one by one while she got left behind.

Sophia gave herself a mental shake. She was happy here in Coral Canyon. This was the first place she'd ever truly made real friends and found that happiness, and she wasn't going to give it up for just anyone.

"There you are," Julianne said as she entered the office. "Celia was just asking where you went. I think she might get on the PA system to find you." She picked up a piece of paper from the desk, a smile on her face. "The cake is ready, and I guess that means it's movie time."

"It does," Sophia said, glad her voice came out normal. Julianne was a very nice woman, and she was the same age as Sophia. She lived with Melinda, the new event coordinator, in the cabin where Elise and Bree had once lived.

Sophia's heart shrank, though she wasn't sure why. She still got to see Bree all the time. She lived here in Coral Canyon. Elise did too, at least in the summertime.

Sure enough, the speaker system that ran through the lodge crackled to life, and Celia's voice said, "The cake is ready, and the kids are telling me the hot bar is too. Let's gather in the kitchen for our celebration."

The Whittakers got together every Christmas season. Since Sophia had no family in town, and no desire to go visit anyone in her family, she stayed at the lodge with them.

She'd enjoyed their family traditions. She loved participating in the good-natured contests they had. Yes, she had to work, because it was a big job to feed thirty people, but she didn't mind. If she wasn't cooking, Sophia wouldn't even know what to do with herself.

She'd always adored cooking, even when her father had warned her against the idea of becoming a chef. *You'll have to work long hours,* he'd told her. *You can't have a family and be a chef.*

Turned out, she didn't have a family yet. She knew she was a great disappointment to him, but Sophia couldn't make a man fall in love with her. If she could, she would've done so with Jake Cyprus, the high school quarterback Sophia had spent the better part of her teenage years crushing on.

She followed Julianne down the hall to the kitchen, others streaming in from downstairs and the living room. The Whittakers had expanded the kitchen and dining room so the gathering area was twice as big now. The guests loved it, and it definitely fit the whole family better than the table for twelve had.

Sophia stayed on the fringes of the family, but she didn't mind. She was loved and accepted here; she knew that.

Celia made a big deal about presenting the triplets with the immaculate cake she'd made. A thread of jealously moved through Sophia. She'd gone to culinary school, and she certainly had a chocolate cake recipe memorized. Celia had never gone to culinary school, and she still made a better cake and better meals than Sophia.

A sense of failure moved through her though she cheered when the triplets managed to get their candles blown out. It wasn't their birthday for another month or so, but their parents were taking them on an extended vacation, and they'd wanted to celebrate at the lodge this Christmas.

She stepped forward to help with plates and forks, trying to strike up a conversation with a couple of the children. But she'd never been all that great with kids, and they seemed to sense her awkwardness. In the end, they usually came around, but today, she found herself with a delicious-looking piece of chocolate cake on a plate, alone.

She looked around at everything going on in the lodge. The dozens of conversations. The laughter. The cowboy hats. The teenagers and children.

And then there was her.

Even Julianne sat next to some of the younger children, happily helping them make bibs out of a couple of napkins she'd unfolded.

Sophia hadn't felt this level of isolation for a long, long time, and she wished she could erase it. She wished she could go back in time and fix some of the bridges she'd burned. Or at least not light those matches.

She turned away from the dining room and headed outside. Down the sidewalk that the Whittaker brothers were religious about clearing for her, and across the backyard, Sophia marched toward her cabin.

Once up the steps and inside, her heartbeat felt like it was trying to flee from her body. She hadn't felt like this in a while.

"Since the day Ames found you on that trail."

She had the sudden urge to call Patsy, but her best friend was gone to Colorado.

Still, her fingers fumbled as she tried to set down her cake and pull out her phone at the same time. She managed to do both without dumping the cake on the floor, and she sent a text to Patsy.

How was the flight? Are you nervous to go to the farm?

She knew Patsy was nervous about meeting Cy's parents as his official girlfriend. She'd met them in group settings before, but this was different, and they both knew it.

You called Ames?

Sophia took a long breath, something steadying inside her. She didn't want to say it was an accident, because what if it hadn't been? What if somehow, the Lord had allowed that pocket dial to happen?

"It's just because his name starts with an A," she told herself, dismissing the feeling of divine intervention.

But it kept creeping back, and Sophia looked down at her phone again, trying to figure out how to answer Patsy.

You don't have to tell me, came in. *Forget I asked. The flight was great. Not terribly long, and Cy had all these treats.*

Sophia smiled, because Patsy didn't leave Coral Canyon very often. She'd grown up here, and been raised here, and she wanted to stay here and raise her family on her generational orchard.

Sophia thought that sounded like a fairy tale. To stay in one place for longer than a year or two, to always have somewhere to belong, to have a place that brought peace to her soul.

She'd never had that, and she'd spent plenty of years bitter about it.

"I'm not bitter," she whispered to herself and to reassure God that she wasn't ungrateful for what He'd done for her. "Thank you for bringing me here and for letting me stay for so long."

She'd been in Coral Canyon and at Whiskey Mountain Lodge for just over six years now, and she didn't want to leave.

What kind of treats? she asked Patsy, because that mattered. As she started an easy, non-important conversation with her best friend, Sophia left her chocolate cake on the side table and settled on the couch.

Every once in a while, when Patsy wouldn't answer for a few minutes, Sophia looked up from her phone, her thoughts centering on one person only.

Ames Hammond.

She'd been so resistant to a relationship with him, because he'd been very clear that he wasn't going to relocate to Coral Canyon. She'd told him about herself, including that she hadn't enjoyed moving often. Even now, her dad and step-mother moved all the time, always searching for the next place to be. Sophia didn't even know where her father lived right now, as she hadn't spoken to him in years.

Sophia had found her place, and it was right here. She looked around the living room. Yes, it was small. But it was hers, and she'd felt the first inklings of God's love here, and she didn't want to leave the cabin, the lodge, or Coral Canyon.

With that between them, her relationship with Ames had become about companionship. Friends. They were friends.

"Maybe I can still be friends with him," she murmured to herself.

Text him then.

The thought appeared in her mind, and Sophia knew exactly who it had come from and what to do with it.

She backed out of her texting conversation with Patsy and started a new one with Ames. *Hey*, she started, trying to think of what else to say. *I sure do miss talking to you.*

Today was an accident, but I liked hearing your voice. Maybe we could be friends?

She read the words over and over again, trying to decide if they were too needy. Too desperate. Too cold. Too much of anything.

In the end, she decided they were fine, and she sent them flying the five hundred miles between Coral Canyon, Wyoming and Ivory Peaks, Colorado.

She drew in a deep breath, feeling strong and sure. The ball was in his court, and Ames was very good at bouncing it back. He was surely still driving, and Sophia would just have to employ her patience until he wasn't surrounded by his family and he could text back.

She could do that....

She could.

SIX MONTHS LATER

Ames ignored his phone when it chimed, because he knew it would be Cy. His brother had an alarm set to text Ames every Sunday evening, and he lived and died by his alarms. Ames was grateful for them, because setting the reminders helped free Cy's mind enough so that he could function.

Hiring a shop manager had helped a ton, and the last eight or nine months since he'd gotten back together with Patsy had completely transformed him again.

Ames was happy for his brother. He was. He absolutely was.

He reached for the next bale of hay he needed to throw down the conveyor belt, grateful for the leather gloves he wore. He focused on the work, because he wasn't the only one in the loft, and he couldn't just be tossing things wherever.

He was grateful for the sun. For the sky above Texas.

For Jeremiah Walker, who had hired him on at Seven Sons Ranch.

Ames's new habit the past few months was to go over all the things he was grateful for whenever the heaviness and enormity of life started to press down on him.

"Just a couple more," Orion said over the walkie on Cub's belt, and Ames met the other cowboy's eye.

"One each," Cub said, his bright blue eyes sparkling with mischief. Ames wondered if he'd ever been as carefree. He'd never been one to pull pranks and laugh at every little thing someone said, the way Cub did.

He'd been told when he was eight that he'd inherit two billion dollars when he turned twenty-one, and that his father expected him to do something with it. The Hammond boys didn't have "the talk" until they were thirteen, but once Wes knew, it trickled down the brothers until Colton had told the twins the day after he'd turned thirteen.

Ames supposed he hadn't been much fun since then. Cy didn't seem to carry the same worry about things that Ames did, and he'd dated a ton in his teens, designed and built tree houses, and then did a welding certificate while he waited for his money.

He'd always known what he wanted to do with his inheritance—open a custom motorcycle shop.

Ames drove one of the bikes his brother personally designed and built, and he was grateful for that too.

He tossed his last bale of hay onto the belt, glad his shoulders didn't ache constantly the way they had when he'd first started at the ranch. He only worked a few days a week, and that was just fine by him. He didn't need the crazy, packed, full-time schedule of a cop, though he had originally come to Three Rivers to join the police force here.

In the end, Texas had experienced some natural disasters in the few months leading up to his arrival that had every county and district across the state tightening their budgets. The position he'd interviewed for and received just after Christmas suddenly wasn't available anymore.

This time, he hadn't kept the secret from his brothers or his parents. He'd told them all—and then surprised everyone once again when he'd announced that he was moving to Texas anyway.

He could still see Gray's drawn face and unhappy eyes as Ames loaded up his truck on the day he'd moved, only six weeks ago.

You don't have to do this, Gray had said. He was much less intimidating than he'd once been—especially when he was holding his little girl.

Ames loved Gray with his whole soul, and he had missed running with his brother. He missed getting Hunter after school and working with the boy on his history homework. He missed driving him out to the farm and staying for dinner. Hugging his mother. Holding baby Jane.

He missed a whole lot of things, and Ames started to spiral as he climbed down the ladder from the loft to the main level of the barn.

Orion stood there, cinching the hay bales onto the trailer. "Thanks, guys. That's it for today."

Cub whooped, but Ames just nodded. He wiped the sweat from his forehead and replaced his cowboy hat. He didn't mind the work, though it was incredibly hot in the Texas Panhandle in June.

But he didn't have much else to do. He'd bought a small fixer-upper in a nice neighborhood in Three Rivers. An older neighborhood, and the woman who'd owned the house before him had lived in it for sixty-two years.

Her kids had finally convinced her to move into an assisted living facility, but they'd promised not to sell the house until she passed away. That had happened a few months ago, and Ames had bought the house as-is, and for cash.

He'd been working on it in every spare moment he had, and if anyone who'd been there before came through the front door, they wouldn't recognize the house.

No one came over, though.

No one here knew that his last name meant anything, and Ames sure did like that. He'd met a couple of women the few times he'd gone to church, but Ames hadn't followed up on the numbers he'd gotten.

Just like he'd never called or texted Sophia back. He wasn't sure why he hadn't. Only that when he'd gotten his phone out to do it, his stomach had tightened, and he'd realized that nothing had changed between them.

"Hey, Ames," Orion said, and Ames turned back to the other cowboy.

"Yeah?"

"Did you want the info about the summer dance?"

"Oh, sure," Ames said. He'd heard the other cowboys

talking about the famous Three Rivers summer dances, and he'd said he was interested. He wasn't sure if he was or not, because Cub had said he'd been going for a couple of years, and he sure did like the "girls" there.

Ames had just turned forty last month, and he wasn't looking for a girl.

The fact was, he hadn't been looking at all, something Cy had called him on last Sunday evening.

"Friday and Saturday," Orion said. "Starts this weekend. Seven o'clock. Come as you are. They put a dance floor down on the grass." He smiled. "I met my fiancée there last year, so they're not all girls."

Ames smiled, and it felt good. Orion wasn't as old as Ames, but he wasn't twenty-two either. "Thanks, Orion."

"Sure," he said. "And if you need someone to go with, I'm pretty sure I heard Micah say he was trying to get Bear Glover to go."

Ames didn't know Bear Glover from Adam, so he just nodded. "I'll have to see how I'm feeling." He tipped his hat and walked away, the path back to where he parked his motorcycle beside the barn with the huge American flag painted on it not that far away.

He did everything by how he was feeling these days, except work. Ames absolutely loved working, because it kept his mind and hands busy.

He needed to figure out what to do with his inheritance, because he was definitely the loser in the family who hadn't done that yet. Everyone around him was so impressive, and Ames felt like he was suffocating almost all the time, pressed down on by all the family expectations.

He'd never told anyone—not Cy and not Gray—the real reason he'd had to leave Ivory Peaks.

Them.

They were so good, and so wonderful, and while Ames definitely had plenty of role models to look to, every one of his brothers served to remind him how little he'd accomplished in his life.

When they'd asked him why he'd quit the force in Littleton, Ames had told them part of the truth. He didn't love the work as much as he once had. He didn't like the pressure or the hours. He needed a break.

All of those were true.

But there was one more piece he'd kept to himself.

He pushed away the last meeting he'd had with his captain as he traded his cowboy hat for a helmet and straddled his bike. Cy had built it for his height, painted it Ames's favorite color—black—and put the Texas star on the side of the gas tank. If Ames put a Texas flag on the back and drove down the street of Three Rivers, he'd fit right in with everyone else who lived here.

He wasn't a born and bred Texan, but he did like it in Three Rivers. It was so much easier to breathe, for one.

At least when he didn't think about the farm and family he'd left behind.

He'd always been so adamant that someone needed to stay in Ivory Peaks, because that was where the Hammond heritage came from. Wes, Colton, and Cy had all relocated to Coral Canyon. Gray lived there in the summer.

Ames didn't want to march to the same beat, even though he hated be the odd man out too.

He sighed as he hit the highway and really opened the throttle. He couldn't have it both ways, no matter how hard he tried.

When he got home, he checked his text, and the one from Cy wasn't asking about Sophia. Thankfully.

No, this one was about his wedding.

"Shoot," Ames muttered under his breath. He hadn't forgotten about his twin's wedding—not exactly. He just hadn't remembered it either.

Of course I'll be there, Ames typed out. *Saturday. I'm planning on coming up on Saturday. Do you need me earlier?*

Cy started typing right away, and *Nope* came through. *You're staying for a while, though, right?*

For their honeymoon, Cy and Patsy were taking an RV up to Glacier National Park and then into Canada. They wanted to see the Rocky Mountains, the touristy town of Banff, and all the bluer-than-blue lakes up northwest of Calgary.

Ames wasn't sure why he needed to stay for a while.

Yes, he typed out anyway. *Two weeks while you're gone. Blue Velvet will be well-taken care of.*

Colton or Wes—or even Gray—could take Cy's dog.

At the same time, Ames needed to go. He'd stay in Cy's house with the dog—and his parents and Grams. Gray was taking them up to the wedding, and then he and Elise weren't going back to Ivory Peaks. They'd stay with Ames until Cy and Patsy returned, and then Ames thought the plan was for them to stay with Wes and Bree for the summer.

Ames would be returning to Three Rivers and his job at Seven Sons Ranch, he knew that.

He showered and surveyed the progress he'd made on installing the kitchen cabinets. Not bad. As he picked up where he'd left off the night before, he thought he probably shouldn't bother with the summer dance this Friday. Even if he did meet someone, he'd be leaving town for a couple of weeks the very next day.

"Seems pointless," he said to himself as he hung the cupboard where he'd most likely put his drinking glasses.

An hour later, things were humming along nicely when pain shot through Ames's fingers and hand. He yelped and looked at his thumb—which he'd literally just nailed to the cabinet and the wall.

He hadn't even been paying attention.

His vision swam, but Ames gritted his teeth and pulled his hand free. Hurrying, he moved to the sink and flipped the water on. He got the nail out, and realized it had just gone through the side of his thumb, not straight through.

Pain radiated up his arm with every pulse of his heart, and Ames grabbed the nearest thing—a washcloth, probably filled with germs—and pressed it to his hand. He leaned against the sink as he closed his eyes, fighting the vertigo and swimming waves in his vision. He couldn't pass out. He lived alone, and literally no one ever came over.

His phone. Where was his phone?

He drew in deep breath after deep breath until he knew

he wasn't going to pass out. He wasn't sure how much time had passed. As he peeled the cloth away from his thumb, he realized it had stuck, so it had obviously been a while.

He didn't have the medical supplies to deal with an injury of this magnitude, but he strode into the bathroom and started digging under the sink to see what he had that he could use while he went to the pharmacy.

His mind raced through what time it was and when the corner drugstore closed. It was a Sunday. He better hurry.

He found only Band-Aids under the sink, so he pulled a clean, dry washcloth from his linen closet and wrapped his thumb in it. "It'll have to do for ten minutes," he told himself as he left the house and got behind the wheel of his truck.

Though his street was residential, it was only a few minutes from downtown, and relief poured through Ames when he pulled into the parking lot at the drugstore and saw a couple of other cars.

The black lab in the back of someone's truck made him smile despite the urgency of his situation. He should've taken his money and opened a dog training facility, because Ames did miss working with his K9 companions. Surely someone had to train those police dogs. Why not him?

Inside, he kept his hand pressed to his chest above his heart, his uninjured one holding the cloth tightly against his thumb. He scanned for the first aid sign, and quickly headed to the back corner of the store.

He wasn't sure if there were other people in the store or

not. His focus was on one thing—getting painkillers and the biggest, baddest gauze wraps he could find.

He found the gauze and tape and more Band-Aids. Ointment and painkillers—but he hadn't grabbed a basket. He had no idea how to get it all to the register while keeping the cloth over his thumb. And he certainly couldn't reveal his wound in the store. Not with the possibility of dripping blood all over.

And passing out, he thought.

"Ames?"

He turned at the voice, something triggering in his memory.

A woman stood there, and he knew her. Her hair was shorter now, and a slightly darker color of brown.

"What are you doing here?" she asked, scanning the floor where he'd dropped all the stuff he wanted as he'd taken it from the shelf.

Ames's brain didn't seem to be working. But his voice said, "Sophia?"

CHAPTER 3

S ophia clutched the handles of the basket she'd been filling. Ames Hammond in Three Rivers had thrown her for a complete loop. The shock running through her echoed on his face, as he obviously hadn't been expecting to see her either.

He held a white cloth to his hand, and it wasn't hard to see the blood staining it. She put her basket down, her instincts kicking in. She could text Marcy from the hospital. Nothing the woman needed was critical—and getting Ames to the emergency room was.

"Come on," she said, stepping over to him. Her foot kicked a box of gauze, but she ignored it. "We're going to the hospital."

"I just need some...." His voice trailed off as if he didn't know where he was and what he needed.

"How long ago did this happen?" she asked, linking

her arm through his elbow as he had both hands pressed to his chest, above his heart.

"I don't know," he said, moving easily with her.

"What happened?"

"I was hanging cabinets in the kitchen," he said. "I nailed my thumb to the wall."

Concern spiked inside her, but Sophia kept her composure. She only increased the speed of her step. She'd been in Three Rivers for a few weeks, so she knew where the hospital was. Only a few minutes from this corner store. She reached her car and opened the passenger door.

"In you go," she said, glad Ames didn't argue with her.

She got behind the wheel and hurried toward the hospital. Ames sat in the passenger seat, his head leaning back against the rest, his eyes closed. "What are you doing in Three Rivers?" she asked.

"I work here now," he said, opening his eyes. He blinked and turned toward her. "What are you doing here?"

"Marcy Walker asked me to be her nanny," Sophia said, trying not to feel too proud of herself. But since she'd never been able to get any of the Whittaker kids to like her, she was dang proud of herself. "Just for the summer. They're coming up to Coral Canyon—like your brother."

Wyatt and Marcy had bought a home in Coral Canyon in the woods, exactly like Gray. She'd just had another baby at the very beginning of January, and she and Wyatt had three little boys under the age of four. Marcy wanted help for summer activities, and Sophia had talked to Graham, Eli, Andrew, and Beau, and they'd decided she could easily do breakfast and dinner at the lodge five days a week and nanny for Marcy during the day.

She'd been putting together summer outdoor activities for the boys for the past two months since Marcy had first called her, and she'd been in Three Rivers for a few weeks to help Marcy get everything prepped and packed. They were leaving in two days to return to Coral Canyon.

Two days.

Her heart pulsed out a few extra beats. Why did God keep bringing Ames into her life when he clearly didn't want to be there? When she had no time for him?

He'd never called over Christmas. He hadn't even texted back.

Sophia had gotten the message loud and clear, though it had come cloaked in silence. He wasn't interested in her. That was fine. She hadn't been out with anyone new, but she'd started to talk to Emily and Eden, Annie's daughters, about the dating apps they'd used in the past.

She hadn't quite signed up yet, but her mind was open to new possibilities for meeting men.

Ames had fallen silent again, and Sophia glanced at him. She was trained in first aid, due to her job around so many other people. Marcy had wanted her to be trained as well, and Sophia was glad to say she already was.

"Ames," she said, maybe a little too loudly. "Tell me about your job."

"Hmm?" His head sort of rolled as he turned toward her this time. "I work on a ranch."

"Which one?" There were at least a half-dozen ranches surrounding Three Rivers.

"Seven Sons," he said.

"Oh, that's the Walker's," she said, glancing at him. Did he see all the similarities in their lives? It was like they existed on two roads running parallel to each other. "I've been out there. It's really nice."

"Yeah," he said.

Sophia turned into the emergency room parking lot, barely watching where she was going so she could keep her eyes on Ames. The last thing she needed was for him to pass out. "What do you do?"

"Ranch stuff," he said, his voice quiet.

"Do you work with Jeremiah?"

"Yes."

"Why aren't you a cop anymore?"

"I worked too much," he said. "No one would go out with me."

Sophia was well aware that he wouldn't be saying any of these things if he wasn't one breath away from losing consciousness. The truth surprised her, though. "So you thought being a cowboy would be less work?"

"I'm only part-time," he said.

"What do you do in your spare time? Hang cabinets?"

He looked at her, surprised. "How did you know I was hanging cabinets?"

"You told me," she said, forgoing finding a parking spot. He was in bad shape, and she pulled right up into the circle drive and said, "Stay. I'm coming around." She jumped from the car and dashed toward the bell to call for help. Then she jogged back to the car and opened his door. "All right, Ames. Up and out."

He stood, but he swayed, and he flung his hand out to steady himself against the top of the car. Two women came outside, one pushing a wheelchair. "What's the situation?" the first one asked.

"This is Ames Hammond," Sophia said. "I found him in the drugstore, trying to buy medical supplies. He said he nailed his thumb to the wall, but he doesn't know how long ago." She eased him into the wheelchair. "I think he's lost a lot of blood. I've tried to keep him conscious."

"Date of birth?"

The other nurse turned Ames around and headed for the entrance.

"Uh." Sophia watched him go. "May something. He just turned forty." She knew that from Cy's birthday last year. Patsy had refused a gift from him that day, and she'd spent plenty of time telling Sophia about it.

"Are you his girlfriend?"

Sophia turned toward the other woman. She couldn't lie about this. She didn't even know Ames's address, and wouldn't his girlfriend know where he lived? *Not if it's new*, she thought.

"Sort of?" she guessed. "We just started seeing each other." That was also sort of true. She knew who he was. She'd kissed him plenty of times. She had been his girlfriend, once.

Maybe. She wasn't even sure about that, though Sophia didn't normally go around kissing men she wasn't dating. Ames seemed to be an exception to everything in Sophia's life.

"Come on in then," the nurse said. "Does he have any family to call?"

"Not here," she said. "They're either in Colorado or Wyoming. I can call them."

"Lora." The second nurse poked her head out of a room down the hall. "He fainted. I need help." A moment later, a red light on the wall above the doorway started to flash. Several people hurried into the room, and Sophia was one of them.

Watching four men and women lift Ames from the slumped position in the wheelchair to the bed made her heart hurt and her fingers shake.

"Let's see what we've got," Lora said, and she peeled the white washcloth away from Ames's hand. The amount of blood there made Sophia's stomach lurch. She couldn't really distinguish his fingers, and she turned away and covered her mouth.

"You can wait outside," someone said, but she shook her head.

"I'm okay," she whispered. "I just don't want to see it."

"This needs stitches," someone behind her said. "It's just the thumb, though. The rest of this is just blood."

"Let's get him cleaned up and sutured," Lora said. "Ivy, the IV. Push a thousand milligrams of ibuprofen. Fluids."

Most of the people cleared out of the room, and when Sophia turned back, she found a woman putting an IV in Ames's arm and another nurse cleaning his wounded hand. It took shape, and Sophia could see the damaged thumb.

Lora re-entered the room pushing a tray. "He's going to

be okay," she said, glancing at Sophia. "Probably eight or nine stitches. Doctor Willis is finishing up with one patient, and then he'll be in."

"How long until he wakes up?" Sophia hugged herself, because she had other things to do that day. But Ames should not have to wake up alone. She wouldn't want to, and she didn't want to leave him here by himself.

"We'll wait to get the stitches done," Lora said. "And then Doctor Willis will probably try to wake him."

"He's not drugged," the other nurse added. "He could wake up any time."

Sophia nodded, and she stayed out of the way as the three of them got him ready for the stitches. They all left the room, and Sophia migrated over to his side. She reached up and brushed his hair back off his forehead. He'd let it grow out since the last time she'd seen him, which admittedly was months and months and months ago.

Nine months.

He'd been a cop then, and he kept his hair shaved and short. Now, it had definitely grown out a few inches, and he was still the sexiest man she'd ever met. Easily.

"Ames," she said. "It's Sophia, and you're in the hospital in Three Rivers. Can you wake up?"

He stirred, and she pulled a chair closer and took one of his hands in both of hers. "Ames, wake up." She squeezed his hand, and he squeezed back. His eyelids fluttered open, and Sophia's heartbeat increased. "You nailed your thumb to the cabinets, and I found you in the drugstore."

Those dark, beautiful eyes found hers, and something powerful hooked them together. "The drugstore?"

"You were trying to buy gauze and Band-Aids," she said with a small smile. "You need stitches, Ames."

He looked around then, more of his awareness returning with every passing moment. "You brought me to the hospital."

"That's right," she said.

"How long was I out?"

"Maybe ten minutes?" she guessed. "Not long. But we barely made it here."

"I'm sorry," he said. "I thought I could just patch myself up."

"You're pretty amazing at a lot of things," she said with a smile. "But even you can't will your wounds to miraculously heal."

He managed a smile in return, and just then, the doctor came in. "Ames Hammond? Good to see you awake."

Sophia pulled her hands away from Ames's and backed up, putting the chair back against the wall where it had been.

"So I heard you nailed your thumb to the kitchen cabinets." The doctor wore a big smile to go with his big personality. He grinned around the room, his charisma palpable. "I'm Doctor Willis, and I'm going to get you put back together right." He stepped over to Sophia. "You're the girlfriend?"

She pulled in a breath, glad she couldn't see Ames past Dr. Willis. "Sophia," she said without confirming. "I'm going to go call his brother."

"Probably best if you're a little squeamish," Dr. Willis said.

Sophia was, but not about the stitches. She stepped past him, unable to make eye contact with Ames.

"Sophia?" he asked behind her, and she turned in the doorway.

"Yeah?"

"You're not leaving-leaving, right?"

"No," she said. "I'll just go call Cy for you."

"Okay," he said. "But maybe try Colton. Cy's getting married in a week."

"Colton," she said. "Got it." Then she got the heck out of there so she wouldn't have to watch the doctor put Ames back together—or face him and admit she'd told complete strangers she was his girlfriend.

———

A COUPLE OF HOURS LATER, SOPHIA HAD MADE MULTIPLE phone calls, sat with Ames for a while, and driven him back to the drugstore. She'd stayed with him while he bought a few things inside, and she turned into a long driveway that led to a home that sat back from the street and parked behind his truck.

He got out and turned back to reach inside and get the painkillers and medical supplies he'd bought at the drugstore while Sophia watched. Marcy had said to take as much time as she needed to make sure her "friend" was okay, and a deep exhaustion pulled through Sophia.

She didn't need to go inside with Ames. The color in

his face had normalized by the time she'd called Colton, Cy, and Marcy and returned to the room. With nurses and doctors in and out, they hadn't spoken about the girlfriend issue, and the only reason she'd followed him home was because she'd promised Lora she would.

Ames glanced in her direction, and she couldn't decide how he was feeling. He wore a dark pair of sunglasses, and with the slightly longer hair and those broad shoulders, Sophia darn near swooned.

She climbed out of the car and closed the door, facing him. "Do you want me to come in?"

"If you want." He didn't move either.

It was far too hot to be standing outside in the Texas heat, Sophia knew that. "Why didn't you call me at Christmas?" she asked anyway. No sense in going in if she was going to get her heart ripped out. Just because it happened in the air conditioning didn't mean it would hurt less.

Ames took a few steps toward her but stopped at the end of his truck. Several feet still separated them. He drew in a breath and blew it out. Said nothing.

Sophia had never known Ames to hold back. He always said what was on his mind, usually in a brisk tone of voice that sent tremors of fear to the recipient. She could still hear him telling Patsy she had no right to hurt Cy.

"Well, you're home," Sophia said. "I don't know if you saw Colton's text. He said he's going to come to stay with you. He'll be here tomorrow." She backed up and reached for her door handle again.

"I don't know," he said. "I don't know why I didn't call."

"It's okay," she said. "You're not interested." She pulled open the door and used it as a shield between her and Ames. "I get it."

"What if I am interested?"

Sophia paused, cursing whoever had invented sunglasses. She needed to see his eyes, because Ames told everything with those eyes.

She didn't want to be the desperate woman who clung to him every time he happened to descend to her level to give her the time of day. Gripping the top of the door until her fingers ached, she lifted her head slightly. "My number hasn't changed. If you're really interested, you can call anytime."

With that, she slid behind the wheel, started the car, and left him standing in his driveway with a couple of bags hanging from his left hand.

CHAPTER 4

Ames dipped the sponge in the water bucket and lifted it back up to the cabinet. He couldn't believe he'd nailed his thumb to the wall. And to make matters worse, he had to run into Sophia at the drugstore?

How humiliating.

At the same time, he was thrilled that she'd been there. Otherwise he might have passed out and been found in the middle of the aisle by anybody. As it was, Colton would be arriving that afternoon, and Ames felt a mountain of foolishness descend upon him. He didn't need his brother to come take care of him. He wondered if this was how Cy had felt when he went to Coral Canyon last year for a couple of weeks. Probably.

Ames needed to swallow his pride and make a plan to become the man he wanted to be. Was that someone who worked another man's ranch? He wasn't even sure if he was in the right place. Three Rivers had felt like home for the past few weeks. But was he in the right place?

He was so far from family when he needed help, and he hated that. Ames had never had this problem before. He knew what he wanted, and he worked to get it, just like Gray had done when it came to the Boston Marathon.

He wanted it. He worked and trained for it. He got it.

The problem was, Ames didn't know what he wanted.

He liked dressing a little eccentrically sometimes. He liked making all kinds of different egg dishes. He loved being in charge of meetings and crews and people. At the same time, he could take directions too.

That was what he did at Seven Sons Ranch, and he had no problem listening to Jeremiah, or Orion tell him what he needed to do. He just did it. He didn't mind putting his head down and getting the work done. In fact, it brought him a great sense of accomplishment, and he craved the feeling that he'd done something good at the end of every day.

"But what have I done good lately?" he asked himself. He also disliked that he was having this out loud conversation with himself as he scrubbed his own blood off the newly painted walls and freshly manufactured cabinets. Worse, he wasn't sure what good he'd done lately.

He wasn't sure he could remember much from last night and the things that Sophia had said, but something triggered in his memory. She wasn't a permanent resident here.

He wasn't sure why she'd come into his mind right now. He rinsed the sponge again, the blood almost gone now. But Sophia wouldn't leave his mind. He'd enjoyed his time with her last fall, and his pulse had acted erratically when she'd called him over Christmas.

He'd said he'd call her back, and then he hadn't. Last night, she'd seemed a little hurt by that, and he wondered if the chemistry and spark between them could be rekindled, or if he'd extinguished it completely when he'd ghosted her over the holidays.

"Probably," he said to himself. "You're not real great at keeping up with what women expect."

When he was a detective with the Littleton Police Department, he knew what he did every day. He knew he kept bad people off the streets. He knew he kept his integrity intact. He knew he had friends he helped. He knew he texted his brothers, kept in touch with his mom, and did all that he needed to do to make sure he was on good standing with the Lord.

Since he quit his job, almost a year ago now, he wasn't really sure what every day would bring. He didn't mind working on the ranch, but he didn't love it. He didn't want his own ranch, that was for sure. He could definitely afford it if he wanted it.

He likes horses—*you like dogs.*

He'd thought about training police dogs in the past, but he'd never pursued the idea. Sophia fostered dogs from a facility in Dog Valley, and she'd told him about what she did. Her job was to socialize the dog and teach it the skills it needed to be placed with a family. The animals were able to get adopted more easily than before if they were potty trained and crate trained and good with kids.

Perhaps he should do something like that. He had plenty of money. He could buy a piece of land somewhere. "Not Wyoming," he muttered.

In Colorado, he oversaw canine officers, so he'd worked with a lot of K9 police dogs. He usually had a German Shepherd that he was training and working with, and he loved them. He himself was not a canine officer, but they were part of his crew, so he needed to know the dogs. He needed to know that the officers and the dogs he paired them with worked well together. Some officers patrolled lonely highways with only their dogs for partners. And if that man got in trouble, his dog would be the one to save him.

"Train police dogs," he said, and the idea had real merit.

His mind moved on to other things, including his schedule for the next few days. A lead weight settled in Ames's stomach. "Cy's wedding."

Come Monday morning next week, Ames would be the only Hammond brother without a wife. He knew he hadn't failed. Intellectually, he knew. But somehow, a heavy weight of failure lingered around his neck.

His mother had stopped saying things to him after he'd sat her down and said, "Mom, I'm doing the best I can."

I know I'm not Wes.

I know I'm not Gray.

I'm not as good as Colton, and even Cy has been able to find someone who can love him and stand by him.

I'm trying, Mom.

It's hard out there, and the last thing I need is you badgering me when I already feel bad enough about myself.

It had been a hard conversation for him to have with his mother, who he loved so much. A sense of fierce missing overcame him, and he knew he needed to call his mom and find out how things were going on the farm.

It was summer now, which meant Gray and Elise had left and gone to Coral Canyon, where they lived for several months out of the year. While it was warm in the Tetons, they took their kids, Hunter and Jane, and experienced life in the mountains.

Ames knew his mom would be lonely, even though she still had her husband and her mother-in-law. Ames was actually surprised Grams was still around. She would be one hundred years old in November, and he couldn't wait for that celebration.

He wondered if anyone was even planning it. He decided he better say something to Colton or Gray so that celebration could happen. In fact, he thought that might be a really great thing for *him* to spearhead to bring the family together.

Ames finished scrubbing the wall and dropped the sponge in the bucket. Then he pulled out his phone to make the call to his mother, but he stalled, staring at the screen. Wondering if perhaps he should make a phone call to another woman instead.

He wasn't even sure if he'd thanked Sophia. She hadn't come in the house last night, and he'd been on some pretty heavy duty painkillers.

Maybe he should just call and make sure that she knew

he was grateful for her help. Even if they couldn't be more than just friends, he should say thank you.

He'd see her at the wedding, because she was Patsy's best friend. And Patsy was marrying Cy.

He looked up, sighing. Ames thought everything would just be so much simpler if the Lord would just tell him what to do.

Ask out Sophia. He could check that box.

Get to know her. Check.

Be patient. Check.

Fall in love. Check.

Ames loved lists. He loved having steps that he should take to get something done. He was very good at following a checklist.

The problem was, Ames didn't know how to fall in love. Sometimes, he barely felt anything, and he'd have to *feel something* in order to fall in love.

He seemed to know when Cy wasn't doing well. He was able to text him and follow up with him. But doing those things for himself was a lot harder than Ames had anticipated.

For so long, he thought he'd been happy by himself, and he had been. He loved running. He loved his job in Littleton, he loved living in the Denver area and driving out to Ivory Peaks to the farm where he'd grown up to visit his family.

But that was when everyone lived in Colorado. That was when Wes ran the company, and Colton did all the social media, and Gray was the corporate lawyer.

That was when there was only one grandchild, and when none of the brothers had wives or significant others.

That was when he fit with everybody else.

Now, Ames was constantly looking for a space where he belonged. Just like he had at Gray's house after Cy's grand opening. His brother had built him a custom motor-cycle, and Ames really needed to be on it. It was a heavy machine though, and he wasn't sure he could handle it with his thumb wrapped up as it was.

He looked at his fingers and a twinge of pain moved up his arm. He wasn't sure how he hadn't felt it last night. He wondered who had put away all the things that he'd franti-cally gathered from the shelves. He probably needed to go back there and apologize for whatever mess he left behind.

He started tapping on his phone and his fingers had a mind of their own, because the next thing he knew, the line was ringing, and Sophia's name sat on the screen.

She picked up with the words, "Ames. Hello," and nothing more.

"Hey," he said, not really sure what to say after that. "I just wanted to say thanks for helping last night. I'm not really sure what happened. But I do know that you were there, and you got me home safe, and I appreciate that."

He nodded to himself and looked out the big windows at the front of the house. "And that's all. I wasn't sure if I said thanks, and I wanted you to know that I appreciated your help."

"Sure," she said. "How are you feeling this morning?"

"Okay," he said. "I feel really stupid. I've never done

anything like that before, and I've built plenty of things over the years."

"Is that true?" she asked. "I didn't know you were a carpenter."

Ames cocked his head, because he thought she might be...flirting with him. "Well, I wouldn't call myself a carpenter," he said, sitting down at the bar. Maybe having a conversation wouldn't be so hard. Maybe he could be like Wes and fall in love on the phone.

When he was face-to-face with Sophia, all he wanted to do was hold her hand and kiss her. He did like talking to her and they had become friends in the few weeks that he'd been in Coral Canyon last year.

She hadn't wanted to relocate, and he'd been vehemently opposed to leaving Colorado, and yet...he'd left Colorado. He suddenly wondered what kind of message that sent to Sophia.

"If you build things with wood, aren't you a carpenter?" she asked, bringing him back to the conversation.

"Yeah, well I don't have any degrees or certifications or anything like that," he said. "I don't have a wood shop, and I don't really have power tools either." His thumb throbbed as a reminder that he was not well-versed with a nail gun, but somehow, he wondered if he could become a carpenter.

He could clearly see what all of his brothers had done. And yet his future, as well as his past, still seemed muddy and unclear to him. What had he really done? Save a few lives on the streets by handing out tickets?

He didn't think that was that great of a legacy. Not

compared to Colton working on the Human Genome Project, and Wes and Gray dedicating so many years of their life to the family company, which would hopefully continue as their family continued to grow. Currently, Ames's uncle's children ran HMC. But he knew that the family ownership shifted every fifteen to twenty years. It wouldn't surprise him at all if he found Hunter at the helm of HMC in another couple of decades.

Hunter was an amazing child who had been through a lot in his short life already and come out the victor many times. Ames had taken him to counseling several times last year. He'd watched the boy come alive as he figured out how he felt, why he felt that way, and what to do about it.

Ames had another realization while Sophia said something about what she wanted to buy when she owned a home of her own.

Perhaps he should go to counseling too.

He'd been pushing Cy to go for so long that Ames had never realized that maybe *he* could benefit from the same type of therapy that his brother did. Compared to Cy, Ames always thought he was the more normal one. He didn't suffer from the same anxiety. He didn't have depression. He didn't worry that much about what others thought about him at all. He didn't really care if he was liked.

He did the best he could, he was kind to others. He worked hard, and he served. He'd always thought that had been enough, and it had been. But maybe he was a lot like Hunter, who'd told Ames that he was worried he didn't feel things the way normal people did.

He'd rather bury himself in a crossword puzzle, or out on the lake while he fished, or even out in the barns working with the calves and the goats than spend time with other people. He had friends, of course, and what had really spurred him into wondering if he was normal or not was when he had his first kiss with his girlfriend, Molly.

Ames hung his head, because even his fourteen-year-old nephew could get a girl and keep her for longer than six months. Ames wondered if he'd ever be able to do that, and he was forty years old.

"I feel like I lost you," Sophia said.

"Sorry," Ames said, rubbing his hand up the back of his neck. "I'm not really sure why I called, but I'm wondering if you have time for lunch." He had no idea what he was doing. Only that the words were there, and he decided to speak them.

"I don't think so, Ames," she said. "We're getting ready to leave for Coral Canyon in the morning, and I've got the boys with me at the park."

"I can come to the park," he said.

Sophia said nothing, and Ames wondered if he should take that for permission. He'd done that a couple of times when he'd leaned down to kiss her in Coral Canyon. Ames knew he liked Sophia. What he didn't know was why he was so resistant to starting and maintaining a real relationship with her.

No end date, he thought.

Ames did love end dates. He loved knowing when things would start and stop, and how long he had to endure something so that he could then get on with his "real life."

It was as if God had opened the heavens and sent lightning bolt after lightning bolt of realization to Ames's mind. He knew now that he viewed Sophia as a complication.

Not her as a person, but a real relationship with her. It would complicate his life. He would have to choose where he wanted to live. He would have to choose what he wanted to do. He would have to be someone that a woman like Sophia would want.

"I think I'm up for the park," he said, making a decision. "I'll bring lunch. Do you have lunch?"

"We were gonna grab hamburgers for lunch," she said. "There's a food truck here."

"Great," he said "I've got a wallet. I'll be there in ten minutes." He almost hung up and then asked, "Wait, which park?"

Three Rivers had a lot of parks, because it was in the panhandle of Texas, and the founders had wanted it to be an oasis in the part of Texas that was mostly desert, dirt, and dust.

———

"WE'RE DOWN AT THE FOUNDERS RIVER PARK," SHE SAID. "There's a little stream here the boys like. We've got both of Jeremiah's dogs with us today. We'll probably be here another hour is all, Ames. You really don't need to come."

"I want to see you," he said, feeling his bravery and boldness rise up within him. "So you tell me if you don't want to see me. Just say, 'I don't want to see you.' And I won't come. But if you wouldn't mind seeing me, I really want to see you." He took a breath and kept going. "I'm really sorry that I didn't call you over Christmas. I had some things I was dealing with."

That I'm still dealing with, he thought.

"But maybe we can try again."

Silence came through the line, and Ames held his breath. She was going to say she didn't want to see him. And then what would he do?

The same thing you've been doing the last six months, he told himself. *You'll be fine.* At the same time, an alarm wailed in his mind, screaming that he wouldn't really be fine.

"You can come to the park," she said. "But honestly Ames, I'm not sure anything has changed. Whatever you were dealing with, I think you're still dealing with. And I'm still not willing to relocate from Coral Canyon."

"You're in Texas right now," Ames said.

"Temporarily," she said. "I'm going to be a nanny for Wyatt and Marcy in the summers, while they're in Wyoming."

"Every summer?"

"Yes, I hope so," she said. "I've always wanted to work with kids, and this allows me to do that. I'll get to keep my job at the lodge and do something a little bit different than I've been doing."

"Do you like it?"

"Yes—well I've only been doing it for two weeks," she

said. "But yes, I like it. Their kids are great. They're great. And they live close to the lodge."

"Is it a full-time position?"

"No," she said. "Only a few hours each day, with a couple hours on the weekends. I have Sundays and Wednesdays off. Marcy said she'd love for me to stay with her when Wyatt travels."

"He's still traveling?"

"Yes. Sometimes," Sophia said. She called to one of the boys, and Ames knew he needed to get off the phone. He still had to call his mother, and he had to be back by two so he could assure Colton he was alive and well.

"I'll let you go," he said, and the call ended.

He didn't want his older brother to know about Sophia, or this new conversation. Colton had asked him about her several times since the phone call at Christmastime.

He thought about Sophia every day, at least once, sometimes more than that. There was a lot of time for a man to think while he was working on a ranch. He liked the quiet time between just him, and the sky around him, and the Lord. It allowed him a few minutes to reflect, where he could find the truth about things, and about himself.

"A lot of good it's done you," he muttered, picking up his phone again. He still didn't know what to do with his life.

But the idea of training police dogs lingered, as did the very hopeful possibility that he could rekindle a relationship with Sophia. His phone rang again, and this time his mom answered with, "Ames, dear, how are you?"

She sounded positive and upbeat, and Ames took that to mean that Grams hadn't died yet, and things were going well on the farm with the man that Gray hired to care for it during the summer.

"Good enough," Ames said, deciding on the spot not to tell her about nailing his thumb to the wall. She'd only worry, and she'd find out soon enough anyway.

Everyone we'll find out soon enough anyway. Before he knew it, he'd be the one they were all laughing at. He deserved it too, because who nailed their thumb to the wall?

He chuckled a little bit and said, "I'm doing great, Mom. How are things on the farm?" as he stood up and headed for the front door. He could connect this call to the Bluetooth in his truck and have it while he drove to the Founders River Park.

CHAPTER 5

Sophia laughed as the two dogs wrestled with each other about thirty yards away. She had her hands full keeping her eye on them, throwing them a ball, and making sure the four-year-old and two-year-old she was in charge of didn't get hurt, lost, or too muddy.

Marcy was pretty laid back when it came to mud and blood and all of that. She claimed she had to be with three boys under the age of four. Sophia had been staying with her and Wyatt for two weeks, and she knew the definition of flexible now.

Sometimes Warren would eat breakfast just fine. Other mornings, he seemed to have woken up on the wrong side of the bed, and no matter what Marcy put in front of him, he wouldn't eat it.

Cole had an affinity for sugar, and Sophia had caught him eating the powdered gelatin from the pantry. His hands and face, chin and neck, had been bright green. She could still see Marcy shaking her head and saying, "Yeah, that one will sniff out sugar like a bloodhound. The Jell-O goes in the top cabinet," as if little boys getting Jell-O boxes and eating the powder was normal.

Sophia had quickly learned that the boys did not eat at any time except when Marcy or Wyatt deemed it mealtime. Otherwise, they were stinkers at mealtimes, and no one could enjoy their food.

She loved them with a fierceness she didn't understand, though. So when Cole got out of the lazy stream and started toddling up the bank, she said, "Come get a drink, baby."

He did what she said, and Sophia held the water bottle for him while she dug a couple of beef training treats out of her pocket for Winston and Willow, one of whom had brought the ball back for her to throw again.

"Hungry," Cole said, and Sophia smiled at him.

"Yeah, it's almost time for lunch," she told him. She scanned the grass beyond where they were playing, reached for the ball when she didn't see Ames or his big, black truck anywhere, and tossed it again for the dogs.

They both took off after it, and Sophia enjoyed watching to see which one would end up with it. If it bounced just right, Willow could leap into the air and catch it. Winston was faster than her, but he wasn't as coordinated, and he sometimes bobbled the ball when he tried to catch it, which opened the door for Willow to steal it from him.

Winston got it this time, and Sophia called, "Good catch, Winsty," as if the dog cared that she'd been watching. Warren and Cole cared. Besides being told they were hungry, the boys' favorite words for Sophia were, "Watch me, Sophia. Watch me."

They were the cutest boys on the planet, so she had no problem watching them. Warren had definitely inherited more of his mother's fair features, while Cole had a dominant Walker gene in his blood. He was Wyatt's twin, and Marcy said they had the same rebellious streak and tendency to cause trouble.

Sophia had never seen Wyatt Walker cause trouble, but when the Walker family got together...Sophia couldn't look away. She couldn't hear afterward either, that was for sure. They were a fun-loving group, with a lot of children, more on the way, and dozens of dogs and horses—some of the miniature variety.

Warren especially loved his grandfather's miniature horses, and Sophia had been down to Gideon Walker's little farm at least three times in the two weeks she'd been in Three Rivers.

"Hey," a man said, and her heart leapt into the back of her throat.

She spun around to find Ames Hammond standing there, just as tall, just as dark, and just as delicious as he'd always been. "Hey," she repeated back to him.

He didn't smile at her, which set Sophia's nerves on edge. She reminded herself that Ames could come across a bit cold. She pictured him holding his hand to his chest, and that he was just a human. A mighty fine specimen of a male human, but a human nonetheless. When he got cut, he bled red just like everyone else.

Winston and Willow came trotting back to Sophia, and they got Ames to crack a smile. The foster dog she'd had last fall had loved him too, and she watched as Ames bent down to give the canines a quick pat.

"Let me round up the boys, and we'll go over to the food truck," she said, turning away from him.

"Okay," he said. "Can I ask you something first?"

She turned back to him, not willing to give him the easy way out by looking somewhere else. She had plenty to dominate her attention too, but she kept her gaze leveled on him. "Okay."

"Would you go to Cy's wedding with me?"

Sophia blinked at him, surprise rendering her mute for a moment. "With you?"

"Yeah." He bent and picked up the slobbery ball.

"You use this," she said, handing him the throwing stick. "Then you don't have to touch that." She eyed the gross ball. "And I'm already going to the wedding." Her best friend was getting married, for crying out loud. "I wouldn't miss it for the world."

"Right, I know," he said, throwing the ball for the dogs again. "Oh, wow. Look at them go after that thing."

Sophia did, and joy filled her when Willow leapt and caught it above Winston, who didn't seem to know where the ball even was.

Ames laughed, the sound rich and full. "Did you see that?"

"I've seen it," Sophia said, trying not to show how impressed she was. She took a few steps toward the river.

"Come on, Warren. We're going to go get hamburgers now."

"Hungry," Cole said again, and Sophia swept him up and into her arms.

"Yes, baby," she said, smiling at him. "I'm hungry too. We'll get you a cheeseburger, okay?"

Cole smiled and pressed one of his chubby cheeks right against hers. Love filled her for this boy, and she was well-aware of the weight of Ames's eyes as he watched the exchange. Warren came running up the bank to the grass, soaked from the waist down.

"Good thing is so hot today," she said when she saw him. "You'll have to see if you can get a bit dry before we get in the car. Your dad won't be happy if you get in soaking wet."

"Okay," Warren said. "Can I get a cwili cweese dog?"

Sophia grinned at him and bent to pick up her bag while still balancing Cole on her hip. She now kept everything under the sun in it, from a pair of nail clippers, to Band-Aids, to a portable charger for her phone. "Do they have chili cheese dogs at the hamburger truck?"

"I don't know," Warren said.

"Let's go find out," Sophia said. She glanced up to look for the dogs, yelling at them to come back. They did, and Ames grabbed the ball with the throwing stick.

"I have their leashes in my purse," she said, turning toward him so her purse was within his grasp. He only dug around for a moment before finding them, and he clipped the leashes to the dog's collars and fell into step beside her.

"So is that a no on the date to the wedding thing?"

She glanced up at him, not truly allowing herself to meet his eye. "I'm already going to be there. I'm the Maid of Honor."

"Okay," he said.

"You know she's my best friend, right?"

"Yeah, and he's my twin," Ames said, a flash of his attitude rearing its head. "I just thought it would be nice to go together."

She heard more than he said, something she'd always been very good at when it came to Ames. What he was really saying was that if he had a date, he'd have somewhere to belong. Someone to belong to, among a crowd of people who already had a place to be and someone to be with.

For some reason, though, her annoyance with him kept her from readily accepting his invitation to be his date to his twin's wedding.

Not for some reason, she thought. *He ghosted you at Christmas, and he still wouldn't be talking to you if you hadn't rescued him in the drugstore last night.*

She kept all of that to herself, though, because there was no need to drag it all out into the open. The feeling of helplessness she'd felt last holiday season still stung, and she still felt it keenly. He didn't just get a free pass on that because he'd "been dealing with some things."

What things? she'd wanted to throw back to him on the phone. She had experience giving Ames's bad boy attitude right back to him, and it usually didn't go in her favor. He was extremely intelligent, and incredibly well-spoken, and before she knew it, she was the one who'd done something wrong by questioning the mighty Ames Hammond.

Sophia was surprised at the bitterness coursing through her, because she didn't normally hold on to friendships anyway. She'd moved a lot growing up, and she'd learned how to fit in, how to make new friends, and how to let go of old ones easily. If she hadn't, she wouldn't have survived her teen years.

Those years were also why she steadfastly wanted to remain in Coral Canyon. She had connections there. Real friends she didn't want to lose. It had gotten harder and harder to say goodbye, and if she stayed in Coral Canyon, she didn't have to use that word.

They arrived at the food truck, and Sophia took a few seconds to study the menu board. "You're in luck, Warren," she said. "They have chili cheese dogs."

The little boy cheered and asked her to read him what they had to drink. When she got to lemonade, he said, "That, Sophia. I want lemonade."

"All right," she said, stepping up to place their order.

Ames crowded in beside her as she finished and said, "This is all together. I'll have the double bacon cheese with sweet potato fries. And another lemonade."

"You don't need to pay for our lunch," she said. "Marcy gives me money for that."

"I have plenty of money," Ames said, almost out of the corner of his mouth.

"You're kidding," she said dryly, and she walked away, because she didn't want to argue with him in public. She'd said he could come to the park, but now she wished she'd told him she didn't want to see him anymore.

Then you'd be bitter and a liar, she thought.

Ames finished paying and stepped over to where she waited with the boys and the dogs. The big cypress trees in this park provided a lot of shade, and it was needed on these hot summer days.

"I'm sorry about Christmas," he said. "I know you're still mad at me, and I'm sorry. If I could go back in time and call you, I would."

She looked at him again, studying that handsome face. He wore anxiousness in his eyes today, and he hadn't shaved that morning. "Would you really?"

"Yes," he said.

"What *things* were you dealing with?"

He looked away, and Sophia nearly scoffed at him. She pulled the sound back down her throat and waited for him to explain. "You've met my brothers," he said. "That alone should give me a pass for at least a month."

Sophia let her smile come out, but she shook her head. "Nope. But nice try."

Ames grinned too. "How about if I told you you were the only one who knew I'd quit my job? Well, I did tell Gray a couple of days before Christmas. Everyone else found out literally moments before you called me. I was stressed."

"You didn't tell them you quit your job?"

He shook his head. "Didn't seem relevant."

"You didn't think your brothers and parents would

want to know you quit your job? That wasn't *relevant* to you?"

"They're always giving me advice," he said. "I don't need their advice."

Of course he didn't. Ames Hammond knew all. "And now you're here in Texas. How did that happen?"

Ames gritted his teeth, which made his jaw jut out on the sides. She told herself that she was allowed to ask him questions. He was the one who'd come to the park to see her.

"Felt like the right thing to do," he said.

"Okay, no," Sophia said, having heard enough. "I've heard that from you so many times, and it's hardly ever true." She adjusted the shoulder strap on her bag so it wasn't digging into her collarbone. "If you're not going to at least tell me the truth, I've changed my mind. I don't want you here at the park with me."

Of all things, Ames grinned at her. "There's the Sophia I know."

"Don't do that either," she said. "You don't know me."

Surprise crossed his expression. "I don't?"

"Coming to my cabin and eating my food for two weeks doesn't count," she said. "And besides, Ames, that was nine months ago. Nine. You don't think I've changed in nine months?" Exasperation filled her, and thankfully, the kid in the truck called her name.

"Food's ready, guys," she announced to the little boys. "Let's find a patch of grass to sit on while Ames picks it up." She didn't look at him to confirm, but he went to get the food.

She pulled a small blanket out of her bag and spread it on the ground several feet away from the main activities surrounding the food truck. Ames brought over their burgers and hot dogs, and with the boys eating happily, Sophia dared to look at the cowboy billionaire who'd shown up in her life again.

"I came to Three Rivers to get away from Denver," he said. "That's the truth."

"Why'd you need to get away from Denver?" He'd told her he felt a responsibility to be the Hammond that stayed in Colorado. It was where generations of Hammonds had been born and raised and lived. And yet, she'd found him bleeding in a drugstore in Texas.

"Everything felt stale," he said. "I was stale. I was… nothing." His voice quieted to the point that she could barely hear the last word he said. "I wanted something new. A fresh start, in a fresh place."

"How long have you been here?"

"A couple of months," he said. "Five or six weeks, actually."

"Not long," she said.

"Not long," he repeated. He took a bite of his burger and then another. After swallowing, he said. "I came to join the police force, but they put a hiring freeze on a week or so before I was set to come." He looked out across the park, his thoughts clearly somewhere else. "I came anyway."

"Hmm."

"I came to find myself," he said quietly. "For a while there, I thought I'd just be happy if I could find a girlfriend. Maybe someone I could fall in love with and start a future together with. But…I don't know."

"Sure, you do," she said, repeating something he'd said to her in her cabin in Coral Canyon. He was good at seeing when someone was hiding something, which had made him an extraordinary cop.

His eyes met hers, and she nodded at him, hoping to encourage him. "What I thought I wanted wasn't really what I wanted."

"So that's why you didn't call. You didn't want a girl-friend anymore."

"I want…all of that," he said slowly. "I do. I just want to know that I'm in the right place for it. I need to be ready for the girlfriend and the wife and the family. And I wasn't." He finished his bacon burger and wadded up the wrapper. "Again, I'm sorry I didn't call or text."

She nodded, because she heard sincerity in his voice. "Apology accepted."

Ames smiled at her, and that crackling chemistry that had first brought them together definitely hadn't faded. Sophia wondered if it came from Ames, and if he could feel it as strongly as she could.

"At the risk of being pushy, I'm going to ask again—will you be my date at Cy and Patsy's wedding?"

Sophia helped Cole with the last bite of his hot dog and handed him a napkin with the words, "Wipe your face, bud. You've got ketchup everywhere." She helped the little boy with that too, trying to decide if there was anything else she needed to know before she said yes to Ames's invitation.

When she couldn't put it off any longer, she raised her eyes to his. "Maybe."

"What are your conditions?" he asked.

"I just need to know the parameters of...us," she said. "Is this a one-time 'date' to a wedding so we don't have to sit alone? Or is this you trying to start something real for the second time? Or...something else entirely?"

Ames thought about it for a few seconds, and then he said, "All of the above."

"It can't be all of the above," she argued. "If it's a one-time date, that's not a second chance at a relationship."

"Sure it is," he said. "I don't want to be alone at the wedding. I do want a second chance with you—at a real relationship. Those are both true."

Sophia cocked her head at him. She wished she could get inside his mind and see how it all worked in there. "And the something else entirely?"

"Now, that, I don't have a definition for," he said with a cheesy grin. He reached over and took her hand in his. He rubbed her fingers, and with the gentle movement she'd felt from him before, Sophia started to melt.

"It's something else entirely," he said. "I don't know what it is. I don't know how to define it. I just know I want to see if we can."

Sophia wanted to say no as much as she wanted to say yes. She just had one more question. "Have you found yourself, Ames?"

"Almost," he said quietly.

Sophia hesitated for another moment. "All right," she said. "I'll be your date at the wedding."

CHAPTER 6

C olton Hammond pulled into the driveway at the address Ames had texted him that morning. His brother's motorcycle sat up by the house, in the carport, but his truck wasn't there. Instant worry hit Colton's gut, and he hurried to put the rental car in park and get out. He left his suitcase behind and went to the door in the carport. Once up the five steps, he knocked at the same time he twisted the doorknob.

The door didn't open, which didn't surprise Colton. He still rammed it with his shoulder, because he'd been hoping to get lucky. Nope.

"Leave it to Ames to lock his house tight when he lives in a small town." Three Rivers, Texas had charm, Colton would give it that.

American flags hung from every streetlight on Main Street, and the fire hydrants had been painted to look like trolls. They were cute, and Colton had smiled his way through town to his brother's house.

He was secretly thrilled he could come help Ames before they'd both fly to Coral Canyon for Cy's wedding. He could easily get time off at Springside, the lab where he worked a couple of days a week. Other than that, Colton had simply adjusted his workout schedule and how often he got to take his dog to the dog park—something that Coral Canyon had just opened two weeks ago—to get on a plane with only a few hours' notice.

He went back down the steps, his pulse still bobbing somewhere in the back of his throat. Around the corner of the house and down the sidewalk sat the front door. The roof sloped over the front porch, which wasn't very big. Maybe two people could stand there, if one of them wasn't tall and broad-shouldered like Colton.

He rang the doorbell and knocked again, calling, "Ames?" this time. His brother didn't come. This door was also locked, and the Texas heat and lack of his brother drove Colton back to the rental car.

He started the ignition again, because he'd bake to death in the car without air conditioning. In that moment, he was grateful for the cooler mountain temperatures, as he'd never felt heat like this before. "It's humid too," he told himself, as humidity wasn't something he'd ever dealt with in Colorado or Wyoming.

When he'd lived in Virginia, he had experienced some humidity, but Texas seemed to be one degree away from the sun. He called Ames, his concern amplifying with every ring of the line.

He didn't answer, and that only drove frustration through Colton. What was the point of him rearranging his life to come help his brother if the man wasn't even around? If he'd gone to the grocery store or driven himself somewhere, he certainly didn't need Colton.

"You aren't giving anything up," he muttered to himself. "Other than dealing with your jealousy." He looked out the windshield, his heartbeat settling back to normal. He loved his new niece and his new nephew. He absolutely did, and he enjoyed spending time with Wes and his family. Some of the best times in Coral Canyon happened at Gray's house in the woods, and Colton had never turned down an invitation to go there in the summer.

They'd returned to Coral Canyon for the next few months, and they had a seven-month old baby girl, who was literally the most adorable human on the planet.

Colton simply found himself wanting one of those tiny, precious, adorable humans for himself. Annie had noticed the change in him—he had a terrible time hiding anything from her as it was. She'd asked him about it, and he'd confessed his feelings to her, the same way he had Wes and Hunter last fall.

What should we do? she'd asked.

Colton had no answer for her. She didn't want another baby, and he had never had one. Her daughters were grown and married, and he completely understood why she didn't want to start over with an infant.

She had also told him that she was too old to physically

have a baby, and Colton had assured her once that he was fine with it.

But now, he wasn't sure he was. They'd been talking about becoming foster parents or even adopting. *It wouldn't need to be a baby*, he'd told her. *There are kids of all ages who need a good home.*

They'd taken no steps yet, because neither of them really knew what to do. Colton didn't even know what he wanted. Sometimes he watched Wes and Gray, and he didn't want their lives. Other times, *all* he wanted was to snuggle with his wife and child on the couch.

Basically, he was a mess.

He leaned his head back and closed his eyes. "Clear my mind, Lord," he murmured. He'd been praying for some version of having a clear vision to know what to do for some time now. The pathway before him still felt shrouded in darkness.

His phone rang, and he opened his eyes to see who it was. Annie. He tapped to connect the call. "Hey, love," he said. "I just realized I never called you when I landed."

"That's why I called."

"I'm alive. It's hot here. And guess what? Ames isn't even home."

"He's not home? Where is he?"

"I don't know. He wouldn't answer his phone."

"You don't think he's hurt again, do you?"

"I hadn't even thought of that," Colton said. "Should I go check the hospital?"

"You can call, at least," Annie said.

"I'll do that as soon as I hang up here," he said.

"I have some news."

Colton forced himself to take an extra moment to take a breath. "Oh? Good or bad?"

"Good," she said, and he could hear the smile in her voice. It made him smile—as did his whole life with Annie. He'd told her over and over that his unrest had nothing to do with her. She was enough for him.

"All right," he drawled. "Lay it on me, hon."

"Emily is pregnant." She squealed, and a loud laugh came through the line afterward.

"That's great," Colton said, and he meant it. Annie had wanted to be a grandmother since the day her oldest daughter had said I-do.

"She's not due for six more months," Annie said. "But they're moving back here, Colt. I'm so happy."

"I'm happy you're happy," he said.

"And you know," she said. "Maybe this is the way you'll get to hold that baby you want."

Colton straightened and looked out the windshield, that clarity he'd been seeking illuminating his mind one degree at a time. "You know what? I think you might be right."

Annie said nothing, and motion behind Colton caught his eye. Ames pulled into the driveway. "Tell her congrats from me, sweetheart. I have to go. Ames just pulled in."

"Okay, love you, Colt."

"I love you, too, Annie." He ended the call, turned off the car, and got out again. Ames had already gotten out of his truck too, and he seemed perfectly fine. "Why didn't you answer your phone?"

"I had it on silent," Ames said. "Sorry." He headed for the side entrance in the carport, and Colton followed him, sensing something was off. Way off.

"Where were you?"

"The park." Ames fitted the key into the lock.

"Why do you keep your house locked? You realize your biggest threat here is an elderly woman walking by."

Ames tossed him a slightly sour look and went inside the house. "I hope you weren't here long."

"Long enough to be worried—and call my wife."

"I'm fine, Colt. I told you you didn't need to come."

"I thought you were drugged." Colton closed the door behind him and paused, taking in the complete chaos that was Ames's house. "What are you doing here?"

"Renovating," he said, reaching to open the fridge.

"I can see that." He moved over to the fridge too, crowding into his brother's space. "I meant, what are you doing *here*? You don't belong here."

Ames glared at him, and they were so close in height, they practically stood nose-to-nose. "I'm a grown man."

"You're stubborn," Colton said. "And hot-headed. And unreasonable." He backed up, because Ames could sometimes come at a person swinging. He hadn't for years, but Colton didn't really want to find out how short his fuse was right now. "Oh, and I know you're not telling me something." He folded his arms and kept backing up until he touched the wall behind him, then he cocked his eyebrows as if to say, *So start talking, bro.*

"I'm in a lot of pain right now," Ames said. "I missed my mid-day dose."

"Yeah, because you were hanging out at the park," Colton said dryly as Ames shook a pill onto the counter. He put it in his mouth and lifted the bottle of water he'd gotten out of the fridge to his lips, doing everything quite well with only one hand. "Do you have a girlfriend here already?"

Ames coughed, choked, and sputtered as water came shooting out of his mouth. He flew over to the sink while Colton watched, dumbfounded. The moment his brother calmed, he said, "Oh, my holy heaven. You do."

"No," Ames barked, his back still to Colton. "I don't have a girlfriend."

"You're a bad liar."

"You should go home."

"You should come with me."

Ames turned around, fire blazing in his eyes. "I am *not* moving to Coral Canyon."

"Why not? You moved to Texas, and this is way farther from Ivory Peaks than Coral Canyon." Colton was probably the only brother who could talk to Ames like this. Cy said hard things to his twin, but Ames was head-strong and confident, and he *always* did what he wanted.

Ames's fists clenched, and then as if Colton had blown out a flame, he deflated. "Thank you for coming." He crossed the ripped up kitchen to Colton and hugged him.

Colton knew then that something was seriously wrong with his brother. Still, he hugged him tight and clapped him on the back. "Do you have a couch in this house? Let's go sit down and talk like normal people."

Ames fell back a step and nodded. He led Colton out of

the kitchen and around the corner to the living room at the front of the house. "I'm going to knock down that wall and open everything up," he said as he sat on a bright blue couch.

Colton just looked at him. He was far too big for such a tiny couch. "I have literally never seen a couch this color."

"Nice, right?" Ames grinned at the couch like they were best friends. "It came with the house. It's sixty years old. Vintage."

Colton sat on the other end of it. "Feels like it's sixty years old." He glanced to his left and saw a hallway. "Tell me the mattresses here aren't six decades old."

"I got new beds when I moved in," he said.

Colton focused back on his brother. "All right. Get talking."

"About?"

"Don't be cute with me," Colton said. He leaned back and pushed his cowboy hat forward, very nearly covering his eyes. "I know you were at the park with Sophia. Just admit it."

Ames drew in a long breath and held it. "Fine," he said in one burst of air. "I was at the park with Sophia. But it's not what you think."

"No?" Colton turned his head toward Ames and watched him in his narrow range of vision. "What is it then?"

"A cruel trick?" he guessed. "I don't know. She found me in the drugstore after I nailed my thumb to the wall. She got me to the hospital. I just went to thank her."

Colton watched his eyes drop to his lap. "Again, not a

great liar. You'd think you'd have learned something about lying from all your years with the department."

Ames lifted his eyes to Colton's, somehow finding his under the cowboy hat. "I asked her to be my date at the wedding," he said. "But only because all of you will have someone to be with. You have no idea what it's like to show up to a family function and have nowhere to belong."

Colton wanted to argue back, but he couldn't. In this case, Ames was simply right. Colton could always retreat to Annie's side. They could leave together. They arrived together. He hadn't walked in alone to a family party in years now.

"Okay," he said. "Do you like her?"

"What do you think?"

"I think you just avoided the question." Colton had a close relationship with all of his brothers. Wes had told him once that Colton was his best friend, but Colton knew Gray thought they were best friends. The fact was, he was very good at reading people, and he cared about them deeply—especially his brothers.

"What are you feeling?" Colton asked. "Is it that nothingness again?"

Ames simply nodded, his eyes back on his hands in his lap, and Colton's heart tore a little bit for him. "Hunter's doing great with the therapy," Colton said, making his voice light.

"I'm not going to therapy."

"It's not a failure," Colton said. "You're the one who

told Cy that over and over. Heck, look at him. He's doing amazing."

"Patsy has something to do with that."

"Just think," Colton said. "If you went, maybe you'd learn how to embrace what you feel, and maybe this time, you'll be able to keep Sophia in your life. Then you'll have someone like Patsy that will help you do amazing too."

Ames said nothing, and Colton's eyes grew heavy. He didn't want to sleep though. Ames had told him about Seven Sons Ranch, and how wonderful it was. He forced himself awake and got to his feet. "All right," he said, extending his hand to Ames. "Let's go."

"Go where?"

"You can show me the ranch, and then take me to the best restaurant in town." He grinned down at his brother. "And I'll just say this once, I swear. I won't badger you to death about it."

Ames grabbed his hand and Colton pulled him up. With their hands still clasped, Colton looked right into his brother's eyes and said, "You should consider coming to Coral Canyon for the summer. You can live with me. We'll go running in the morning, and you can go fishing with Hunter and Gray. You can see Cy's therapist—or get one of your own. You'll be closer to Sophia too. Then you can see if a relationship with her is worth relocating for. Or not."

Colton shrugged like he didn't care one way or the other. He did, though. Something in his gut gnawed at him, and he'd learned not to ignore those feelings. They usually came from the Lord, and they nagged at him until he did something about them.

"So I'm offering just this once. You don't have to decide until we leave for the airport on Sunday. Come stay with me and Annie for the summer. If things go well, great. If not, you can come right back here to this blue couch. No harm, no foul."

"I'll think about it," Ames said, and Colton couldn't ask for more than that.

CHAPTER 7

Ames let Colton lift his suitcase into the back of the
rental car. He could use his left hand to do it, but
Colton had come to help, and he seemed to genuinely
want to. He'd woken the day before to find Colton in the
kitchen with a bag of bagels and far too much cream
cheese to go with them.

They'd gone to Middlestreet Barbecue for lunch, and
Colton hadn't stopped talking about the sweet 'n spicy
sauce that he'd literally drenched his brisket with. He
wanted to go back today and buy a bottle to take home to
Coral Canyon.

"Do we have time to stop at that barbecue spot?" he
asked when he got behind the wheel.

"Yes," Ames said, staring straight ahead. "It's literally
on the way out of town."

"Great," Colton said, putting the car in reverse. He
either didn't hear the clip in Ames's voice or he didn't

care. Ames wasn't sure why he'd suddenly slipped into this grouchy mood. He was the one who'd announced over his second bagel that he wanted to go to Coral Canyon for the summer, and they didn't need to wait until the weekend.

He'd spent a lot of time on the phone yesterday in between all the eating—Colton could literally eat a meal and then want another one an hour later. He'd first called Jeremiah Walker and explained about the thumb injury and the need to be closer to family this summer. The man was seriously a saint, because he didn't even get the slightest bit upset. He'd said, "Let me know when you're back in town. There will always be a place for you at Seven Sons, Ames."

That had made him feel good. He did know how to work hard, and it was nice to be validated. He'd then called Skyler Walker, who had admired his motorcycle on several occasions. Another explanation of the situation, and that he didn't want to leave his expensive, custom bike in a carport without anyone living in the house.

He'd come last night to take the bike out to the ranch. "I will take such good care of it," Skyler had said. "Thank you, Ames." He'd hugged Ames, and he'd oscillated again. At the same time, he'd heard and felt the truth and power in Colton's voice when he'd asked him what he was doing here.

Ames had been wondering that himself. Maybe he did belong in Coral Canyon. Maybe he should go back to Ivory Peaks. He wasn't sure, but he felt confident this summer would shed some light on the situation. It had to, because he couldn't keep living in this limbo for much longer.

"How often is Jenn going to come take care of the house?"

"Every week," Ames said. "She'll check on the water, the air conditioner, and take care of the lawn." He looked out the window on his side of the car, frustration still his dominant emotion. He wished he could feel sad about leaving Three Rivers behind, but he didn't. He didn't know what that meant.

He stayed in the car while Colton went in Middlestreet to get his barbecue sauce, and he was grateful when his brother let him stay silent on the way to Amarillo. The flight from Texas to Wyoming happened quickly, and before he knew it, he was walking outside to the view of the majestic Teton Mountain Range.

The thing that had been teeming inside him quieted instantly, and Ames couldn't ignore that anymore. He let Colton get their luggage, let Colton load the truck, let Colton drive through somewhere for lunch.

They had another hour-long drive ahead of them from Jackson Hole to Coral Canyon, and Ames should've known his brother wouldn't give him another sixty minutes of broody silence.

"Annie's daughter is pregnant," he said.

"That's great," Ames said, and he sounded cheerful. Deep down, though, he didn't care about Annie's daughter. He did care about his brother though, and he looked at Colt. "You're going to love that baby, aren't you?"

"I want a baby of my own," Colton said, shifting in his seat.

Ames didn't quite know what to say, because he hadn't known that about his brother. "You'd be a great dad," he said.

"Thank you," Colton said, glancing at Ames. "What about you? Do you want kids?"

"Yes," Ames said. "Maybe. I don't know." He looked out the window again. "I can't answer questions right now, Colt. I'm literally lost."

"I'm sorry, brother," Colton said quietly. "I won't ask you any more questions."

"Just not hard ones," he said. "I can handle stuff like what do you want for lunch? or how many miles should we run today?"

"How many miles do you run?"

"Usually not more than five," he said. "I just do it to get rid of some of the negative emotions building up inside me. I'm not trying to stay fit or lose weight or run a marathon."

"Negative emotions," Colton mused. "Interesting."

"Why do you run?"

"Gotta keep up my stunning physique," he said, a wide grin on his face.

Ames burst out laughing, and his spirit soared with the sound of it as it moved through him and came out his mouth. He hadn't laughed like this in a long, long time. This alone was worth being in the company of his family.

The ride was much more comfortable after that, and Colton jabbered about Wes and Bree and the backyard project at their place. "He's forgotten how old he is," Colt said, shaking his head. "And Bree's about to have another baby, and there's no way Wes is finishing that yard himself."

"He doesn't even need to," Ames said. "What? He doesn't have enough money to pay someone to do it?"

"Right?" Colton laughed and shook his head. "Hunter comes to stay with us sometimes. Boy, do I love that kid."

"He's a good kid," Ames said. "I wonder what he does with his girlfriend over the summer." He'd have to ask his nephew when he saw him next.

"Are you going to take advice from a fourteen-year-old?" Colton asked.

"Hey, he's had more luck with the girls than I have," Ames said.

Colton laughed again. "I think Molly is coming for a couple of weeks this summer."

"You're kidding." Ames looked at Colton. "Is she staying with them?"

"I think so," Colt said with a shrug. "Gray mentioned something about it, but we didn't talk long, because Jane started screaming after that. She'd been sick, and Elise was in town getting medicine, so Gray had to go."

"Fascinating." Ames didn't understand relationships these days. His parents would've never let his girlfriend come on a family trip. He couldn't believe Molly's parents were okay with it.

They arrived at Colton's house, and Ames managed to take in one of his own suitcases. He'd stayed in the guest room at the top of the stairs several times, and he got set up in there again. When he came downstairs, the scent of marinara filled the house, and he found Annie in the kitchen stirring something.

"Hey, Ames," she said over her shoulder. She left the stove and approached him. She gave him a hug, and Ames didn't know what to do with it. "Thanks for coming. Colton is thrilled to have you. We both are." She smiled at him warmly, but Ames had heard something in her voice.

He glanced around, looking for Colton. "How is Colt?" he asked. "He seems…a bit off."

"Oh, he's okay," Annie said lightly, turning back to the kitchen. "We're dealing with some things. We'll be all right."

Ames watched her, and she seemed to really believe that they'd be all right in the end. Ames wanted to believe that too.

"Dinner will be ready in about ten minutes," she said over her shoulder.

"Thank you," he said. Ten minutes. Just enough time to text Sophia and find out where she was. She'd left Three Rivers today too, but she, Marcy, Wyatt, and the three boys were driving. They were stopping in Fort Collins tonight, and he'd said he'd check in with her.

He went out onto the front porch and sat on the bench there. He sent her a quick text that said, *How's the day been? Have you stopped yet?*

She didn't answer immediately, and he told her that he'd been in Coral Canyon for a couple of hours, and then he added, *I sure do like it here.*

Checking in now, she texted back. *I'll call you in a few minutes.*

He may not have spoken to Sophia much over the past ten months, but he'd heard her say "a few minutes" before, and it was never just a few minutes. She'd call in a half an hour, if then. Probably more like an hour.

He gazed out across the front yard and took in the neighborhood. He allowed himself to envision himself living here, maybe even on this street. To his surprise, he could see it clearly in his mind.

He drew a breath, and everything he'd been fighting against finally settled.

———

A COUPLE OF DAYS LATER, AMES RAN WITH COLTON IN THE morning. He fished with Hunter and Gray before lunch. He took sandwiches to the park and met Wes, Bree, and Michael. By afternoon, he was peopled out. He retreated to the bedroom on the second floor and lost a couple of hours to social media.

He'd kept in touch with Sophia, and he knew she wasn't working tonight. Cy was busy with Patsy getting ready for their wedding in just two days, and Ames decided he couldn't spend another minute staring at a screen.

He went downstairs, but the house was still empty. Annie ran her own housekeeping business, and Colton worked in the lab on Fridays. It was easy for Ames to slip out of the house without having to explain himself to anyone, and he made the drive up the canyon to Whiskey Mountain Lodge in under thirty minutes.

The parking lot held more cars than he'd seen before, and he supposed summertime would be busy at this luxury lodge nestled in the most beautiful canyon on the planet.

He took a spot far from the entrance of the lodge but closer to the cabin where Sophia lived. It sat in the back corner of the yard, and Ames had found it cozy and charming when he'd been there last.

Emerald green grass shone all around it, and Sophia had put bulbs in the ground last fall. He'd been there while she'd done it. The daffodils and tulips had grown properly, and the red and yellow pops of color surrounding the cabin brought him a healthy dose of cheer.

He went up the steps and knocked, but he didn't expect her to open the door. He hadn't seen her car in the parking lot, and he assumed she hadn't made it home yet.

Sure enough, no one answered the door, so he turned around and settled on the top step to wait. The wind whispered through the trees, and with the sunshine making everything glow with golden light, Ames experienced a sense of peace he hadn't before, probably ever.

He wanted to bottle this feeling and open the lid every time he started to get stressed. "So I guess I need to be here, is that what You're telling me?" He looked up under the brim of the cowboy hat Colton had loaned him until he could get his own.

The heavens didn't open, and Ames hadn't expected them to. He'd never been able to hear the voice of the Lord very well, and getting promptings and feelings didn't seem to happen for him.

"Maybe I should start seeing a counselor," he said to himself. He'd never thought of himself as broken, the way Cy had, and he didn't have trauma in his past the way Hunter had. He simply wasn't an overly emotional man. That didn't mean he was a terrible person.

It did make dating and relationships harder. "Help me to simply work harder at it," he said turned toward the parking lot, wondering how long he should wait to see Sophia.

CHAPTER 8

S ophia hugged Warren tight, her heart expanding as the four-year-old clutched at her neck. "You be good now," she said to him, pulling back and touching her forehead to his. "No crying when your daddy asks you to pick up the toys. It's not that hard."

"Okay, Sophie," he said, and she grinned at him.

"Just sing that song I taught you." She straightened and nudged him back to Marcy. He went, and the other woman picked him up and hugged him too. He really was a sweet little boy. He was simply four, and head-strong—just like both of his parents.

She grinned at Marcy and said, "I'll see you on Monday."

"We'll be at the wedding, too," Marcy said, returning the smile. "Thank you, Sophia."

"Oh, right. The wedding." She hadn't forgotten about that. Oh, no, she had not. She'd simply forgotten that the

Walkers were part of the Hammonds now. They were a lot like the Whittakers in that regard—taking in anyone who allowed them to.

She wondered why she was so resistant to being welcomed to their family, but she literally refused to dwell on it. She'd spent so much time thinking about Ames Hammond that she couldn't obsess over his family too.

She stepped out the front door of the immaculate mountain home that Wyatt and Marcy had purchased and moved into a couple of days ago. They'd driven Wyatt's truck from Three Rivers, Texas, to Coral Canyon, with a trailer attached with everything they needed to survive for the first few weeks.

Marcy and Sophia had spent the last couple of days getting the boys' rooms set up and ordering furniture, rugs, curtains, and other household items.

Wyatt had spent that time looking at and ultimately buying toys. He'd bought two four-wheelers, a boat, and even a little side-by-side for the boys. He'd started teaching Warren how to drive it, and Sophia had never seen anything like a four-year-old motoring around the mountain in a vehicle by himself.

She'd never met anyone like the Walkers at all. They were so far away from her reality that everything they did surprised her. Marcy didn't even look at prices. If she liked something, she bought it. No haggling. No back and forth about whether she should go with something cheaper. Nothing.

Wyatt had called Marcy at least a dozen times while he'd been at the outdoor adventure shop in town to get her opinion on things, and Sophia liked that. They were a functional couple, with a family they were doing their best to raise.

Sophia had never truly experienced that either. Her father had been in the military when she was growing up, and she'd barely known him. He was gone all the time, and her mother ran a tight ship. She'd clipped coupons and refused to let her children do anything after school until they'd done their household chores and their homework.

Sophia had thrived under the rigidity of her upbringing, but her two brothers had not.

Both Ryan and Keith had left home the day after their high school graduations, and neither had gone into the military the way their father had hoped.

Sophia's mother had started complaining about her husband in Sophia's senior year of high school. They both ended up leaving the house the next summer, and Sophia now had four separate cells of people she tried to interact with.

The Cooke family did not get together for holidays. They didn't have family video calls the way she'd seen the Walkers do. Wyatt would gather his whole family around the computer to talk to his parents, and most of the time they were out at Seven Sons Ranch, so Skyler, Micah, and Jeremiah participated in the call. They all lived on the ranch property, in separate residences.

In the two weeks Sophia had spent in Three Rivers, sorting through clothes and closets with Marcy as they anticipated what they'd need for the summer—and what they'd need for an entirely new residence—Sophia had been out to Seven Sons more than once.

It was definitely a place like Whiskey Mountain Lodge, where everyone seemed to gather without a formal invitation.

She didn't mind the crowds, but she craved the tranquility and silence of her tiny cabin on the edge of the woods too. She still lived alone, and Graham Whittaker had said that would probably stay that way. They'd hired a gardening service instead of a full-time employee, and the cabin was so small....

Sophia hadn't minded the smallness of the cabin when she shared with Patsy. She and Patsy had become close quickly, as Patsy dealt with a tough family situation too, and one of their first encounters had been when Sophia had arrived at the lodge only to overhear Patsy arguing with her sister.

"Sorry," she'd said with a sigh. "My sister thinks she was the one who created the heavens and earth in only six days."

Sophia had gaped at her for about two seconds before she'd burst out laughing. "I have a father and a brother like that," she'd said, and they'd both giggled.

Patsy sat on the steps of the cabin, and Sophia had sank down beside her. That was it. They'd bonded instantly, and if Sophia let herself dwell too long on the absence of her best friend, she did not have a good day.

In her car, she drew a deep breath and released it. She was happy for Patsy. Thrilled, even. She'd found a wonderful man to love, and Cy adored her with his whole soul. He'd take good care of her, and that was all Patsy had ever wanted. That, and her orchard. After some rough times down a dark road, she'd gotten both.

Hope and faith filled Sophia. She wanted a good man to love her and adore her and take care of her too. She didn't have a family legacy like an orchard she wanted, but she did want to feel important and needed.

She knew the Whittakers loved and appreciated her. But she also knew Celia would always be "the chef" at the lodge.

Marcy and Wyatt treated her like gold, and Sophia could admit that had a lot to do with her decision to pull back at the lodge and nanny for them four days a week.

The moment she turned into the parking lot at the lodge, she saw the big, black truck. Her heartbeat started to race, and she peered through her windshield like Ames would be striding toward her across the asphalt.

She didn't see him, and irritation threaded through her at her excitement to see the man. They had enjoyed a fairly decent lunch in the park earlier in the week. He'd been on his best behavior, Sophia knew. She could see it wear him down as time went on, almost as if it required such a great effort from him to speak in a softer tone and put a smile on his face instead of a frown.

He still accelerated her pulse in a way no one else ever had, and she pulled in to park next to his truck.

She hoped he wasn't expecting to be entertained, because she was exhausted. He'd come over before after a long day of her cooking at the lodge, and she'd enjoyed his company in the small cabin then.

She collected her bag, which had grown in size since she'd started spending time with children who needed distractions and sippy cups and snacks, and got out of the car.

The air was crisp and fresh, and Sophia was reminded of why she lived in and loved Coral Canyon, Wyoming. Why she didn't want to leave. Why she felt like she belonged here.

"Thank you for a good day," she murmured as she started down the skinny sidewalk that led to the cabin. "Thank you for a safe trip from Texas." She caught sight of Ames's cowboy hat above the railing on the steps, his head bent down as he looked at something, probably his phone. "Thank you for this man on my front steps."

She shook her hair over her shoulders, wondering why she hadn't colored it yet. She hated the nondescript color of it, and Patsy had told her she should pick a color and go with it. Sophia had liked that idea, but she hadn't been able to decide if she should go lighter or darker.

"Hey," she said as she arrived at the bottom of the steps. "Are you lost, cowboy?" She grinned as Ames lifted his head and their eyes met.

He smiled too, and he was devastatingly handsome. How he hadn't found someone to be his wife was a complete mystery to Sophia, and she started up the steps toward him.

She groaned and sighed as she sat next to him. "Been here long?"

"A little while," he said.

"I didn't get a text or call," she said. Not that it

would've mattered. She worked for Marcy and Wyatt until six on Fridays.

"I didn't text or call."

She didn't want to dance with him tonight. She pressed her shoulder into his bicep and laid her head against his shoulder. "It's good to see you here."

"Yeah?"

"Yeah," she said. "A sight for sore eyes." She reached over and took his hand in hers. "You want to come in? I've been out of town, and the place is a mess, but I probably have something in the freezer I can heat up for dinner."

He squeezed her hand. "Too tired to go to dinner with me? Then you won't have to cook."

That sounded appealing too. Sophia couldn't decide if she'd rather spend a quiet evening in with him or go on a date.

"You choose," she said.

He looked at her, his chin tilted way down to see her. "I don't want to share you with anyone tonight." He started to stand, and Sophia let him pull her to her feet too. "If you point me in the right direction, I can get the food heated up."

"Okay," she said. He'd done that before while she'd showered the day off her skin and changed into a set of more comfortable clothes.

She went inside, and the cabin still harbored a musty smell from the time she'd been gone. "Could you open a window too?"

"Sure." He did while she put her purse on the small

table outside the kitchen where she and Patsy had kept their keys and mail.

"I wanted to ask you about the dog fostering you do," he said as he joined her in the kitchen.

She glanced at him, pulling her attention from the labeled containers in the freezer. "Yeah, sure. But do you feel like pulled pork or chicken enchiladas?"

"Pulled pork," he said, and he leaned against the counter beside the fridge.

Sophia pulled the plastic container out of the freezer and handed it to him. "Thaw that in the microwave. There are some rolls in here too…." She pulled them out and put them on the counter behind her.

Ames hadn't moved, and when their eyes met again, life on Earth could've ended, and Sophia wouldn't have known.

He'd captured her completely, and she felt the barriers she'd put between them start to collapse. She wasn't sure what she was doing by allowing him to break down every-thing she'd built. All she knew was she was tired of trying to keep him in a place she couldn't get to.

He reached past her and set the container of pulled pork on the counter beside the rolls. "I've missed you," he whispered, gathering her into his arms. They breathed out together, and Sophia felt things shift in her life again.

She wanted Ames Hammond, and she'd never admitted that to herself before.

How far are you willing to go to be with him? she asked herself. She didn't have an answer to that question, and within the safety and warmth of Ames's arms, she didn't need one. She simply clung to this moment and the way he made her feel worthwhile, beautiful, and when he breathed in her hair and sighed, she felt cherished.

No one had ever made her feel like that before, and a door in Sophia's heart opened that she'd kept steadfastly closed when it came to Ames.

CHAPTER 9

A mes thought he could stand in Sophia's kitchen with her in his arms for the rest of his life and die happy. He knew he needed to move, but Sophia didn't, so he stayed.

When her stomach growled, he stepped back. "I'll get this going," he said. "You go take care of yourself."

"All right," she said softly, and she flicked her gaze to his for half a second before turning and leaving the kitchen.

He watched her go, marveling at the way she prompted him to be a softer, kinder version of himself without saying a single thing. She had told him in the past when she'd thought he was speaking to her in a harsh tone. He'd realized then that his normal speaking voice, especially when he spoke about something he was passionate about, could come across as mean.

He'd dialed that back in the few weeks he'd spent with

her last year, and now, when faced with her, he automatically slipped into a calmer state of mind.

He turned away from the wide, arched entrance to the kitchen and got busy heating up their dinner. He couldn't stop his thoughts from revolving, and they switched from Sophia, to the therapy he'd been considering, to getting a rescue dog to occupy his time while the microwave whirred.

A tiny piece of his heart had come alive when Sophia had initiated the physical contact between them. He wasn't sure if she'd ever done that as blatantly as she just had, and Ames's pulse skipped a beat just thinking about kissing her again.

"You're an idiot," he muttered to himself. "Why didn't you call her at Christmastime?"

He felt like he'd wasted the last six months of his life. If he'd been talking to her all this time, who knew where their relationship would be?

He probably wouldn't have taken a job in Three Rivers, moved there, and bought a house. If he didn't go back—and Ames couldn't believe he was even thinking about not going back—what would he do with that house?

He'd already started demolishing it. He was in the middle—literally, the very middle—of a kitchen remodel. Who would buy a house in that state?

Hire someone to finish it, he thought. Just like he'd told Colt that Wes should just hire someone to finish his back yard, Ames could certainly afford to hire someone in Three Rivers to finish the house. List it. Sell it. Heck, he could just keep it and live there in the winter, the way Wyatt and Marcy Walker did.

"Why not?" he asked himself.

"Talking to yourself again?" Sophia asked from behind him, her words full of a tease.

Ames smiled and turned toward her. "Yes. What did you hear?"

"Just your voice." She reached for the rolls and untwisted the tie keeping the bag closed. "What were you telling yourself?"

"Nothing," he said. It was far too soon to talk to her about leaving Three Rivers. He'd just gotten there, and Ames felt like he'd made a mess of everything. Literally everything.

"Do you ever think God just lets you do what you want?" he asked, watching her for her reaction.

"What do you mean?" she asked.

"Sometimes I feel like I pray so hard for direction. I don't get it, so I end up making a decision and acting." His parents had taught him to do exactly that. Whenever he had a major decision to make, he should consult with the Lord first. If there was a strong feeling or prompting to take one path over another, follow it. The Lord would never lead him astray.

If not, make a decision and act on it.

Ames had often operated from that state of mind, because he struggled to get promptings or direction from the Lord.

"And then, I find out later, I should've made a different decision. Like, why didn't God just have me do that in the first place? Seems like it would save a lot of time." Not to mention his mental energy, his money, and the way he'd started to second-guess everything he'd ever done in his life.

"Life would be easier," he said.

"I don't think that's the point," Sophia said, looking up at him.

"To make life easy?"

"Right," she said. "I think sometimes, it really *doesn't* matter what a person does, or which road they're on. It's about the journey, and learning something while you're on it."

Ames nodded, wondering what he was supposed to learn by moving to Three Rivers. Foolishness stabbed through him. He shouldn't have moved there and started that job at Seven Sons, only to leave six weeks later.

What am I supposed to learn from that? he thought, hoping his thoughts would make it through his thick skull and up to the Lord's ears.

Behind him, the microwave beeped, and he turned to get the food out. He removed the container and set it on the counter so he could put the rolls in. Sophia handed him the bag, and he got those going while he stirred the meat.

"Almost ready," he said.

"Coffee?" she asked.

"No way I can drink coffee this late in the day," he said. He could barely drink it in the morning, as Ames seemed to have plenty of pent-up energy from the moment he woke until the minute he laid down at night.

"Oh, that's right," she said. "I forgot that about you."

Ames disliked that he was forgettable, but he said nothing. He hadn't forgotten anything about Sophia, and he once again wondered why in the world he hadn't called her when he'd said he would.

He'd probably regret it for the rest of his life.

No, he told himself. "So tell me about the rescue dogs," he said out loud. "I need something to keep me busy this summer."

She smiled and sat at the small breakfast bar that could house two barstools. "They'll love you, because you won't be afraid to take the big dogs."

"I only want a big dog," Ames said.

She grinned at him, and he thought she was the most beautiful woman he'd ever seen. "It's up in Dog Valley," she said. "If you want me to go with you, I can. Introduce you to Lindsey and have her show you everything."

"You're not too busy?"

"I don't cook here on the weekends," she said. "And Marcy and Wyatt want their weekends to be just theirs. I'm off tomorrow, and I have the daytime on Wednesday to myself too."

"We could go tomorrow," he said.

"Let me text Lindsey," she said. "She might not be available, and we want her to show us everything." She pulled her phone toward her and started tapping away. "She leads the dog foster program, and she doesn't do as many tours as she used to. But if you're really interested in fostering, you'll want her to know your name and face."

"Okay," Ames said, because he trusted her. "Will she let me take more than one dog at a time?"

"Maybe," she said. "If they do, she'll be the one that has to sign off on it." She glanced at him. "She's off tomorrow. She said Wednesday would be great."

"Wednesday it is," he said, smiling at her. Silence filled the space between them, and a sense of awkwardness descended on Ames. He was entirely too old to feel this way, and he cleared his throat and turned back to the microwave just as a flash of light came from within.

"Whoa," he said, grabbing for the door to get it open and stopped. He yanked the bag of rolls out of the microwave. "This caught on fire."

He examined the bag, but he couldn't see why it would cause anything to light on fire. He turned back to the microwave, and a definite wisp of smoke lifted from the appliance.

"You can't use this anymore," he said, turning back to her. "I'll get you a new one."

"It's had some problems," she admitted.

Ames reached to unplug it while she told him he didn't need to replace her appliances. "Graham will do it," she said. "I just need to tell him."

Ames didn't want to push her into a place she didn't want to be in, so he didn't insist he go to the department store tomorrow and get her a new microwave, even if that was what he wanted to do.

He joined her at the breakfast bar and said, "Okay. So you're off tomorrow, and I don't do anything. Want to show me the best thing about Coral Canyon?"

She giggled as she finished slicing the rolls. "The best

thing about Coral Canyon? That might be hard to do in one day."

"There's more than one thing?"

"Ames," she said, a hint of exasperation in his voice. "Yes, there's more than one thing."

"Okay," he said. "I want to see them all this summer." He'd texted her the moment he'd decided to spend the summer in Coral Canyon, and neither of them had said anything about his departure date. It was months away, and as Ames enjoyed Sophia's leftover pulled pork, he actually seriously considered moving to Coral Canyon for the first time in his life.

He kept that close to his heart, though, and didn't say anything to Sophia. He enjoyed listening to her talk about Wyatt and Marcy Walker and her new adventure as a nanny. He told her how his thumb was healing and all about a woodworking class he'd learned about that took place at the community center on Tuesday and Thursday evenings.

By the time he wrapped Sophia in another hug, the sun had long since set and Colt had called him twice. "I'll see you tomorrow morning," he said, forcing himself to back up without kissing her. His eyes dropped to those perfect lips, but he'd already decided not to kiss her right up front.

They'd done that last time—something she'd initiated —and while Ames had liked it, he wanted more time to think through his actions and what path they put him on.

"See you." Sophia curled her fingers around the door just above her head and smiled him out of the cabin.

He went, pushing his cowboy hat lower on his head as

he turned to go down the stairs. He wanted a longer relationship with her this time, and that meant he had to take her out and really get to know her better before he got to kiss her.

———

THE FOLLOWING MORNING, AMES WENT DOWNSTAIRS TO Colton's kitchen to find him and Annie sitting at the table, a couple of file folders open in front of them.

Colton said something in a low voice that Ames couldn't decipher, and then he turned toward Ames. "Morning," he said, his voice a false chipper version of his normal tone. "What time did you finally get home?"

"I texted you when I left the lodge," Ames said. "I got back thirty minutes after that."

"I didn't get your text until this morning."

"Yeah, because you're an old man now and need to be in bed by nine-thirty," Ames teased him. He bypassed the coffee, his nerves buzzing from the text Sophia had sent five minutes ago.

On my way to you. Do you have water shoes?

No, he'd said.

We'll stop at the sporting goods store. Swimming trunks?

Back home, he'd said.

Bring a towel, she'd said, and he'd confirmed, but she hadn't responded.

"What are you smiling about?" Annie asked.

"Sophia," Colton said before Ames could answer. "You're seeing her today, right?"

"Yes," Ames admitted. "And no, I didn't kiss her last night," he added in a hurry when Colt opened his mouth again.

"Wow, kissing already," Annie said, lifting her mug to her lips as they started to curve upward.

"I don't believe you," Colton said. He turned back to his wife. "Last time, they were kissing before he even took her out."

"*She* kissed *me* last time," Ames said.

"Yeah, I'm sure." Colton laughed.

Ames didn't correct him again. He didn't care what Colt believed. Ames knew the truth, and that was Sophia had kissed him on that hike, after he'd spoken to her for ten minutes.

His lips tingled, and he got to his feet. "Well, she's coming to pick me up, so I'm going to grab a protein shake and wait out front."

"I'll put it on your tab," Colton joked as Ames went into the kitchen. He'd offered to buy his own groceries, but Colton had said that he just needed to write down what he wanted on the pad on the fridge, and they'd get it all.

Ames took his chocolate shake out to the front porch and shook it up. A blue sky stretched before him, and in Texas, he'd be sweating already.

Here, the air held a coolness he'd only felt in Colorado in the springtime, and Ames took a big lungful of it in. As he breathed out, the overwhelming sense of gratitude that he was there, in this place he'd thought he'd never want to spend a significant amount of time in, caused emotion to grind in his throat.

"I'm willing to go where You want me to go," he said to himself. "Guide my feet. Soften my heart. *Open* my heart."

That last statement was the one Ames really needed help with, as he'd decided a long time ago that he would absolutely *not* be moving to Coral Canyon.

Sophia pulled into his driveway, her window rolling down. "Towel, Ames. You need a towel."

"Oh, right," he called to her. "Just a sec." He ducked back into the house, wondering where she was going to take him that required him to have water shoes, swimming trunks, and a towel.

He couldn't wait to find out.

CHAPTER 10

C y Hammond paced up and down the sidewalk in front of his house while Blue Velvet barked somewhere in the orchards that stretched in front of him.

"Come on," he called to the dog, but Blue would just ignore him. He needed to get his anxiety out before Ames showed up, though, so Cy walked back toward the trees and turned around again.

His twin had been in town for a few days, but Cy hadn't seen him yet. He and Patsy had been so busy getting all the last-minute details of their wedding together that Cy had only managed to text Ames.

"Today," he said to himself as his pit bull came galloping toward him. He was getting married today.

He'd been at the orchard until almost midnight last night, helping Patsy get the lights hung in the trees, tying ribbons to the backs of the chairs where the audience would sit, and setting up tables where the buffet would be.

The entire event was taking place at Foxhill Farm, in Patsy's favorite section of the orchard that was a couple hundred yards south of the main entrance and farmhouse that sat on the property.

The wedding felt huge to Cy, because the Foxhills had lived in Coral Canyon for many generations. A lot of people from town had been invited, and most of them had RSVP'ed in the positive. When they'd put in their final numbers for the food last week, Patsy had recorded three hundred and fifty placements.

Cy had invited the family that shared his last name and the family he'd built at Rev for Vets.

Patsy had invited her family, the family she'd become part of at the lodge, and anyone who knew her family from town.

A ball of emotion lodged in his throat, and if Ames didn't show up in the next five minutes, Cy was going to be late.

He couldn't be late.

Patsy's mother had arrived in town last night, and she'd gone to Jackson Hole to pick her up. Cy was meeting her that morning, and then he and Patsy would separate again, only to meet again later at the altar.

He breathed in, reminding himself that today was the hinge-point of his whole life. He wanted what was on the other side of the door, and he wanted it badly.

The sound of an engine hummed on the air, and he faced the narrow strip of land that separated his property from the more commercial parking lot he'd poured for his motorcycle shop. Three rows of apple trees that were fully leafed out prevented him from seeing much of Rev for Vets, which had been his goal.

A truck came around the corner, and relief filled Cy. He lifted his hand to wave to Ames, and he went to the other side of the drive so he'd be on the right side to get in the passenger seat.

"Come on, Blue," he said to the dog, and he opened the back passenger door so she could jump inside.

When he got in, Ames was chuckling as the pit bull tried to lick his face. Their eyes met, and Cy joined in the laughter.

"It's good to see you, brother," Ames said. "You look ready to get married."

"Do I?" Cy asked. "What does that look like anyway?"

Ames put the truck in drive and started forward again. "I don't know. You're glowing or something."

"Glowing?" Cy thought that was probably a fine sheen of sweat, because he couldn't believe he was about to do this again.

He wanted to do it, but getting married was something a person thought they'd only do once in their life. Cy was going to do it twice, and he hoped he and Patsy would be able to enjoy a long, happy life together.

"Something," Ames said, glancing at Cy.

"You have that something too," Cy said, watching Ames as he drove. "Have you texted Sophia yet?"

Ames started laughing and shook his head. "You're worse than Mom."

"You should text her." Cy didn't understand why Ames was being so stubborn about this. Since Patsy and Sophia were best friends, Cy knew when his brother didn't call Sophia over Christmas. He'd heard from Patsy that Sophia had been upset about Ames's silence. Cy had found so much happiness in Coral Canyon, with his new shop, with Patsy, and with himself. He just wanted that for Ames too.

One look at Ames, and anyone would know that he wasn't happy. He'd tried running away to Texas, but thankfully, Colton had convinced him to come to Coral Canyon for the summer.

Cy had been praying for the last few days that a summer was all Ames needed to realize how happy he could be with Sophia and with all the other brothers in this mountain valley.

"I don't need to text her," Ames said. "I'm going to see her at the wedding today."

"And then what?" Cy asked.

"I don't know," Ames said. "I'm handling it."

"Handling it?" Cy shook his head, a vein of disgust flowing through him. "Ames, she's not a criminal."

"Relax, Cy," he said. "Today is about you. It's your wedding day."

"Yeah." He looked out the window, his right hand moving to his left wrist, but he hadn't put his rubber band on today. He hadn't worn it for months now, actually, because he took his medication every day, and he'd learned other ways to bleed his anxiety out of his system.

"Are you excited?" Ames asked.

"Yes," Cy said. "You're still okay to stay at my place with Blue?"

"Yep," he said. "Thanks for letting me take care of the house and your dog."

"You're doing me the favor."

Ames chuckled, but the sound was a little darker than normal. "Trust me, you're saving me—and Colton's life."

"Colton?"

"He's definitely worse than Mom. He's always on my case about what time I get up and what time I get home at night. You'd think I was fourteen and not forty."

"You're sleeping in?" Cy asked, swinging his attention back to his brother. He'd never known Ames to get up later than the sun, other than when he worked the overnight shift on the police force.

"I get in a little late," he said, his voice a light type of forced casual. "It takes me a while to settle down, so I'm not going to bed very early. Not nine-thirty like Colt."

"Why are you getting in late?" He hadn't heard of his brother getting a job or anything like that.

"Well, Sophia works during the day," Ames said. "So I can't see her until evening. I mean, I guess we spent all day together yesterday, but you know." He shrugged one shoulder, his words sinking into Cy's ears and mind slowly.

Ames gave him plenty of time to absorb what he'd said, a smile spreading across his face at a slow rate.

"You're already seeing her," Cy said, a frown pulling at his eyebrows. "Why didn't you just tell me?"

"It happened really fast," he said.

"Keep talking," Cy said. "I want all the details you can

give me in the five minutes it'll take us to get to the orchard."

"Five minutes?"

"Go," Cy said.

Ames complied, and he told Cy about Sophia finding him in the drugstore, taking him to the hospital, and going to her cabin on Friday night.

They'd gone to the watering hole yesterday, and Ames had just said, "I did the rope swing a bunch of times. Have you been?" when he pulled off the highway and the site of Cy's wedding spread before them.

Patsy's car was there, and Cy found her standing with another blonde woman near the back row of chairs they'd set up last night.

Cy swallowed, his mind being split into two trains of thought. "Good for you, Ames," he said. "I'll take my alarm off, so I don't text you about stuff you're already doing."

"That would be great," Ames said dryly.

"You should've just told me," Cy said. "Then I wouldn't have done it."

"It happened after your text on Sunday," he said. "I figured I had seven more days before you'd text again. And honestly, if you had texted tonight—your wedding night—I'd seriously be angry with you."

He pulled in next to Patsy's car, and both women turned toward the truck. Cy nodded and got out, ready to do his best to charm Patsy's mother.

"Hey," he said as he came around the front of the truck, a smile already on his face.

"Mom," Patsy said, her pretty face all lit up. Cy hoped that meant she'd enjoyed her evening and morning with her mother, someone she hadn't seen in a long time. She'd told Cy that she hadn't spoken much to her mother over the years, and their relationship was somewhat strained.

"Here he is. My fiancé, Cy Hammond." She took his hand in hers. "Cy, my mother, Edith."

"Ma'am," Cy said, reaching to take her into a hug. "That's right, I'm a hugger." He chuckled as he embraced her mother, glad when Edith gave him a healthy pat on the back.

"How was the flight?" he asked as he stepped back.

"Good," she said. "A couple of layovers, but nothing too major." She looked at Patsy, and he knew where she got the sparkling sapphire eyes. "It's so beautiful here. I've forgotten what it's like to look outside and see such huge mountains."

"I love it here," Cy said. He fell back to Patsy's side and indicated Ames. "This is my twin brother, Ames. I've got to give him all the instructions for taking care of the house, so he's tagging along this morning."

Ames shook Edith's hand, and Blue came trotting over to them after running off into the orchard for a moment. "And my dog, Blue Velvet."

Edith bent down as she spoke to Blue in a high-pitched voice women reserved for babies and pets, and Cy met Patsy's eyes. She nodded, and happiness burst through him. He'd wanted the reunion with her mother to go well, because it had happened so close to their actual wedding.

"Well, let's get to breakfast," Patsy said. "Then I have to get to the salon to get my hair and makeup done."

"Cy needs to do that too," Ames said, and everyone laughed. Patsy had actually cut his hair last night, into the perfect "wedding day" cut, and all he needed to do was change out of his jeans and motorcycle boots and into his tuxedo and cowboy hat.

Patsy had insisted he wear the cowboy hat, and Cy would do anything to make her happy. He'd gone shopping with Colt and Wes, and they'd all paid far too much for the nicest dress hats the shop in town could order.

They'd come in last week, and Cy could admit he liked the hat more than any other he'd worn in the past couple of years.

"Yes, let's go," Edith said. "Is everyone okay with Breakfast Plate?"

HOURS LATER, CY HAD GIVEN AMES THE DIRECTIONS. HE'D showered and changed into the right clothes. He'd taken the custom pair of cufflinks from his father and put them on.

All of his brothers stood in the tent with him, waiting for the signal that Patsy was ready for this shindig to begin. No one seemed as nervous as him—except for Ames.

He manned the doorway, constantly parting the drapes that hung down to check for something.

He recognized Ames on the outside, because Cy saw

him every time he looked in the mirror. But there was absolutely something different about him too.

"He seems happier, doesn't he?" Wes asked.

Cy looked at him to find him nodding toward Ames.

"I don't know," Cy said. "He still seems like the on-edge, might-go-crazy-if-this-doesn't-start-on-time police officer I'm used to."

"No way," Colton said. "He's much calmer now."

Gray turned from the fan, which he'd been standing in front of. He still ran a lot, but he wasn't currently training for a marathon, so he'd put on some bulk in his shoulders and chest.

"He's quieter," Gray said. "I know that."

"That's not hard in this crowd," Cy said. The Whittaker brothers were really loud, and with the number of chairs they'd set up for this ceremony, everything felt too loud for Cy.

Ames lifted his left hand and gestured the rest of them forward. "We're on, boys."

Wes grabbed onto Cy and said, "Love you, little brother."

Colton went next, holding Cy in a tight grip. "This is amazing. I'm so happy for you."

Gray hugged him too, saying, "You're perfect for each other."

One by one, they left the tent, and Cy caught Ames's eye. "You better go," Cy said. "You're first down the aisle."

Ames grabbed onto him, and the two clapped each other on the back. Neither said anything, because they didn't need to. They had a sense for the other, and Cy definitely knew there was something different about Ames. Different in a good way, too.

He determined he'd have to find out exactly what it was once he returned from his honeymoon, because Patsy deserved his full attention for the next couple of weeks.

Finally, it was just Cy and his father, and Cy's pulse bobbed in the back of his throat.

"You're a good man," his dad said. "I'm so proud to be your father."

"Thank you, Dad." Cy hugged him the longest, because his father had done more for him than anyone else, except maybe his mother. And Ames.

"Hug your mother when you get out there," Dad said. "She hates that I get to be in here and she doesn't." He smiled and left the tent.

Cy took one more deep breath and then he left the tent, took several long steps, and drew his mother into a hug. He bent down and hugged Grams.

Then he took his spot at the altar and turned to look down the aisle that ran through the middle of all the chairs.

He was ready for this next step of his life. Beyond ready. He just needed Patsy at his side, and he could get through anything.

CHAPTER 11

S ophia stood at the front of the line, her arm linked through Ames's. The nearness of him made her blood feel like someone had poured popping candy into her veins. He smelled amazing, like fresh air, warm cinnamon, and a forest-y element that made her want to pull him close, breathe him in, and kiss him until she couldn't think straight.

Just the scent of him caused her thoughts to scatter.

They'd had an amazing day yesterday. Utterly amazing. One of the best of her life. He'd been flirty and fun, soft and strong, adventurous and encouraging. She'd enjoyed lying on a blanket with him while the summer sun dried them off, and she'd started slipping down a steep slope of being in deep with him as they'd gone to dinner together.

He'd come up to her cabin after he'd run back to Colton's to shower, and she'd made caramel-swirl brownies and homemade vanilla bean ice cream for the two of them.

He'd groaned when he'd eaten it, and Sophia loved eliciting that response from someone—especially him.

He'd held her hand, and they'd snuggled on the couch together while they talked late into the night. But he'd once again left without kissing her, and Sophia needed to find out what that was about.

Tonight. She'd ask him tonight, after the wedding.

Her desire to kiss him seemed to double with every second that passed, and she hoped she made it down this aisle without embarrassing herself.

"He looks so happy," she murmured. "Doesn't he, Ames?"

"That he does," Ames said, his voice just as low as hers. He'd kept his wardrobe conservative this time, and he spoke to everything female in her in that dark tuxedo, with that pure black cowboy hat on his head. He looked exactly like Cy down on the other end of the aisle, except Cy wore sunshine on his face, and Sophia knew if she looked at Ames, she'd find a storm.

Finally, the music started, and Ames's arm tightened against hers. "Ready, sweetheart?" he asked.

"Yes," she said without moving her mouth, and she repositioned her bouquet as she took the first step down the aisle with Ames as her escort.

She knew a lot of the people in the audience, because the entire Whittaker clan had come. She beamed at them, and waved her flowers slightly to Averie and Chrissy, two of the older children whom she'd spent a lot of time with over the past few years.

She caught sight of Marcy and Wyatt—which wasn't hard, because Wyatt Walker was the tallest man in the crowd. "Sophie!" Warren called, and Marcy immediately shushed him. Sophia giggled quietly, and she was surprised to hear Ames doing the same thing.

They reached the end of the aisle, and he went left with her, taking her to the end of the marked area where the bridesmaids were supposed to stand.

He circled around the back of the altar and took the spot closest to the aisle. Sophia turned so she could watch her best friend walk down the aisle with her father.

Once everyone in the wedding party had taken their spot, Patsy took her first step. Each one after that seemed to take a very long time, as her father had been fighting cancer for a few years now. She seemed to be gripping his arm with everything she had to keep him upright, but the smile on her face did not slip even once.

Sophia admired Patsy on so many levels, and she drew from her strength over and over.

Ames stepped forward once Patsy's father had pressed a shaking kiss to her cheek and handed her to Cy. He escorted the older gentleman to the first row, where he sat next to Patsy's brother.

Once Ames had re-taken his spot in the wedding party, Cy nodded to the pastor, who welcomed everyone to the "happiest event happening in Coral Canyon today."

Sophia felt that joy streaming through her, filling all the empty spots inside her. Patsy deserved the whole world, and if there was anyone who could give it to her, it was Cy Hammond.

She watched her friend for the first few minutes, and then she found her gaze wandering to Ames. He didn't look at her at first, and then the next time she let her eyes dart toward him, he was looking at her—and he didn't look away.

A smile sprang to her face, but Ames didn't return it. He was always so stoic. He kept everything he felt behind a cage, and Sophia wished he could just let go and allow himself to get caught up in the magic and joy of his twin's wedding.

She lifted her eyebrows, silently asking him why he looked like a serial killer at a wedding. She broadened her smile, and Ames finally ducked his head slightly—but not before she saw the first inklings of a smile.

Ah, so his bad boy exterior could be cracked. Sophia stifled a giggle and focused on the ceremony.

Patsy had just finished reading her vows for Cy, and he turned toward her and said in that loud, Hammond voice, "Patsy, it's true that you almost ran me over when we first met. I think I may have fallen in love with you a little bit then. Every day since has been an exercise in falling, and I'm so glad and grateful you said yes into that speaker system at Whiskey Mountain Lodge."

Sophia could remember that day keenly, and she pressed one hand over her heart as a silent *aww* moved through her. Cy had always adored Patsy, and anyone with even one good eye had been able to see it.

"I can't wait to ride into the sunset with you, side-by-side on our motorcycles. Which are not horses." He chuckled. "I love you, and you've made me a better man, a better friend, and a better brother."

Sophia could not imagine anything more romantic, and the next thing she knew, Cy and Patsy were pronounced husband and wife, and she cheered along with everyone else as they sealed their union with a kiss.

The roar filled the trees, then the sky, then everywhere. Sophia basked in the good energy here, with so many good people who'd come to celebrate this day with Patsy and Cy.

She'd always wanted a big wedding too, and she'd never thought she'd get it. She wasn't even sure her family would come if she told them she was getting married.

The wedding party started to move again, and Sophia inched forward until she could loop her arm through Ames's once more and go down the aisle again. She smoothed down her pale green dress once she reached the last row of chairs and exhaled.

"That was amazing, right?" she asked Ames.

"Yes," he said, turning back to watch Cy and Patsy parade down the aisle while another round of applause went up. "Completely amazing." He started to clap too, his smile finally appearing on his face.

She stuck close to him while the event transitioned from ceremony to dinner, and then to party. She ate with him, laughed with him, and danced with him. Along the way, Sophia had never been more grateful to be at her best friend's wedding with a date.

"You were right," she told him much later that night.

Her feet hurt from all the walking and dancing in heels, but she didn't want the day to end. "It was much better being here with a date." She beamed up at him, and he gazed down at her.

She could not think of anything more romantic than a kiss under a summer, starry sky, while she wore a dress she felt beautiful in, and he wore a tuxedo with the tie loosened. He was always just one step away from perfectly polished and buttoned up just right. That was the rebellious streak in him. The bad boy he simply would not tame.

She let her eyes drift closed as she settled her cheek against his chest. They swayed together, and Sophia thought she could float away on these feather-light clouds of happiness drifting through her.

The song ended, and he said, "My feet are killing me. I've got to sit the next one out."

Sophia was about to tease him, but a commotion started, and she turned toward the deafening sound of two motors revving.

Wes sat on one motorcycle while Gray sat on another. Ames slipped his hand in hers and led her through the remaining crowd until they could see clearly.

The crowd parted, and Cy and Patsy came forward, but they'd changed their clothes. They both wore jeans and leather jackets now, and gone was Cy's cowboy hat. He'd tied a blue bandana around his head, and he carried a small saddlebag that he attached to the bike where Gray sat.

He and Patsy turned back to the crowd, both of them

wearing wide smiles. Cy held up his hand, and Gray and Wes stopped the obnoxious revving. "Thank you so much for coming," he said. "We love you, and we'll see you in two weeks."

The crowd clapped again, and Gray turned his bike over to Patsy, who climbed on as easily as breathing. Sophia didn't know how she rode a motorcycle. The machines were huge, and they scared Sophia.

Cy took charge of Wes's motorcycle, and a moment later, they left their own wedding in favor of their honeymoon.

Sophia sighed again, wondering what it would be like to go on a romantic vacation with the man she loved. She had no idea, because she'd never done anything like that.

Ames led her away from the crowds while they started gathering up their loved ones. She had no idea who would clean up and put everything away, but no one had asked her to, so she went with Ames, though he was leading her away from his truck, not toward it.

"Where are we going?" she asked, glad to be out of the fray and somewhere a little quieter.

"Are you in a hurry to get home?" he asked.

"Not really," she said, though she did have to work in the morning. "Breakfast is at eight-thirty, though. So I need to be up and at the lodge by seven-thirty to start cooking." Saying it out loud made a measure of exhaustion fill her. "And I have a forty-minute drive up the canyon from here."

"I won't keep you long," he said, and he took her straight into the orchard. The summer sky was fairly dusky, but she could still see where she was going, even under the canopy of the trees.

"Are you okay in those shoes?" he asked.

"I'm managing," she said. "You're the one who said you couldn't dance another song."

"I don't wear cowboy boots often, believe it or not."

"Even in Three Rivers?" she asked.

"I did there, sometimes," he said. "There wasn't a dress code, and I found my work boots more comfortable." He glanced at her. "Don't tell Wyatt I'm not a real cowboy." He gave her a quick grin, and Sophia laughed lightly.

"I barely see Wyatt," she said. "He and Marcy are working on a new product line this summer, and Marcy has daily calls with her team in Texas. She owns a crop-dusting business."

"Yes, I heard that when I lived there," he said.

Sophia wondered how much farther they had to go, and then, in just three steps, they reached the edge of the orchard on the other side, and the whole world opened up in front of them.

"Oh, wow," she said, her voice made of mostly air. "This is amazing." The orchard sat on the road that led to Dog Valley, and Sophia didn't realize how much elevation she'd gained. They stood up above the town of Coral Canyon, the tops of the closest houses at least a mile away. They didn't obstruct the view of the Tetons in the distance, or the glorious sunset as the last light of the day spilled over the tops of those mountains.

She pressed one hand to her heartbeat, drinking in the glory of God's creations.

"Cy told me about this place," Ames said. "He said he likes to come here to watch the sun set. Sometimes to bask in the light of the moon."

Sophia could imagine this scene under the complete cover of night. With all the houses asleep, and the deep darkness that settled over Coral Canyon when the lights went out. It would all be guarded by the silver light of the moon, and she wanted to experience it.

"Will you bring me on the next full moon?" she asked.

"Absolutely," Ames said, his voice hushed.

Sophia took another moment to truly breathe in the beauty of the place she lived, and then she focused on the beautiful man beside her. He still clutched her hand in his, but he didn't look at her. "You don't seem as happy as one might expect. Your twin brother just got married."

Ames nodded. "Trust me, I know." He spoke in that gruff, grouchy tone that told everyone to approach with caution.

"Why is that?" she asked.

"Because now I'm the only one who's *not* married," he said, his voice even harder and sharper.

Sophia had felt alone for most of her life. Left out. Left behind. Adrift. "I know exactly how you feel," she said, surveying the land before her again. She leaned her head against his bicep and curled the fingers from both hands around his single one. "But I'm here with you, and I think we had a great time together."

"We did," he murmured. He shifted, and Sophia lifted her head from his arm. They seemed to move in sync, and she turned toward him as he did the same to her. She reached up, her movement slow, as if her hand had been encased in quicksand.

Her fingers touched the brim of his cowboy hat. They pinched it and removed his hat from his head.

He gazed down on her, and she couldn't tell if he was upset or frustrated or simply looking at her.

She closed her eyes and tipped her head back slightly, her invitation for him to kiss her crystal clear.

She waited.

She sensed the very millisecond when Ames entered her personal space. She pulled in a breath, and when his lips touched hers, the flame that Sophia had kept going just for him roared into an inferno.

She raked her fingers through his hair, pressing closer to him as he kissed her like the cowboy bad boy that he was at his core. She never wanted to kiss anyone else, and the prayer that she'd never have to started on a loop in her mind.

CHAPTER 12

A mes had kissed Sophia Cooke before. Many times. None of them held this much passion, this much desire, or this much care.

She *cared* about him, and he could feel it in her touch. He'd started the kiss like an explosion, and he forced himself to slow down. She didn't seem to want to go slower, but Ames insisted.

She matched him, and though a river of excitement flowed through him, giving him a healthy buzz, he still managed to be a gentleman and pull away before he took things too far. He couldn't seem to get a proper breath, and thankfully, neither could Sophia.

He tucked her into his side and gazed out over the town of Coral Canyon again. "I think I could potentially move here one day," he whispered, afraid to give full voice to the confession.

"You do?" Sophia asked. "For real?"

"Yes," he said. He couldn't explain more right then, but he truly did feel that perhaps God had heard his prayers for the past year and He was finally going to answer them.

"Don't you get my hopes up, Ames Hammond," Sophia said. "Don't say things like that unless they're true."

He shifted his feet so he could look at her. "I won't."

"You said *potentially move here one day*," she said.

"Yes," he said.

"How far away is this 'one day'?"

"I have no idea." He sighed, because he knew he wasn't being fair to her. "I'm trying to go slower this time, Sophia. I had made up my mind before I ever came to Coral Canyon that I would never move here. It's going to take some time for that mindset to change."

She nodded, a shiver running through her. "Can we head back now, please? I'm tired, and it's getting late."

"Sure."

She moved first, and Ames got the hint by the way she huddled into her own arms as she picked her way through the orchard. She didn't want to hold his hand. He wouldn't be kissing her before she got in her sedan and drove back up the canyon.

He'd messed up—again.

You're so.... He didn't even know how to finish the thought. He wasn't stupid, and he was tired of beating himself up that way. He was inconsistent. That's what he was. And Sophia obviously didn't want a man who changed his mind about where he'd live every six weeks.

If only she knew he didn't want to be that man either.

He followed her all the way back to her car before he realized he'd left his cowboy hat on the edge of the orchard. Part of him just wanted to leave it, but Cy had spent hundreds of dollars on the matching cowboy hats for his wedding, and Ames couldn't just leave it to rot in the mud.

Sophia already had her hand on the door handle when he reached her car, and he decided to be bold by putting his hand over the seam where the door pulled away from the car. "Can you wait a second?" he asked, hearing the bite in his tone.

She looked up at him, the fire flashing in her eyes. "I suppose," she said coolly.

"Look, I obviously messed up back there," he said. "I don't know what you want me to say."

She cocked her hip and folded her arms. "I don't want you to say anything."

"That's just not true." He could fold his arms too, but he deliberately kept his hands at his sides. He didn't need to turn into the big, bad cop who huffed and puffed and ruined everything.

"No, it's one hundred percent true," she said. "Don't tell me you're going to move here unless you're absolutely, positively, without a doubt going to move here. Like, don't even start to say it until you have the truck packed and you're on the way." Her words carried plenty of frustration, and Ames thought he detected an undercurrent of hurt.

"Okay," he said. "Fair enough. I can do that." He'd just thought he could talk to her about it, but this was probably a better topic for someone like Colton, or Wes, or Gray.

His mind seized onto Gray. He'd decided to make a home in Colorado *and* Coral Canyon, and Ames wondered why he couldn't do the same. He blinked, and he was looking at the reason why. The beautiful woman in front of him would not want to leave Coral Canyon and her job at Whiskey Mountain Lodge, even for a few months out of the year.

"Thank you," Sophia said, and Ames acted out of bravery once more by embracing her. He lifted her right up off her feet, which caused her to squeal and giggle.

"Forgive me?" he asked while she wrapped her arms around the back of his neck.

"Yes," she whispered, and he set her on her feet and gave her a moment to find her balance before he released her.

"Thank you, Sophia," he said. He stepped away from her car, because he'd already shared the most amazing kiss with her, and he wanted that to be the thing he thought about as he fell asleep that night. "I left my cowboy hat out there, so I've got to go grab it. Good-night."

"Good-night, Ames," she said.

He quickly retraced his steps through the small patch of orchard, collected his hat, and hurried back to where the wedding had taken place. He was supposed to take Blue Velvet with him back to Colton's that night, and then tomorrow, he'd move over to Cy's with the dog.

The festivities had mostly been cleaned up, and Ames thought that had happened really fast. A few workers loaded up the chairs from the party rental store Cy had used, and Patsy's sister stood at the dessert table, loading the leftover cookies into plastic zipper bags.

He went that way, and as he approached, he asked, "Have you seen Cy's dog?"

Her sister—Ames could not think of her name to save his life—looked up at him. She did a double-take, which Ames was actually used to. He put a smile on his face and said, "I'm Ames, his twin. I was supposed to take his dog home with me tonight."

"I think Colton took her," the woman said.

"Thanks." Ames cursed himself for forgetting about the canine. Now he'd have to answer his nosy brother's questions—or worse, endure his teasing for how he stayed out until all hours of the night with his girlfriend.

He took his phone from his pocket and looked at it. Colton had not called or texted. It was definitely far past nine-thirty, but the wedding celebration had only ended about twenty minutes ago. He probably couldn't even get back to Colt's in that amount of time.

As he strode toward his truck, he dialed his brother.

"There you are," Colton said, clear relief in his voice. "I've called you five or six times. You just disappeared, and I was worried something had happened to you."

"I didn't get any calls," he said.

"Sometimes the service is patchy up there," Colton said. "I have Blue here with us. You're still coming here tonight, right?"

"Yes," Ames said. "Sorry, Colt. I just...." He couldn't say he'd wanted to get Sophia alone so he could kiss her, though that was exactly why he'd taken her through the orchard to the overlook. That, and he'd wanted to see it. Cy had told him about the spot at breakfast that morning with Patsy's mother, and he'd said it was a beautiful place to let go of all the stress he carried.

Ames needed to do that too, especially after watching his twin tie the knot for the second time and then ride off into the sunset—literally—with his beautiful wife.

"It's fine," Colton said. "Are you on your way back now?"

"Yes." Ames reached his truck and got behind the wheel. "I'll be there soon." He ended the call and drove a little faster than the speed limit back to his brother's house. He was constantly teased about his adherence to the speed limit, and he wanted to put on the family text that he'd gone five over the speed limit just to see what all the brothers would say.

He could hear them in his head already.

I don't believe it, Gray would say. *Did you get a picture? No picture, didn't happen.* The lawyer always wanted proof.

Wes would laugh and say, *About time, Ames. You quit the force a long time ago.* Wes acted like moving on was something that a man could achieve overnight, if he simply put his mind to it.

Colton would send a dozen cop car emojis, and he'd probably say something like, *Welcome to the dark side, Ames.* He was always a bit ahead of the technology curve, as Ames couldn't remember the last time he'd used an emoji. He honestly didn't understand them, and he thought they were pretty lame all around.

Cy would say, *I don't even know who you are anymore.* He'd be kidding, so he'd send a smiley face with all its teeth showing in the smile.

Ames wasn't sure he knew himself anymore either, and he thought about it as he took Blue outside so she could go to the bathroom. The dog then followed Sparky, Colton's dog, into the master bedroom, and Ames hesitated in the kitchen.

"Ames?" Colton called, and he turned toward the hallway on the other side of the house.

"Yep."

"She can sleep in here, if you don't care." Colton appeared at the end of the hall, already in his gym shorts and T-shirt.

"Sure," Ames said. "I don't care." He touched the brim of his cowboy hat, glad he'd gone back to get it. "I'm headed to bed. I'll be out of your hair tomorrow."

"You're not in the way," Colton said, taking a few quick steps to intercept Ames before he could reach the staircase that went upstairs. His dark eyes searched Ames's, something urgent in his expression. "Okay, Ames? You can stay here and look after Blue just as easily as you can at Cy's."

"I know," Ames said. "She'd probably be happier here too." He didn't really want to go to bed alone tonight, and he'd been looking forward to having Blue Velvet as a friend and companion.

"Take them both," Colton said.

"I'm going to get my own dog on Wednesday," he said. "Sophia and I are going up to the place where she gets her foster dogs."

"Oh, good idea," Colton said.

"What about you?" Ames asked. "Are you and Annie going to do the foster parent classes?"

Colton ran his hand up the back of his head and sighed. "I don't think so."

"She doesn't want to?"

Colton shook his head. "I don't want to. Fostering...it's not permanent."

"You want your own child."

Colton nodded. "Everything is back on hold," he said. "We just decided not to foster this morning."

Ames hugged his brother, wishing he could remove the hurt and unrest in Colton's soul. Heck, he'd love to pluck it out of his own.

"Are you going to adopt?"

"We don't know," Colton said. "Annie doesn't really want another child at all. She's almost fifty years old and has two grown daughters."

"Wes is that old."

"Wes married someone a decade younger than him," Colton said. He shook his head. "I'm fine, Ames. Don't worry about me."

Ames nodded, and the brothers parted ways. Ames brushed his teeth and put on his own pair of gym shorts. As he knelt beside his bed, his thoughts dried up.

"I just want everyone to be happy," he said. "Myself, Sophia, Colton."

With nothing left to say, Ames slid between the sheets, his mind suddenly whirring again. He noticed the difference between when he was praying and when he wasn't, and he closed his eyes and tried to focus on the Lord.

He fell asleep faster than he ever had before.

————

Ames stayed out of Sophia's way over the next couple of days. He didn't text her first but waited for her to message him. He didn't drive up the canyon to her cabin and wait on her front steps. He didn't try to see her during the day while she was with the Walkers.

He'd gone to Cy's on Monday, as planned. He'd visited the shop to see if he could get a motorcycle to ride that summer. He'd left his in Three Rivers, and the roads through the mountains here practically begged him to get out of the truck and experience Wyoming from the back of a motorcycle.

Marissa, Cy's shop manager, had told him that Cy had at least five motorcycles in the garage on his property. Ten minutes later, Ames had lifted the door on the garage to find his brother had *seven* motorcycles stored inside.

He didn't want to bother Cy on his honeymoon either, so Ames hunted around in the kitchen, opening drawers, until he found the one with all the keys in it. Grabbing them all, he returned to the detached garage and started trying keys in ignitions until he got one to start.

The bike rumbled beneath him, and Ames felt something calm and perfect move through him. This was exactly where he needed to be, and he was doing exactly what he needed to do. He aimed the bike north, the wind in his hair and his mind blissfully blank about anything that didn't have to do with riding the motorcycle.

Cy had often told him that riding a motorcycle was the only thing that settled him, and Ames understood his brother on a deeper level during his ride. He wasn't exactly sure where the dog rescue operation was up here, but he had plenty of time to ride around, and he could read street signs as well as the next person.

His thumb had healed enough to be able to manage the bike, and Ames loved the scent of the mountain air as it brushed past his face.

He and Sophia would come together tomorrow, but today, Ames parked his bike and looked around. No one came to greet him, though he could hear plenty of barking from somewhere on the property.

He couldn't seem to take the first step toward the door of the nearest building. He didn't want to be here right now. He and Sophia were coming together tomorrow.

So he got right back on the motorcycle and got out of there. He drove too fast back to Coral Canyon, and he didn't stop when he passed the orchard where he should've turned off to get to Cy's house nestled in a grove of trees.

He just kept going, turning right and heading for Jackson Hole. Maybe he could just ride and ride and ride. No one would even know that he'd left until tomorrow morning, when Sophia expected him to pick her up.

Then he remembered Blue Velvet, and he slowed to turn around and go back. He knew better than to try to outrun his problems anyway, but it sure had been freeing to try, even for a few minutes.

"If you could just give me a hint," he said, the air flowing past him almost muting his voice. "Doesn't have to be huge. I can take a hint."

In the very next moment, his phone buzzed in his back pocket. He couldn't pull it out to see who'd texted, but when he got back to Cy's place and had put the motorcycle back in its rightful spot, he remembered his phone.

"Sophia," he said, remembering exactly when this text had come in—right after he'd asked the Lord for a hint and promised Him that he could take it. He spun toward the house, the word, "Blue," coming from his mouth.

He jogged toward the back door and yanked it open. "Blue," he said again as the dog spilled outside. "Come on. Hurry up and take care of your business. Then we're going up to the lodge to see Sophia."

CHAPTER 13

Bree fought back the tears as she listened to Wes's line ring and ring and ring. "Why isn't he answering?" she asked, the first tear sliding down her face. She swiped at it, because she was tougher than the pain searing its way through her shoulder.

Echoes of it moved into her back, and panic struck her in the chest. If she'd hurt the baby because she'd stumbled down the last few steps, she'd never forgive herself. She'd gone upstairs to get the blanket she'd taken with her last night, when she'd gone to lay with Michael.

She and Wes were trying to transition him from his crib to a toddler bed, and his adventurous spirit wouldn't allow him to go to bed and stay there. He'd been coming downstairs every ten minutes in the past week, and Bree was exhausted.

She ended the call when her husband's voice came on the recording. She tried Gray next, as she'd called Wes three times now without getting him. Maybe he'd left his phone somewhere, as he did sometimes. Gray never went anywhere without his, and Bree drew in a deep breath and held it as the line sat there, silent.

When it didn't ring, she pulled the phone from her ear and looked at it. Gray's smiling face sat there, along with his name, but the call hadn't connected. Desperation choked her, and a sob rolled through her chest. She tried to swallow it but failed, and a fresh wave of tears rolled down her face.

She paused and took breath after breath, trying to calm herself. "You're okay," she said, putting her hand on her stomach. She was five months pregnant, so there was definitely a belly for her to rest her hands on. She wished she could feel the baby's heartbeat through the layers of her skin and muscles.

The baby had started kicking and moving recently, and she pressed her eyes closed and whispered, "Let him kick. Please, Lord, don't let him be hurt."

She and Wes hadn't learned the sex of the baby yet, but Bree still used the male pronouns for some reason.

The baby did not kick.

She tried to lift her right arm, and a sharp, slicing pain shocked her. She gasped, and she knew she needed help. She'd slipped on the steps, and when she'd come to a stop, her right arm was still up a few stairs, her shoulder rotated way too far. Her right leg was at the bottom of the steps, and she'd strained the muscle that ran up her shinbone. Her left leg was still on the fourth step, and she didn't normally stretch her legs in that way.

She'd sat on the steps for a moment, the blanket tangled around her, to catch her breath. Then she'd gotten up and limped to the couch, where she'd been trying to get in touch with Wes for ten minutes.

"Elise," she said, and she tapped to get her friend's number on the screen. She watched the screen, relieved when the call connected and the line started ringing. But she didn't answer either, and Bree's whole face squinched up as she let herself cry fully now.

Wes had taken Michael to Gray and Elise's for the night, because Bree just wanted to lay in bed and sleep, and he was so kind and mindful of her mental and physical health. They might have been in Gray's basement, and because his house sat halfway up the mountain, the service wasn't great.

Colton only lived a couple of miles away, but Bree hesitated to get him on the line. He and Annie were dealing with their family issues, and Bree knew Colton wanted kids of his own, and Annie was done having babies. The last thing she wanted to do was rub her pregnancy in Colton's face.

He was one of her best friends, and she could not stand to hurt him.

Her baby still hadn't moved, and though Bree hadn't landed on her stomach at all, she had practically done the splits, and she'd stretched some things down there that she didn't normally stretch. She wanted to go to the hospital and make sure she was okay, and that the baby was okay.

She couldn't get in touch with Wes, Gray, or Elise, and she wouldn't call Colton or Annie. "Ames," she said, her mind seizing onto another Hammond who'd recently come to Coral Canyon.

She got his number pulled up, and she tapped on the green phone icon, glad when the line started ringing immediately.

"Bree?" Ames asked, his voice far away and slightly tinny. "What's going on?"

"I'm so sorry, Ames," she said, her tears starting anew. "I need help, and I can't get a hold of Wes or Gray or Elise."

"Are you at home?" he asked.

"Yes."

"I'll be there in a few minutes. I'm already in the truck on the way to town."

"Are you sure? Where are you going?"

"To your house," he said. "Be there soon." He ended the call before Bree could protest again.

She wiped her face, trying to erase the evidence of her pain and stress. Using her right hand, she tried to lift her left hand above her head, but she couldn't do it as pain ripped down to the very tips of her fingers, down her side and across her ribs, and spread through her back.

Ames hadn't even asked what kind of help she needed. He'd just come, and Bree leaned back, the pressure from the couch against her back easing some of the pain. She tried not to move her left hand, elbow, arm, or shoulder at all, because she'd hurt herself badly there. She couldn't pretend like she hadn't.

She tried Wes again, but his phone didn't even ring

before the voicemail picked up. He was definitely some-where without service.

A knock sounded on the door, and almost immediately after that, Ames called, "Bree?"

"I'm right here," she said, pushing herself up with her good arm. She heard his footsteps behind her, and then he was there. "I slipped on the steps, and I hurt my shoulder." Her leg, her ankle, and maybe the baby wasn't okay. But Bree couldn't say any of that as more emotion choked in her throat.

A slip of embarrassment moved through her, because she was unshowered, without makeup, and wearing a pair of black leggings with an oversized T-shirt. "I need you to take me to the hospital."

Ames pushed the coffee table out of the way and knelt in front of her. "You think it's that bad?"

Bree nodded. "It's that bad, Ames. I can't move my shoulder at all. I think I dislocated it." She wiped her face with her right hand. "And I sort of did the splits, and I want the doctor to check on the baby."

Ames's eyes immediately came to hers. "You're pregnant?"

She nodded, her eyes filling with tears again. "I'm sorry to take you from wherever you were going."

"Don't," he said, standing. "It's nothing. I'm doing nothing." He put both hands under her right arm and helped her stand. "Can you walk? Do I need to carry you?"

"I can walk," she said, because this was embarrassing enough. If he were Wes, she wouldn't feel so self-conscious, and she told herself that Ames didn't care what she was wearing or how she looked. He cared about her too.

He helped her into his truck, and he took her to the hospital. Along the way, he tried Wes twice, with no success. "What the heck are they doing?" he grumbled. "I'll send Colt up there."

"You don't—"

"Your husband should be here," Ames said, giving her a look out of the corner of his eye. "Call Colton."

The truck dialed Colton, who picked up with a, "What's up, bro?"

"I'm in the truck with Bree," Ames said. "She fell, and I'm taking her to the hospital. We can't get in touch with Wes or Gray or Elise. She said Wes took Michael to Gray's, and they're probably in the basement watching a movie."

"I'm already heading out the door," Colton said. "Is she okay?"

Bree glanced at Ames, and he told her story to Colton. "We're almost there, and I'm taking her to emergency," Ames said.

"Okay," Colton said. "Bree, my best friend on the planet. You hang in there, okay?" His voice pitched up and caused Bree's face to tense up again as she tried to hold back her tears.

"Thank you, Colt," she said, not caring that her tears were evident in her voice. "Tell Wes I'm okay. There's nothing life-threatening." She felt Ames's eyes on the side of her face, but she didn't say anything else.

"Keep me updated," Colton said.

"Will do." Ames turned into the hospital parking lot

and ended the call at the same time. "You're more worried about your baby than you let him know."

"You told him I wanted the baby to be checked," she said, pulling in a long breath to try to calm herself. She was about to go into public, and she didn't want to be a blubbering mess. "We haven't told anyone about the baby."

"News is out now," Ames said. "Congrats, by the way."

"Don't congratulate me." Bree sobbed and shook her head. "What if I lose the baby?" She looked at Ames as he pulled into the circular driveway in front of the emergency room door.

Ames jumped out of the truck and ran around the front. He opened her door and crowded into the space there. He looked her right in the eye and said, "You're not going to lose this baby. Okay?" He wiped her face for her and added, "Let's do what Colt said, all right? Let's hang in there and not worry about what-ifs until we have facts."

He stepped back and let her slide out of the truck. She cried out as her shoulder got jostled and a flash of pain moved through her entire left side.

"I can get a wheelchair," he said.

"I'm okay." She gasped and panted, but she managed to get inside on her own.

Ames took charge then, and together, she got checked in, and because it wasn't very busy, she was taken back almost the moment the nurse finished putting her information into the computer.

"What's your pain level?" the nurse asked as she took her back.

"My shoulder is at a ten," Bree said. "But I'm most worried about the baby."

"We'll get everything checked," the nurse promised as she led Bree into a little room. Ames was right there with her, and he helped her get up on the table. By the time she was situated, another nurse had entered the room. He put a clip on her finger to check her pulse while the woman that had walked back with them started talking about the painkillers they needed for the IV drip.

"I'm Phil," the man said. "Let's get this up, and get you to lie back. Then we can listen for your baby's heartbeat."

"Our doctor tonight is Doctor Banks," the woman said. "I'm Jennika, and Phil and I will be with you tonight. I'm just going to get this IV in." She did that, and then Bree let them both help her slide up on the table as Phil made it more into a bed.

"I don't want strong drugs," Bree said.

"We've got acetaminophen," Jennika said. "I'll give you a low dose."

Bree nodded and breathed in through her nose.

Phil and Jennika left, and she looked toward Ames, who'd somehow made himself invisible and small against the wall. He came forward and took her hand. "It's okay, Bree," he said. "It's going to be okay."

She nodded and gripped his hand with all the strength she could muster, because she wanted him to be right so badly. "Will you pray for me?"

"Absolutely." Ames swiped off his cowboy hat and pressed it to his chest. "Dear Lord, we ask Thee to comfort Bree. She's in pain and scared and worried, and if possible, please help her to be calm and to accept Thy will. Bless her baby that he'll be okay, and please bless Wes and Gray and Elise to get here soon and safely." He paused, and several seconds later, he said, "Amen."

Bree kept her eyes closed as she said, "Amen," too, and felt a drape of comfort and calmness come over her. "Thanks, Ames."

"Of course," he whispered, and while he put on a tough front and was definitely the most mysterious of the Hammond brothers, he was exactly like them in a lot of ways. He loved the Lord, and he had faith. He worked hard, and he cared about his family. She was sure she'd pulled him from Sophia that night, and she'd have to apologize to her friend too.

Phil returned, and he said, "I'm just putting the acetaminophen in now, Bree. You okay?"

"Yes," she said. "When will the doctor be in?"

"She's just finishing up with another patient," Phil said, and Bree nodded. It still took ten more minutes before the dark-haired woman wearing a white coat came in, and she actually wore a smile.

Bree was annoyed instantly, and she knew that was due to her pain and worry. Still, she couldn't get herself to smile back.

"You're pregnant?" she asked, looking down at the clipboard in her hands with Phil and Jennika crowded into the room too.

"Yes," Bree said. "Five months."

"How many weeks?"

"Twenty-one," Bree said.

She set the clipboard down as she said, "I'm Doctor Banks, and let's see if we can hear this baby's heartbeat." She glanced at Ames. "Are you the dad?"

"No," he said quickly. "I'm the brother-in-law. The dad is on his way."

Dr. Banks looked at Bree. "He's okay to be here?"

"Absolutely," Bree said.

The doctor smiled again, and she unlooped her stethoscope from around her neck. She put the appropriate pieces in her ears and Bree pulled up her shirt. She definitely had a baby bump there, and a flash of love for her unborn child filled her.

Dr. Banks put her stethoscope on Bree's stomach, and the chill of it made her flinch. She smiled and focused on something on the floor. She moved the stethoscope around for couple of seconds, and then she grinned. "Good news, Bree. Your baby's heartbeat is strong and steady."

"Really?" Bree's relief made her sigh, but it took a few seconds for her to process what the doctor had said. "He's okay?"

"Perfectly okay," the doctor said.

"What if there's another complication?" Ames asked, glancing at Bree. "Some other issue that wouldn't make the baby's heartbeat change?"

"We can order an ultrasound to be sure, if you'd like." Dr. Banks looked from Ames to Bree.

"Yes, please," Bree said.

She nodded to Phil, who made a note in her chart. "Let's look at this shoulder." She moved the bed to sit Bree upright more, and Ames backed up as the doctor moved to the left side. Her fingers felt like needles, and Bree was panting by the time the doctor said, "Yes, I think that's separated. We'll need an x-ray of that too, so we can see the extent of the damage."

"Do separated shoulders heal on their own?" Ames asked. "Or is this something she'll have to have surgery for?"

"We won't know that until we see the x-ray," Dr. Banks said. "So we'll get both of those done, and then we'll know more. We can keep giving you the pain meds, Bree, if it gets to be too much for you."

She nodded, and the doctor started to leave.

Thankfully, she didn't have to wait long to be taken for the x-ray, and Ames was able to go with her. She did wait in the room for the ultrasound for another ten minutes, during which Ames sent a bunch of texts to his family string.

"They'll all know," he said.

The door opened, and a man walked in. "Bree Hammond?"

"Yes," she said.

"I'm Doctor Rock, and I'll be doing your ultrasound." He shook her hand, and then Ames's, and he got down to business. Bree had not had her ultrasound yet, so this was actually semi-exciting for her, and she wished Wes were with her.

"Let's see," the doctor said. "I understand you had a little spill, and you want to make sure everything's okay in here." He started the ultrasound, and the baby's heartbeat filled the room with its special, echoy sound that was unlike any other.

"Oh, wow," Ames said, his voice made mostly of air. "Is that…that's the baby?" He came to stand beside Bree so he could see the screen too.

"Yes," the doctor said. "Everything looks good. I don't see anything here…or here…." He pressed harder on her left side. "I don't see any bleeding or any trauma. I can tell what the gender is. Do you want to know?" Dr. Rock looked at her, and Bree hesitated.

She did want to know, but she wanted Wes at her side.

The door opened, and a nurse said, "She's right here."

Wes entered the room, and everything in the world got better. "Baby," he said, and Ames melted out of the way, and Wes took his spot. He cradled her face in his hands and kissed her. "You're okay? Really okay?"

"I'm okay," Bree said, closing her eyes and basking in the warmth of her husband's touch, and breathing in the smoky, leathery, spicy scent of him. "He just asked me if I want to know the gender of the baby."

Wes spun around and looked at the screen, but Dr. Banks had taken the instruments off Bree's belly. "Yeah, we want to know that."

"Where's Mikey?" Bree asked.

"Gray kept him," Wes said.

"Okay, continuing," Dr. Banks said. "Everything looks good here, guys."

The baby's heartbeat came back to life, and Wes reached over and squeezed Bree's hand. "I love you."

"And you two are having a little boy," Dr. Banks said.

Bree grinned, and when Wes turned toward her, a look of wonder on his face, Bree fell in love with him all over again.

The ultrasound ended, and Wes stood to embrace Ames. "Thank you, Ames. Thank you so much."

"Yes, thank you, Ames," Bree said as she tried to get up off the table. She'd forgotten about her shoulder, and she cried out as another wave of pain kept her on the table.

"Anytime," Ames said. "I'll head out now. Let me know if you need anything." He made a hasty exit, and Wes turned to help her up.

"I'm so sorry," he said. "We took Hutch up on a trail, and there was no service."

"It's fine," Bree said. "I was kind of freaking out, and Ames was so calm."

"He is good under pressure," Wes agreed. A smile slid across his face. "Another baby boy, Bree."

She smiled too, because she loved Wes's excitement over the baby. "We better start thinking of names. I have a feeling it's going to take a while for us to find one we both agree on." Michael had taken forever for them to decide on, and that was such a normal name.

He laughed and kissed her, and she knew he'd take good care of her...and let her name their baby whatever she wanted.

CHAPTER 14

S ophia looked up as someone knocked on her front
door. She abandoned her bowl of cold cereal and
stood up as Ames said, "It's just me," and came into the
cabin.

"I'm ready," she said, putting her half-eaten bowl of
cereal in the sink and turning to meet him. He grinned at
her from the living room, and he had to know what that
grin did to a woman.

"Eating cold cereal again?" he asked, plenty of tease in
his voice.

"Yes," she said. "I made breakfast burritos at the lodge,
but they didn't sound good for some reason."

"That's because you love those sugary flakes you hide
in the cupboard above the fridge." He took her into his
arms and held her close. She hadn't seen him since Cy's
wedding, and she wondered if he'd kiss her before they
went up to Ruff Rescue.

She liked holding him too, but she didn't stay in the embrace for long. "We don't want to be late."

"No, we don't," he said. "What time do we have to be back?"

"Whenever," she said. "Julianne is ordering pizza tonight, because it's a guest's birthday and they specifically requested it. That means I don't have to cook."

"So we can go to dinner," he said.

"Sure," she said, and she saw the whole day and night with Ames flow before her eyes. She picked up her purse and turned toward the door, but Ames blocked it. The man had sobered in the two seconds she'd turned her back on him, and he wore a brooding look that was as sexy as it was concerning.

"What?" she asked.

"I just want to make sure we're okay," he said. "Last time I saw you, you drove away upset with me. We've texted since, but I just want to make sure you know I didn't mean to upset you, and I won't say things I don't absolutely mean."

Sophia sure did like it when he simply said what was on his mind. He didn't play games with her, and she appreciated that.

She'd had plenty of time to think about Ames in the past two days. No, she had not liked him using words like "potentially" and "I think I could." She didn't want to get her hopes up that he would stay in town when he only thought there was the *potential* of it happening. At the same time, she really wanted to explore a real, long-term relationship with him.

She thought she'd been clear enough on that point, but she decided to be as bold as he was. "Thank you," she said. "I would appreciate that. In that same spirit, maybe I should explain why what you said upset me."

"Go ahead."

"I really like you, Ames. I don't want this to be a summer fling. I want the *potential* of a real, long-term relationship with you." She nodded like that was that, and just by her saying it she could make it so.

"Is that true?" he asked.

"Ames," she said, a vein of exasperation pulling through her. "Of course that's true. You were there when we kissed the other night, right?"

He ducked his head, the brim of his cowboy hat hiding his face. "I was there."

"Then you seriously can*not* have doubts that I like you."

He glanced up, and a sparkle resided in his eyes. "Long-term, though?"

"Yes," she said boldly. "I'm not interested in the same thing we did last time. I'm really not." She couldn't believe she was having this conversation, but it felt like something crucial that needed to happen. "If that's what we're doing, I'd rather you just go up to the dog rescue alone."

She felt sure she'd cry the rest of the day if he went to Ruff Rescue alone, but she'd rather know now than later.

"I don't want to go to the dog rescue alone."

"You know what you're saying, right?"

"Yes."

"Say it using regular words," she said.

He chuckled and shook his head, and though she heard a bit of annoyance in the sound, it was mostly happy. He looked away from her and then back into her eyes. "I'm thinking long-term with you too, Sophia. I just don't know exactly what that looks like, or where it puts me in the end."

"You don't have to know exactly," she said. "I just need to know we're on the same page."

"I think we are," Ames said, taking a step forward and slipping his fingers between hers, oh-so-slowly and so deliberately. His touch brought something to life inside her that laid dormant when he wasn't around, and she couldn't ignore that.

She didn't know exactly what would happen with them either, but she wanted to find out. Her heart might get beaten up and bruised and broken, but if she could spend more time with Ames, the risk was worth the reward.

"We better go," she said as he took another step toward her. "We'll be late."

"I think we'll be fine," he said.

"You hate being late."

"I'll drive fast," he said, leaning down.

She giggled, because the man never drove over the speed limit. She reached up as his cowboy hat bumped into her forehead. She slid her hands up the sides of his face, noticing the way his eyes closed in bliss.

She felt powerful in that moment, as she could make this handsome, strong man soften and sigh with her touch. Hers.

It seemed impossible, but the evidence of it was right before her eyes. She ran her thumb over his eyebrow and pushed his cowboy hat off his head so she could kiss him. She had to tip up onto her toes to get to his height, even with his head bowed, and he steadied her with both hands on her waist.

She touched her mouth to his, and Ames's grip on her body tightened. She slid her fingers around to the back of his neck and enjoyed this slow, sweet kiss. He let her set the pace and dictate the direction of the kiss, and she pulled away when what she really wanted to do was keep kissing him.

"We really will be late," she said, ducking her head so she didn't have to look him in the eye.

"Let's go then," he said, moving out of her personal space and taking her hand again. Things between them turned light and casual once they climbed in the truck and started down the canyon to Dog Valley.

"You've never really said much about your family," he said. "And mine is a circus you can't look away from." He glanced at her, but Sophia kept her gaze out the windshield. How did she start this story?

"It's complicated," she said.

"Start with something easy," he said. "Siblings?"

"Yeah," she said. "I have two older brothers. Ryan and Keith."

"Parents?"

"Divorced," she said, all of the members of her family flashing through her mind like a bad slide show. "My dad was in the military when I was growing up. We moved all over the place, sometimes year after year." She was aware that her voice had slipped into somewhat of a monotone, and she pushed out her breath in a long exhale. "We're all spread out now," she said. "I don't talk to any of them all that much. It was like once I graduated and my dad retired from the Army, we just...fell apart."

"I'm sorry," Ames said.

"It's been fifteen years," she said.

"That doesn't mean it doesn't still hurt."

He was right, and Sophia knew it. Her throat closed, and it was just as well, because she didn't know what to say. She'd gotten along the best with her father growing up, but he'd thought she had sided with her mom in the divorce, and while he hadn't cut her out of his life completely, he never initiated a conversation.

Her mother had gotten as far from the military base as she could, and she lived in California now. At least she had the last time Sophia had checked with her. She got the feeling that her mother had given all she could, for many long years. Almost thirty years of marriage to Sophia's father. Thirty years of raising children alone. Thirty years of being responsible for every little thing, down to paying every bill, cleaning every toilet, and managing every schedule.

In California, she'd been living a life Sophia suspected she'd always wanted—and that didn't include her, Keith, or Ryan.

Something pinched in her chest, and when she breathed in, it actually hurt so much she gasped.

"You okay?" he asked.

"Sort of," she said. She didn't try to cover over her feelings with a smile, because it wouldn't have worked anyway.

"You can tell me about them, if you want," he said.

Sophia shook her head. "Maybe another time, okay? I want today to be fun."

"They're not fun?"

"Not at all," she said.

"Is this why you stay at the lodge during the holidays?"

"Yes," she said. "And Ames, it's why I don't want to leave Coral Canyon. I moved all the time, and I never truly had a place to belong. Then my family dissolved right when I needed them to rally around me, and it's just been me for the past fifteen years. I've had to rely on myself for everything, and when I came here—I didn't. I'm part of that lodge family, and it feels good. It feels right. I belong there." She looked at him then, desperate to make him understand.

He nodded, one hand lazily draped over the wheel as he drove. "I understand better now."

"I didn't tell you last time, because we weren't serious."

He glanced at her. "Thanks for telling me now."

She nodded, and she needed the spotlight off of her. "Okay, you have to tell me something you didn't last time."

"Oh, is that how this works?"

"Yes," she said, deciding on the spot. "That's how this

works. So let's see...I want to know why you're not married."

He looked at her despite the fact that he was driving. "I've never asked anyone to marry me."

"Have you been in love before?"

He finally put his attention back on the highway. "No," he said, his voice very low.

"I find that so hard to believe," she said. "You're good-looking. You're rich. You're smart and hard-working. You can literally do anything. You're—"

"I cannot literally do anything," he said, shaking his head.

"Seems that way," she said. "Cop, cowboy, carpenter. That's a lot."

"You're a cook and a nanny. Oh, and a dog foster mom."

She smiled, because she did miss having a foster dog. She toyed with the idea of getting one today if there was one under thirty pounds. Realistically though, she didn't have time to foster right now, not with Marcy and Wyatt in town. She'd have to wait until the fall when they returned to Three Rivers.

He cleared his throat, and Sophia tensed. "I never really dated much," Ames said. "So despite the good looks and the money, I've never fallen in love."

"So you never tried to find someone to marry," she said.

"Right."

"And now you're trying?"

"Yes," he said simply.

"Why's that?" she asked. "What changed?"

He shrugged one boxy shoulder. "I don't know. Maybe seeing Colt and Wes find wives and settle into families. Somehow, in my head, I thought we'd all just be brothers forever."

"You're still brothers," she said, not quite getting what he was saying.

"It's different now," he said. "Yeah, we're still family, but they have people that are more important to them than I am. Not that I need to be the most important, but...yeah. And they're so happy. I was watching Wes one day last year, and I just thought, I want that. I want a woman who makes me smile in the morning and makes me laugh at lunchtime and makes me want to be the absolute best man I can be, just so she'll stay with me." He glanced at her, and Sophia gaped back at him.

"Wow, Ames. I didn't know you felt like that."

"I didn't either," he said. "I always thought I was fine by myself. And the truth is, Sophia, I *was* fine by myself. I still am, most of the time. I don't really care what other people think of me, and I don't need their approval or validation."

"Mm, yeah, I can see that about you." She called that confidence, and it contributed to his bad boy persona that he wore so well.

"Then I see Gray with Elise, and my heart tells me I want that kind of close friendship, that bonding love, that companionship. I see Wes holding his son, and my heart screams at me that I want a family too." He cleared his throat and shifted in his seat. "So I decided to try."

"You've dated a lot lately, then?" she asked, trying not to let the jealousy rear up inside her.

"Not as much as you'd think," he said. "In Colorado, the Hammond name is everywhere. It was hard to get a date with a woman who didn't have an ulterior motive for saying yes."

"I see."

"And I was a cop, and no one wanted to date a cop."

"Really?"

"Really."

"Is that why you quit?"

"No," he said, but it came out as a bark, and Sophia thought it had definitely contributed to his decision to leave the Littleton Police Department. After all, he'd used that as a reason why he didn't want to relocate to Coral Canyon. He'd worked for years to move up the ranks in Littleton, and he didn't want to start over somewhere else.

Of course, then she'd found out he'd already quit that job before he'd come to stay with Cy in Coral Canyon. Before the kiss on the hillside above the lodge. Before the three-week relationship between them that had ended as abruptly as it had started.

When she'd learned that he'd already quit before his visit in the fall, it felt like part of her heart had been surgically removed with a butter knife. And then, when she'd seen him in Three Rivers and knew he'd left Colorado?

Her heart struggled to beat right now. She reminded herself of the two kisses they'd shared recently, and that things in Ames's life were currently in a state of flux. It sounded like they had been for at least the past ten months.

"I quit because it was time to quit," he said. "I knew I wasn't supposed to be there anymore."

"And you went to Three Rivers."

"I bet that made you mad," he said. "When you found out I was in Three Rivers."

"A little," she said, though it had been more than that.

He glanced at her again. "I'm sorry," he said. "The truth is, I don't know where I'm supposed to be, or what I'm supposed to be doing. I'm trying to figure it all out, but it's not happening as fast as I'd like, and I find myself constantly second-guessing every decision I make."

He slowed and turned off the highway and onto the dirt road that led to Ruff Rescue.

"And that gets us to where we are right now," Sophia said.

"About," Ames confirmed as he pulled up to the tiny administration hut that marked the entrance to Ruff Rescue. Lindsey came outside, as she'd probably been watching for them to arrive, a smile on her face.

Sophia couldn't help smiling back at the woman who'd become a good friend over the years. "Okay, Ames," she said. "Let's go have some fun and find you a rescue dog to foster." She looked at him. "No more serious stuff today, all right?"

He wasn't too sure about that, Sophia could tell. But he nodded, and he said, "All right," as he reached for his door handle. She got out of the truck too, squealing, "Lindsey," and dancing over to her friend to hug her.

She did want a fun day with Ames, but she'd enjoyed the more serious conversation too. She couldn't believe he hadn't really ever tried to find someone to fall in love with and spend his life with. Even more shocking was that when he'd finally decided to do so, he'd chosen her.

Bless us, she prayed silently. *If we're meant to be, please bless us to find a way down whatever paths we're on to one we can walk together.*

CHAPTER 15

A mes smiled at Sophia's excitement to see her friend, and when it was his turn, he stepped forward and shook Lindsey's hand.

"My boyfriend, Ames Hammond," Sophia said, beaming up at him. Heat exploded through him, and his smile got a bit wider. She turned back to the brunette. Lindsey was at least four inches taller than Sophia, and she had wide, dark eyes to go with her hair. She'd pulled that hair into a ponytail and put a visor on to keep her face shaded.

"Nice to meet you, Ames," she said. "Tell me a little bit about what you're looking for."

"I used to be a captain in a police department," he said. "I oversaw officer and K9 pairings, and I've trained police dogs before."

"Wow," Lindsey said. "Sophia said you wanted a big

dog. I take it you're not afraid of one that's maybe a little more aggressive?"

"That would be fine," Ames said. He could usually tell if he and a canine would get along within the first few minutes of meeting it, and the size and breed didn't matter to him. "I'd actually like two dogs. I find they work better and learn faster in pairs or packs."

Lindsey looked at him, keen interest in her eyes. "You really do have experience with dogs."

"Tons," he confirmed.

"Are you looking for a job?" she asked, laughing afterward.

He smiled too, but he didn't answer. Sophia caught his eye, her eyebrows raised, but he shook his head slightly.

"We're always looking for good people," Lindsey continued, unaware of the exchange between him and Sophia. "Especially with our bigger dogs. Everyone loves the small lap dogs and the cats. The big dogs need as many advocates as they can get."

"I'm sure that's true," Ames said, not committing to anything.

Lindsey talked about the facility and the dogs they brought in as they walked down a path between two huge kennels. The chain link on both sides of the path stood at least eight feet tall, with a gate every so often.

Some of the dogs they passed just came over to the fence to see them, but some barked their welcome. Ames couldn't help the joy moving through his soul, and the heavens opened up right there on the hot, dusty path.

He needed to be working with dogs every day. He

needed his own facility. His mind started running down a set of greased tracks, and he could barely hear one thought before another took its place.

He needed land.

He needed someone to help him design the facility.

He needed to contact the new captain over the K9 units in Littleton.

He needed to find the right puppies for the program.

He needed to establish himself as a credentialed police dog trainer.

"Here we are," Lindsey said, and Ames compartmentalized everything quickly. He could think about this later. "We've got several different breeds in here, and this is our shelter for dogs over sixty pounds."

Four or five of them had already approached the gate, but they backed up as Lindsey opened it. The gate swung in, and she followed it closely, talking to the dogs. They clearly knew her and listened to her. Ames followed her, reaching for Sophia's hand to bring her behind him.

"This is Norman," Lindsey said, bending down to pat a big black, gray, and white Akita. "He's an Akita, and he's got a heart of marshmallow." She grinned at the dog as she scrubbed him around his jowls.

Ames joined her and extended his hand toward the canine. Norman sniffed him, and then he touched his nose right to Ames's palm. He crouched down and looked into the dog's eyes. He saw intelligence, and confidence, and loyalty there, and he wanted this dog to come home with him.

"He's been here about nine months," Lindsey said. "He

was abused, and he bit some children in the neighborhood. We went to pick him up in Glendale so he wouldn't get put down."

Ames slid his hand along the side of Norman's face, reading his whole history in just a few moments.

"This is Jones," Lindsey said, introducing him to a brown and black boxer. Ames liked him too, but there wasn't the instant connection there had been with Norman. He met a hairy black mutt that looked more like a Newfoundland than anything else, though he definitely wasn't pure.

He met a Doberman named Bonnie, who had some seriously high energy. Ames wanted to work with the dogs and help them be able to integrate into a family, but he wasn't sure he had the time to dedicate to Bonnie.

"Oh, look at that," Lindsey said as a Belgian Malinois came right up to Ames. The other dogs had parted as this one came forward, and it was clear he was the pack leader. Or the other canines were simply afraid of him.

"She likes you," Lindsey said. "This is Florence. She's a—"

"Belgian Malinois," Ames said with her. "I recognize them. We had six in Littleton." He smiled at Lindsey as he crouched down in front of this dog too. He held up his hand, palm forward and about a foot away from the animal.

"She used to be a police dog," Lindsey said. "But she attacked without being commanded, and she caused some serious damage to a witness the police needed. We got her after that. She's been here a while—a long while—and she doesn't like anyone."

Her nose worked great, and Ames watched her sniff and sniff and sniff, her neck stretching out to find the scent she'd picked up. He saw pure intelligence in her eyes, and she burrowed her way right into his heart.

"She always stays in the shadows," Lindsey continued. "She avoids the other dogs. They avoid her. I barely know her." She sank to Ames's level too, looking from him to the dog.

"I want her," he said quietly, though the dog had not let him touch her yet, and she hadn't touched him.

"I don't know if—"

"I want her," Ames said, looking at Lindsey. "And not as a foster. I want to adopt her."

Surprise made Lindsey's eyes widen. "Wow. Uh, okay."

"I want to foster too," he said. "I can handle her—and them."

"He's got Cy Hammond's dog for the next couple of weeks too," Sophia said. "He's brilliant with dogs, Linds."

Lindsey looked doubtful, but she didn't say anything as she got to her feet. A dog nudged his elbow, and he swung around slowly, knowing quick movements startled dogs. Norman sat there, and Ames smiled at the dog. "Yeah, buddy, I haven't forgotten about you."

He looked at Florence, who flicked her gaze to the Akita too. They both sat down, and Ames reached out to Norman with his injured hand, because if Florence snapped, he didn't want to get another injury on his right hand.

Slowly—only moving an inch every few seconds or so —he moved his left hand toward Florence. "*Sitz*," he said to her, using the German words they'd used for their police dogs in Colorado. "*Platz*."

Florence looked at him, the seconds ticking by. Then she sat—*sitz*—and she went all the way to the ground—*platz*.

"That's a good girl," he said, reaching out to touch her shoulder. He knew better than to go for the face as he had with Norman. Florence's eyes drifted halfway closed, and Ames chuckled as he moved his hand up to her ears, and finally to stroke along her nose, down the sides of her face, and under her chin.

He stood up and snapped his fingers. Both Norman and Florence came right to his side, all three of them looking at Lindsey.

"I have never seen *anything* like that in my entire life," she said, pure awe in her voice. "That was *incredible*." She looked from Ames to Sophia and back. "I will hire you right now. Name your price."

"I just want to foster right now," Ames said quietly. Norman nudged his hand again, and he patted the dog. "You're coming with me, bud. It's okay." He met Lindsey's eye again. "I want Florence as mine. I want to foster Norman, but I want the option to adopt him if I find I can't give him up."

"Done," Lindsey said.

"I want one more foster," Ames said.

"I think I'm fairly useless here," Lindsey said. "You can walk around and find that dog that speaks to your soul."

"Thanks." Ames turned away from Lindsey and Sophia, and he started walking around the enclosure. There were plenty of trees here, which he liked. The water looked fresh enough in this heat, and the dogs had healthy coats and clear eyes.

There were easily fifteen or twenty dogs in this area, and there had to be more in another enclosure. Sophia said the bigger animals were harder to adopt or foster out, and they certainly had more than twenty of them.

An English setter perked up as Ames went around the corner of a small shed, and she barked once as if Ames had startled her. "Hey," he said, well-aware that at least six dogs had become his shadow. The others had lost interest already. He bent down as the cream dog with the long hair started trotting toward him. She looked like someone had spilled dark brown dirt all over her, and he found her spots classic and beautiful.

"What's your name? Huh?" The setter came right up to him and sniffed his neck, licking him in the next moment. He was shocked this sweetheart hadn't been adopted a long time ago. Maybe she hadn't been here that long.

"Come with me," he said to the dog, and he started back to where Lindsey and Sophia stood chatting. "What's this one's name?"

Lindsey looked at the English setter. "That's Cocoa. Someone found her on the streets in Jackson Hole. She was pregnant at the time, and she had nine puppies about six months ago. We adopted them out in less than a few hours."

"But not her? Seems hard to believe," Ames said.

"She had some complications in labor," Lindsey said. "She requires a lot of medical attention, and I guess no one was willing to incur those costs."

"I want her as a foster too," he said. "Same conditions as Norman."

He looked around at the dog pack still with him. "I think that's it for now. Sorry, friends." He patted the other dogs who'd clearly taken a shine to him. "I'll need more dogs soon, okay?" He wanted to take them all, and he found it a little shocking that he could feel so much for these animals in such a short time when it took him so long to connect to humans.

He didn't have to pretend to be someone or something he wasn't with dogs. They knew who he was, and they either accepted it and liked him, or they didn't.

"I'm not going to stop asking you to work here," Lindsey said. "You have eight dogs following you around as if you rolled in steak-scented cologne before you got here."

"I wish I could work here," he said. "But I have some prior obligations." He flashed her a smile and added, "Do we need leashes for them?"

"Yes," she said. "Not that they need them. I have a feeling they'll follow you anywhere." She took down a couple of lead lines and handed them to him. She looped one around Cocoa's neck while he did Norman and Florence. "I can't *believe* Florence came out of the trees to meet you. I just can't believe it."

Sophia started talking to her about her family's ice cream shop, and Ames glanced at his girlfriend to let her know he appreciated it. He didn't need Lindsey fawning over him or offering him a job every five seconds. The dogs were put in an indoor kennel while Ames started the paperwork to do the adoption and the fostering.

Forty-five minutes later, he had all three large dogs in the back seat of his truck, Cocoa sniffing Sophia's hair and the other two sitting demurely next to the open windows on both sides of the truck.

"Thank you," he said to Sophia as he reached over and took her hand in his. A twinge of pain moved through his hand from his injured thumb. He pulled away and added, "My thumb hurts today. Maybe I should unwrap it and check it."

"Did they say to do that?"

"I honestly don't know," he said. "I was really out of it at the hospital. Do you remember?"

"I think they said to keep it dry and then yes, check it after a few days."

"It's been a long time since I rewrapped it. Before the wedding." He determined he'd do it after he dropped off Sophia, took the dogs back to Cy's, and got all the things they needed. Bowls, food, leashes, collars, and anything else he saw at the pet supply store. Cy sometimes put sweaters on Blue Velvet in the winter, but Ames had learned that he'd done that because Patsy loved sweaters.

Ames didn't want to dress up his dogs. He wanted to make them feel loved and safe. He wanted to exercise them and teach them to do what they loved best—work and love their master.

"Down," he commanded Norman, and the Akita went straight to his stomach, his tongue hanging out of his mouth as he panted. Florence knew the English and German commands for down, and she trotted up after Norman and sank all the way down too.

Blue Velvet hadn't even run after the ball this time, as she didn't have quite the stamina of Norman and Florence. Likewise, Cocoa had retreated to the shade about ten minutes ago. Ames knew the other two dogs would go and go and go until he told them they could stop.

The summer sun was hot here despite the elevation, and he picked up the ball and dropped it in the bucket. "All right," he said. "We're done." He stepped over to the house and turned on the hose. "Come get a drink."

Norman and Florence followed him, and they both drank from the water spouting from the hose. Blue Velvet waited, and then she drank too. Cocoa drank last, and Ames filled the big plastic bin they used as a water bowl outside with fresh, cold water too.

"I think we've all earned a nap. Let's go inside." He went up the front steps and opened Cy's door. All four dogs filed in, and Ames grinned at each one as they did. Blue Velvet probably couldn't wait for her real master to get home, as Cy didn't make her run four miles in the morning, play fetch an hour later, and then train in another language right after lunch.

He'd been throwing them a ball in the afternoon too, before taking all of them up to Sophia's in the evenings. Cy and Patsy would be home on Monday, only five days from now, and Ames really needed to find a place of his own.

Colton had said he could come back to his house, even with the three big dogs. Ames simply didn't want to. So while the dogs jumped up on the couches or flopped on the bare floor, all of them still panting, Ames pulled out his phone and got back to work.

He'd marked four homes he could rent, and he wanted to set up a time to see them. "This is Ames Hammond," he said when the first woman called. "There's a house on Merchant Street for rent? I'm interested in seeing it."

Half an hour later, he had appointments to see all four houses. Two that evening, and two in the morning. The dogs would be thankful he wouldn't be running them tomorrow, and Ames was glad he might have his own place by the weekend.

He had at least two more months of summer before he had to decide if he was going to stay in Coral Canyon or go back to Three Rivers, and he didn't want to buy another place and regret it.

The way his relationship was going with Sophia, he had the very real feeling he'd need to figure out how to get his house in Three Rivers fixed up and up for sale from Wyoming.

He sighed and looked out the big windows that framed the front of Cy's house. All of the dogs had fallen asleep, and a feeling of serenity and peace filled the house in the silence he'd left in the wake of his phone calls.

"What do I do with the house in Three Rivers?" he asked, looking up at the ceiling now. Just like that, like someone turning on a switch to flood a room with light, Ames knew the answer.

"Micah Walker," he said. He reached for his phone again, scrolled for Jeremiah's number, and put the phone to his ear once more.

CHAPTER 16

Sophia opened a container of raspberries and dumped them into the colander in the sink. She'd already put in five other containers, and it still might not be enough. She rinsed them all, picking out the leaves and berries that were softer than she'd like. She tapped the colander against the side of the sink and set it on a towel.

She repeated all of her actions with a second colander and half a dozen blueberry containers. She'd been making a patriotic sugar cookie cake for many years, but that wasn't exactly breakfast food.

As today was the Fourth of July, and she was in charge of breakfast today, she wanted to provide something red, white, and blue for the guests at Whiskey Mountain Lodge. The lodge never provided lunch for the guests, but dinner was almost always on the menu. Tonight, though, they'd partnered with the Chamber of Commerce to provide chuckwagon dinner tickets to any registered guest at the lodge.

All of the employees had gotten them too, and Ames had purchased one the moment Sophia had told him she had a free ticket for the big city dinner, complete with Coral Canyon's own cowboy band and silent auction.

The whole town had been draped in Americana for the past couple of weeks, and Sophia loved it. Even Ames had commented on the banners and flags, the way the town had a new announcement about another contest winner that day.

"Baby contests," he'd said. "Garden contests, lawn contests, art contests. How do they keep up with all of it?"

"The committee for our summer season is huge," Sophia said. "I know, because they tried to recruit me one year to judge the kid's baking contest."

"I'm sure they did," Ames said. "I've had your cinnamon swirl bread." He'd grinned at her, and Sophia had giggled. Then she'd made the bread with the streusel topping again the next morning. The guests at the lodge loved it too, and she had realized she'd do whatever she had to for them to like her cooking as much as they liked Celia's.

At the same time, she knew that was an impossible task. Celia was an absolute genius in the kitchen, and no matter what Sophia did, she wouldn't catch up to that reputation.

She'd still managed to find a way to transform her cake recipe into a less sweet version of itself and turn it into a pancake recipe. The cake was decorated with raspberries and blueberries and frosted with white cream cheese frosting to make it look like the American flag.

She couldn't decorate everyone's pancakes, but she would make an example, and then let them do what they wanted with the cream cheese glaze and the berry bar.

With the glaze ready, and the berries washed and drained, she turned to the griddles on the counter. Pancakes were hard for a breakfast that lasted an hour, where guests could come and go, so Sophia rarely did things like this. Casseroles and large batches of sausage or bacon were much easier.

She had half a dozen pancakes on the serving platter when the first guests arrived, and she quickly poured the warm glaze from the pan into the pitcher and the berries into the waiting bowls.

"Sugar cookie patriotic pancakes," she said, her voice quite chirpy. She started pouring smaller pancakes for the children, and the time for breakfast passed quickly. She got several compliments, and she saw more than one person taking a picture of their red, white, and blue breakfast.

She finished, cleaned up, and headed down the sidewalk to her cabin. Marcy and Wyatt had given her the day off, though it was Thursday, and she wasn't surprised when she found Ames sitting in her living room, two dogs on the couch with him. The third sat only a few feet from the door, and Sophia definitely liked Cocoa the best. The other two scared her a little bit, though they'd never given her any reason for that.

Ames had complete control over them, and they adored him as much as Sophia did. At least she suspected they did. He definitely loved them, and Sophia was just glad he'd made room for her in his life too.

The past few weeks with him had been downright amazing, and Sophia really didn't want summer to ever end. Now that July had arrived, she felt like the count-down had begun. She wasn't even sure why—there was plenty of summer left.

She swallowed back her concerns and said, "Hey, you didn't come get pancakes."

"I looked in," he said. "But it looked really busy."

"There was plenty," she said, wishing he'd come right in and wrapped her in his arms, dropped a kiss on her temple, and stood with her as she fed everyone at the lodge.

Ames leaned forward and put his phone on the coffee table in front of him. He grinned at her, and told the dogs to get down. Norman obeyed, but Florence just gave him a baleful look. "I think there's room, even with her still there." He patted the cushion Norman had vacated, and Sophia moved over to the couch and squeezed herself into the small space between him and the large Malinois.

She giggled as he put that arm around her and gave her that kiss she'd been thinking of. "I was thinking you and I could go to breakfast together," he said.

"Today?" she asked, her eyebrows raised. "The grand parade starts in twenty minutes, and everywhere will be crazy right now." She snuggled deeper into his side, throwing her arm around his torso.

"Not in town," he said.

"Yeah, because you hate crowds."

"I don't hate them," he said. "I just don't like them." He ran his hand up and down her arm. "Oh, look at my thumb. It's almost all the way better." He held it out for her to see, and sure enough, his thumb looked really good. The stitches had come out a couple of weeks ago, and he'd been playing doctor with the bandages until now, when he didn't wear one at all.

The skin was still pink, and she could see the smoothness where the stitches had been. "It looks so great," she said.

"I haven't picked up a nail gun since," he said. "And listen, I wanted to talk to you about something."

"Okay," she said, sitting up and looking at him. Florence made a huffing sound, and she jumped down to the floor. She tossed a stormy look at Sophia, but Ames just clicked his tongue at the dog, and Florence went to lay in front of the door. She always positioned herself between Ames and the main entrance to wherever they were, and that spoke of her fierce determination to protect him.

"I called Micah Walker, and he went to my house in Three Rivers to assess it. He gave me a quote last night for what it would cost for him to finish the remodel, and I'm going to take it."

Sophia blinked rapidly, her heart beating the same way her eyelashes did. "Wow."

"Then I'm going to list that house for sale." He looked right at her, and Sophia had a hard time holding a gaze as powerful as his. "I'm not going back to Three Rivers."

"Really?" she asked.

"Really." He reached up and ran his hand through his

hair. "There's no 'I think' or 'potential' here. I'm for sure not going back."

She wanted to ask him if he was going to stay in Coral Canyon, but she couldn't. Just because he wasn't going back to Three Rivers did not mean he was staying here. He had a house in Colorado too, and Sophia knew it. He'd never mentioned it at all, but he'd lived there for almost forty years, and she couldn't imagine that he'd sold his place there to move to Three Rivers.

He had a lot of money, and he could own homes all over the world without it being a problem.

"That's great," Sophia said, leaning forward to kiss Ames.

He kept the union sweet and short, and then he sighed. "Come on. Let's go to breakfast." He got up and reached for the leashes on the coffee table. "Come on, friends. We're going into the mountains."

"The mountains?" She watched the dogs snap to attention and hold still as he clipped their leashes on. He'd take them off once they got up on the trail, because he liked to train them to be off-leash and listen to him.

Ames threw her a grin over his shoulder. "Put on your hiking boots, sweetheart. I've got breakfast for us up there."

"You do? What is it?"

"It's a surprise."

Sophia loved surprises, especially from her handsome boyfriend. Ames wasn't super spontaneous, and he'd never planned a big surprise for her. She jumped to her feet and said, "I need five minutes," before taking the few steps down the hall to the only bedroom in the cabin. She quickly changed into a pair of denim shorts, bypassing the white ones she was planning to wear to the chuckwagon dinner that night, and put on a bright red tank top. That was patriotic enough for now.

She hurried to put on socks and her hiking boots before she returned to the living room. "Ready," she announced, and Ames extended his hand toward her. She took it, and he kept the dogs on his other side as they left the cabin. They crossed the parking lot together and started up the trail that led to the bench where he'd found her last fall, crying over Patsy's departure from the lodge.

Sophia had gone up there the day Patsy was set to move out of the cabin they'd shared for four years, and she'd been distraught. Seriously distraught. The appearance of Ames had been the one bright ray of sunshine in her life that day, and she was so glad to be on this same trail with him again today.

After several minutes, Ames unclipped the leashes and said, "All right, friends. Stay close and come back when I whistle." Norman trotted ahead immediately, but Florence stayed right beside Ames until he said, "Go on, Flo. You can go."

She did then, and Ames chuckled at her. "She's so worried she's going to do something wrong again." He looked at Sophia. "I don't know how to help her get over that."

"Maybe it will just take time," Sophia said. "Look, she's out there, exploring." She watched Florence, and the dog did trot around, sniffing things. In reality, she looked back at Ames every ten seconds or so, and Sophia saw it, which meant Ames did too. The dog definitely had some anxiety about displeasing him.

They hiked for a few minutes more, and then Ames said, "It's right here." He tugged her over to a large rock just off the path, and he pulled out two camp chairs.

"Oh, you're good," she said, giggling as he set up the chairs. He indicated the blue one, and she sat down while grinning at him.

He stepped around the rock again, and this time, he came back with a picnic basket in his hands. "Let's see." He sank into the gray camp chair and set the basket between them. "I got you some orange juice." He pulled the bottle out and handed it to her.

Sophia couldn't stop smiling as he then produced her favorite spinach and fontina quiche from The Rubber Sole in town, as well as a cardboard container filled with thick-sliced bacon.

"You're flawless," she said, holding all of her food on her lap while he pulled out a container that had a chile verde breakfast burrito in it.

"It's probably cold," he said. "Nothing flawless about that."

"Seriously, Ames," she said. "This is wonderful. Thank you." She leaned toward him, glad when he closed the distance between them and kissed her. She curved her fingers up the side of his jaw and along his neck to hold him in place after the kiss ended. "Ames Hammond, I'm falling in love with you," she whispered.

He pulled in a breath, but Sophia kept her eyes closed

and added quickly, "Please don't say anything. I just feel it, and I want you to know I feel it."

She wished he would say what he was feeling, but Ames rarely expressed those types of things—at least in words. His touch often said a lot, as did the way he held her and kissed her. The way he planned Independence Day breakfasts in the mountains with her, because he knew she would be working at the lodge and wouldn't be able to get to town before all the best places to eat were too crowded.

He hadn't bought a house in Coral Canyon, and Sophia had never asked him about his decision to rent. To her, it was a huge flag that he still hadn't decided where his final destination was.

"I can't say anything?" he asked, both of his hands coming up to cradle her face.

"Only say what's real and true," she said.

"I always do," he said. "And what's real and true is that I'm falling in love with you too."

Sophia sucked in a breath and pulled away from him, her eyes flying open. She wanted to ask him if he was kidding, but she could see the depth of seriousness in his eyes.

"I don't know what it looks like or feels like," he admitted. "But I sure like being with you. When I'm not with you, I'm trying to find ways to make you happy, and the moment I leave, I'm counting down the minutes until I can see you again. Is that love?"

"I don't know," Sophia said. "I've never been in love either."

"So I guess we'll figure it out together."

"I guess we will." Sophia looked down at her lap. "Okay, so quiche and orange juice. Who knew that's all it would take to make me fall in love?" She laughed, glad when Ames did too.

"I think it's more complicated than that," he said.

Of course it was, but for right now, Sophia just wanted to believe that the mountains, orange juice, and Ames could fix everything in her life.

Intellectually, that wasn't true, and a thought Sophia had had over the last few weeks came right to the front of her mind again.

Call your mother.

Not today, she told herself. She didn't want to ruin today, which had been so perfect so far.

CHAPTER 17

E lise stirred the corn chowder on the stove, humming to herself as she did. She didn't care that it was mid-July and not really soup season. She loved soup year-round, and besides, it got plenty cool up here in the shady mountains where she and Gray lived in the summertime.

She sometimes wished she still lived in Coral Canyon full-time, but she knew exactly why they didn't. She loved Hunter with her whole heart, and she wanted him to have friends and be happy. He was such a good boy, and he'd made excellent progress in his therapy over the past several months.

He inspired her to be a better person, and when Jane tested her patience with her stubbornness about taking a nap, Hunter would step in and rock his baby half-sister to sleep just to help out.

Today, Gray had taken his son fishing, as they did several times a week in the summer. Her husband and her son loved fishing with their whole hearts, and she loved cooking for the two of them, so they could have lunch together when they returned from the lake.

Gray had bought a new boat this summer, and while Wes had gotten Hunter a new fishing pole for Christmas, Gray had had to buy his own. Elise had actually purchased it for him, after consulting with Wes, and she'd gifted it to him for Father's Day.

No sound came through the baby monitor, and relief pulled through Elise. Jane fought her every step of the way when it came to sleeping, which meant Elise hadn't slept well in almost nine months now. She loved her blonde baby girl beyond anything she'd ever loved before, though, and Elise would happily sacrifice sleep for her.

Hutch barked, and Elise turned as he trotted over to the sliding glass door that led onto the deck. Her silver gold-endoodle loved to chase rabbits, squirrels, and birds, and there were plenty of those in these hills. They owned five acres here, and Elise moved over to the door. "Do you need to go out, bud?"

She glanced up as movement caught her eye too, and Hutch's booming bark filled the house again. Elise froze as she saw someone walking along the trees at the edge of the yard.

Her heart started pounding in her chest, and she couldn't tear her eyes from the figure there. It looked like a male, and Elise's mind fired scenarios at her faster than she could latch onto.

Hutch's barking continued, and it was that obnoxious sound that broke her from her trance. She quickly flipped the lock on the sliding glass door and said, "Hush, Hutch. Stop it." She pushed the dog back, but he returned immediately to the glass, adding a whine to his chorus of barks.

Elise hurried into the kitchen and grabbed her phone from the countertop. She ducked around the corner and into the mudroom off the back of the garage. The washer and dryer took up the back part of the room, and a window sat above them. She dialed Gray as she stood back and looked out the window.

"Come on," she muttered. He'd hired a few people this year to do some work around their property, and perhaps this man skulking around the edge of her back yard was there treating the lawn or spraying for pests.

"Hey, sweetheart," Gray said, his voice deep and even and full of happiness. "What's going on?"

"There's a man in the back yard," Elise said. "Hutch is going nuts." Even now, the dog barked. "Did you hire anyone who'd be coming today?"

"I don't think so," Gray said. "The guy I talked to about doing a fire pit said he'd be there on Friday."

"Dad," Hunter said, his voice animated. "I've got one."

Elise pulled in a breath as the man stepped onto the lawn and started toward the house. She couldn't be trapped in the mudroom when her baby girl was asleep in the nursery off the master suite. "Gray, I need you to come home right now," she said. "I'm going to hang up and call 9-1-1."

"9-1-1?" Gray asked. "Elise, who's there?"

"I don't know. That's what I've been trying to tell you. There's a strange man in the back yard, and Hutch is going crazy. He never barks, Gray. Ever." She entered the kitchen, and the barking only intensified. "Hutch," she commanded. "Come."

He didn't, and his bark definitely sounded scared as it echoed up to the vaulted ceilings.

Elise ran through the dining room and living room now, tears pressing against the backs of her eyes. Panic fueled her movements, and she said, "I'm hanging up Gray," as she ducked into the hallway that led to the master suite.

"Elise—" he started, but she hung up the phone.

"Hutch," she called back down the hall. "Come on." Much quieter, she added, "Please," as her first tears fell. Behind the closed door she'd just arrived at, Jane fussed.

Elise ducked into the room, and quickly closed the door, sealing Hutch out. Her chest wasn't nearly big enough for her heart to beat as violently as it was. Her hands shook as she dialed 9-1-1 on the way across the nursery to Jane's crib.

"Shh, baby," she cooed at the girl. "Shh, mama's here." She scooped the baby into her arms, glad the nursery was located at the front of the house, not the back.

"Nine-one-one, state your emergency," a woman said into Elise's ear.

"There's a man on my property," Elise said, pulling back on her emotions. This was why she didn't like living alone. Those fears and unreasonable imaginations usually came at night, and Gray made sure she wasn't alone at night.

"Do you know him?" the woman asked.

"No," Elise said, ducking into the corner with Jane in her arms. The little girl had quieted, thankfully. "I called my husband, and he hadn't hired anyone who was supposed to stop by today. My dog is barking like he's never barked before, and I'm in the house alone with my nine-month-old baby daughter."

"Has he tried to get in the house?"

"I don't know," Elise said. "I locked the back door and ran into my baby's room." It was then that she realized Hutch had stopped barking. "My dog is being quiet now," she whispered into the phone. "He's so friendly. If that guy came in, Hutch might think he was a friend." Or the man had injured her dog.

Elise started weeping silently, because she didn't need to alert anyone of her whereabouts.

"I have police on the way, ma'am," the woman said. "Your address is up the hill, so they're about fifteen minutes away."

A sob worked its way up her throat, and Elise couldn't confirm. She barely weighed a hundred and ten pounds, and she couldn't protect Jane from a grown man. Even fourteen-year-old Hunter could overpower Elise.

She let the tears stream down her face, and the woman on the other end of the line said, "Tell me your daughter's name, ma'am. What does she look like?"

Elise looked down at Jane cradled in her arms. "Jane," she whispered. "Her name is Jane Beverly Hammond. She just barely started growing in some white-blonde hair after being bald for months. She has these beautiful blue eyes, but they're much darker than mine, because her father has dark brown eyes. She has the shape of his nose, and wow, she's as headstrong as he is." She half-laughed and half-cried, and the operator giggled with her.

The doorbell rang, and Hutch started barking again. His voice came closer and then passed by, and Elise got back to her feet. "Someone rang the doorbell," she said. "Is that the cops?"

"No, ma'am," the operator said. "They're still nine minutes away from your property."

Gray had installed security cameras on all the entrances to the house, and Elise put the woman on speaker and balanced Jane in one arm while she frantically tried to tap and swipe to get to the Eyewitness app.

It recorded any movement and ten seconds afterward.

"It's my husband's brother," Elise said, pure relief filling her. She watched as Ames rang the doorbell and then opened the front door.

"Elise?" he called, and she spun toward the door.

"I don't think we need the cops to come," she said.

"They're on their way, ma'am. They'll want to check the property."

"Ames is a cop himself," Elise said.

"I'm still going to send them," she said.

Elise didn't want to argue. She stepped over to Jane's door and cracked it.

"Elise," Ames called again, and he appeared at the end of the hallway. She waved the phone at him, and he turned toward her, Hutch coming down the hall right at Ames's heels.

He squeezed through the door and closed it behind

him. "Are you okay? Gray called and said there was someone here."

"There was," Elise said. "We have the Eyewitness app. I saw someone in the back yard. We can see who it was."

He looked at her phone. "You called nine-one-one?"

"Yes," Elise said, her face cracking as the salty tears dried. "There was someone here, and Hutch was going crazy."

"Yeah, I heard him," Ames said. "He's not hurt." Ames scanned her. "You and baby Jane are okay."

"Did you see anyone around?" she asked. "Any vehicles?"

"No," Ames said. "But I wasn't really looking. Gray just said you needed help as fast as possible, and I was at Wyatt's house just up the road."

"Thank you, Ames," Elise said. He was here now, and if there was someone in the house, as least there was someone here who could protect her. She tapped on the back door camera, and there were three recent recordings.

The first showed a man coming toward the deck from the tree line, just as she'd seen him. "See?" Elise said, tilting the phone toward Ames. "That guy was there."

The recording continued, and the bearded man wearing a ball cap came right up on the deck and all the way to the sliding glass door. Elise tucked Jane tighter into her arms as Ames took the phone from her. He frowned as he kept watching, but Elise couldn't see the footage.

As she laid in bed that night, all she'd be able to see was that man striding right up to her house, with just her and her baby inside.

The doorbell rang again, and Ames tapped again and again. "It's the police," he said. He took her phone with him as he left the bedroom, and he closed the door behind him, which was a signal for Elise to simply stay where she was.

She swayed with Jane, smoothing down her daughter's wispy hair. She didn't want to hide behind closed doors, so she cracked the door and listened to the voices coming from the foyer. She couldn't make out what they were saying, and she inched out into the hallway. At the end of that, she turned left and went into the huge, arched walkway that led to the foyer.

"I called the police," Elise said as an answer to one of the police officer's questions. "There was a man on my property."

"I showed them the recording," Ames said.

"Ma'am," the male officer said, stepping around Ames. "I'm Officer Burke. We know who that man is. He's David Mills, and he lives down at the mouth of the canyon. He has some mental disabilities, and he's probably lost."

"Mental disabilities?"

"His parents are getting older," Officer Burke said. "I'm sure he just wandered off. He's no threat to anyone. He gets panicked when he gets lost, and since this neighborhood is new, he probably just got confused."

"Okay," Elise said, foolishness filling her. "Are you going to try to find him?"

"He went west from the back deck," the woman on the other side of Ames said. "Fifteen minutes ago now, Burke."

He cocked his head as the radio on his shoulder

beeped. "Unit seventeen-A, we just got a call from Loretta Mills. She said her son is missing again."

"I can help," Ames said, turning toward Officer Burke. Panic built inside Elise again, and she shook her head. Ames saw her, and thankfully, Officer Burke said, "We've got it, sir. But thank you."

"Thank you," Elise said as Ames came to stand beside her. The officers left, and Elise started to come down from her adrenaline high. That allowed room for her to start to feel like she'd overreacted, especially when she reached up and felt the dry tears on her face.

"Sorry, Ames," she said. "Really, I am."

"It's no big deal," Ames said. "I was literally three minutes down the road."

"Gray will be on his way back." Elise handed Jane to Ames, who grinned at his niece, and she moved into the kitchen. The corn chowder still sat on the stove, the flame underneath it. It would be scorched, and Elise felt the keen sense of failure ripping through her.

Her tears came again, and she worked hard against them as she picked up the spoon to see how bad the chowder was. The bottom definitely had a film on it, but she kept stirring and stirring, because she couldn't face Ames.

He followed her into the kitchen and opened the fridge, saying, "What does your momma have in here for you, huh? Applesauce? I bet that's for you, right, Janey?" He bent to get one of the squeezable tubes of applesauce, and he took Jane over to the table, where he sat down and settled the baby on his lap.

He chuckled a couple of times while Elise struggled against her emotions. The back door opened, and Gray called, "Elise?"

She pressed her eyes closed and took a quick breath. "Right here," she said, putting on the happiest face she could. Her husband came into the kitchen, frantic concern in his eyes. He looked from her to Ames at the table and back to her. "Baby."

Elise couldn't hold the tears back as Gray stepped over to her and gathered her into his strong embrace. "I'm fine," she said, but she knew he'd seen the tears before she'd pressed her face into his chest.

"Of course you are," he whispered in her ear. He held her tightly, stroking her hair every so often, while Hunter said something to Ames.

Elise stepped back and ducked her head so she could wipe her face easier. "I made corn chowder," she said, forcing her voice into something chipper and excited. "How was the fishing?"

"Elise," Hunter said, stepping next to his dad. His face held such brightness and hope. "I caught the biggest trout ever. And it just came in so easy, like he'd just been at the bottom for a long time, and once he got hooked, he decided to just come on up." He grinned like he'd won the lottery and not caught a fish—something he'd literally done hundreds of times before.

Elise fed off his enthusiasm, and she grabbed onto him and hugged him too. "That's so great, Hunt," she said. "I'm so sorry to cut your fishing trip short."

"It's no big deal," Hunter said, and he'd outgrown her

in the past year and a half. It was no wonder the boy had a girlfriend and that other girls kept putting notes in his locker or texting him.

"Sweetheart, this tastes...." Gray looked at her. "I'm going to call for something. Chinese?"

Elise stepped away from Hunter and nodded. Gray didn't particularly like Chinese food, but Elise loved it, and she loved him even more for his concern for her.

"Ames?" Gray said, moving around the other side of the island in the kitchen. "Wanna fill me in while we run down to town?"

"Sure thing." Ames stood up and handed a very saucy Jane to Gray, who grinned at his daughter. One of Elise's favorite things to do was watching Gray interact with his little girl, and Elise hugged herself, because she didn't want to be alone in the house.

"Hunt, bring in the fish and get them cleaned up, all right?" Gray looked at his son, and Hunter nodded. He ducked back into the mudroom and then out to the garage while Gray cleaned up Jane. "Baby, I'm going to take Jane and Ames with me. Hunter will be here, and Hutch, and all the doors are locked. Okay?"

Elise pressed her lips together and nodded. "Okay."

Gray stopped in front of her and pressed a kiss to her temple. "I love you."

"Love you too," she said, and she caught Ames watching them. He ducked his head and cleared his throat before he turned and followed Hunter into the garage. Elise knew he and Sophia were seeing each other, and she wondered how the relationship was going. She'd been so busy with her own little family that she hadn't kept in touch with Sophia as much as she'd like.

As Gray left and Hunter came in, Elise decided she could call Sophia and invite her to lunch on her next day off. And Bree too, if she could come, as well as Patsy and Annie. They'd all been such great friends in the past, and just because they all had busy lives didn't mean they shouldn't try to maintain that now.

CHAPTER 18

A mes laughed at what his mother had said, the sound filling the cab of his truck. He'd parked up at the lodge and stayed in the truck, because his mom had been talking for at least the last thirty minutes.

Apparently, there had been some shenanigans at the farm this summer. The man Gray hired to tend to it while he and Elise were in Coral Canyon had brought a couple of dogs with him this summer, and they weren't nearly as trained as the ones Ames had been working with the past several weeks.

"I have to go, Mom," he said as he caught sight of Sophia coming down the sidewalk toward him. She carried a baby on her hip, and he recognized it as Marcy and Wyatt's youngest, Harrison.

He got out of the car, the sight of her with that baby warming Ames's heart. He'd spent some time with her at the Walker's chalet in the mountains in the past couple of weeks, and now that August had arrived, Ames was starting to feel desperate. He couldn't wait until evening to see her, and he'd asked Wyatt and Marcy if he could come hang out in the afternoons once or twice a week.

They'd said yes, as long as his presence didn't interfere with Sophia's job with the boys. It hadn't. In fact, Ames had brought balloons and activities for Warren and Cole, and he'd entertained them while Sophia sat in the shade with the baby.

"Why do you have him today?" Ames asked as he approached her. He swept his arm around her and the baby and kissed her.

Sophia kissed him back and giggled when she broke the kiss. "Harrison came to stay with me last night, didn't you, baby?"

He'd been meeting with a real estate agent, so Ames hadn't seen Sophia last night. "Why's that?" he asked.

"Warren is really sick, and Marcy didn't want Harrison around it. I offered to bring him home with me."

"You're a saint," Ames said.

"They've got Warren on an antibiotic now, and Wyatt's coming to get him," she said. They walked over to her car, and Sophia handed Ames the little boy so she could bend down to get his car seat out of her back seat. When she turned back to him, she grinned. "You look good with a baby in your arms."

"Do I?" Ames looked at the little boy, and he didn't look anything like Ames. Marcy was blonde and blue-eyed, and Wyatt had the lightest features of the Walker brothers, and their children definitely had light features and hair.

Everything about Ames was dark, and he absorbed Sophia's lighter features. She still had brown eyes, and lighter brown hair, and he wondered what their children would look like. He'd fallen fast for her, and he was one breath away from being completely gone. At least he thought he was. He'd never been in love before, but the things he felt for Sophia sure felt like love.

"Yes," Sophia said, taking the baby from him. "How do I look with a baby in my arms?"

Ames soaked her in, fighting to keep his foothold on the path he was on. The problem was, he felt like the Earth was shaking and he was about to go over the edge of the cliff. "Amazing," he said, his mouth suddenly too dry.

She cocked her hip and smiled, then turned as an enormous truck entered the parking lot. She gave Harrison to Wyatt, and they chatted for a few seconds. Then she came back to Ames and tucked herself into his side. "So," she said. "What are we doing on my day off?"

"Whatever you want," he said. "We only have a few Wednesdays left. So you tell me."

Sophia flinched, and Ames wondered what he'd said. "Is that true?"

"Is what true?"

"We only have a few Wednesdays left?" She pulled away from him, and his heart dropped to his boots. "What does that mean, Ames?"

"I mean, it's August," he said, his voice weak. "Summer's almost over."

Sophia backed up a couple of steps, and Ames felt her retreating from him physically and emotionally and spiritually. "What are your plans for when September comes?"

"I don't know," he said.

"When are you going to figure it out?"

Ames clenched his teeth and looked away. This was not a conversation he'd wanted to have today. He really did just want Sophia to have the perfect day. She worked so much, and so hard, and he wanted to give her a comfortable place to be.

"I'm trying," he said.

"Are you?"

Ames returned his attention to her, wishing that her eyes weren't shooting lasers quite so strongly. "You don't want me to say things that I don't know. No potential or thinking, remember?"

Sophia took a breath and blew it out in a way that suggested her annoyance with him. "It would be nice if you told me what you were thinking. Even just a little bit."

Ames gazed steadily at her. "Now you want me to tell you what I'm thinking?"

"I always want to know what you're thinking. You just never say. You're like this walled-off city."

"I am not," Ames said. "I've told you all kinds of things."

"But not what you're thinking about where you'll live, and what will happen to us once you make that decision." She shook her head. "I feel like we're living on borrowed time, and I hate it." She folded her arms, but he saw the tremble in her hands. "I hate that you have me on this string, and you can decide to pull, and I'll lose everything."

"Sophia," he said. "I'm not going to do that."

"You aren't? What assurance do I have of that?" Her eyes blazed that fire, but her chin shook. "This whole thing has just been ridiculous."

"Do you really think that?" he demanded. "And I'm not the only one who doesn't talk."

"I talk to you."

"Have you called your mother? Your brothers? Any of them?"

Sophia opened her mouth, the flames in her expression dimming. She closed her mouth again and looked away.

"I'm going to take that as a no," Ames said. "Let's just say that we get engaged and then plan a wedding. Are you going to talk to them then? Are we ever going to visit them? I don't understand how you just don't talk to them."

"Not everyone's family is as perfect as yours."

"Come on," Ames said, well-aware that his voice carried plenty of disgust and bite. "My family isn't perfect, and you know it. But at least we act like adults and *talk* to each other."

"You don't talk to me!"

"You want me to talk to you?" Ames had so much he could say. "I met with a real estate agent last night. That's what I was doing. I didn't want to tell you until things were more solid, but that's the truth." His chest heaved, and he couldn't quite get a proper breath.

"What? Why?" she asked, her expression hopeful.

"I want to start a police dog training academy," he said.

"I've been talking to my guys in law enforcement and learning where they get their puppies. There's an endorsement program to become a certified dog trainer, but there's more you have to do for K9 dogs. I want to do that. Finally, I feel like this is what I'm supposed to do with my life. But there are so many unknowns, and I'm still sorting through so much."

Sophia had softened during his speech. Ames didn't normally say so much at once, but everything had just spilled out of him.

"I wish you would've told me. I can help you."

"You're working two jobs," he said. "The majority of my time is spent throwing a ball for a dog." He shook his head, frustrated and not holding it back. "I don't know what the future holds. The dog training is a year-long program, Sophia, and it's not in Coral Canyon."

There. He'd said it out loud.

"But the facility would be here."

"Maybe," he said. "Apparently, there are permits to have more than four animals on a property." He looked at her, a measure of helplessness infecting him. "Can we just…I don't know. I don't want to ruin anything with you. I'm trying *so hard*." Harder than he'd ever tried with anyone before.

"It shouldn't be hard," she said.

"Being with you isn't hard," he said. "Trying not to hurt you is a little harder." He looked away, because he didn't want to see the hurt in her eyes. "Most of the time, Sophia, I don't really care what anyone thinks about me. I've lived my life just doing my thing. But with you…I'm really thinking about you, and how my choices will impact you, and us, and all of it."

"I'm a big girl, Ames."

This so wasn't going well. "I know." He blew out his breath. "Can we be done talking about this for today? I don't have anything definitive to share with you, which is why I haven't said anything."

"It's okay to talk to me through the process."

"I got a completely different message the night of Cy's wedding," he said.

Sophia nodded. "I suppose you did. Fair enough."

They stood in the parking lot, neither one of them truly looking at the other. Ames didn't know what else to say. He knew the day was getting hot, and he really didn't want to argue with Sophia when she had so little time off.

"Will you still spend the day with me?" he asked quietly. "I promise I won't use that bad boy voice again." He'd let it come out during their conversation, because honestly, his family was *not* perfect.

"Yes," she said, her voice a pinch too high.

"Great." He folded her into his arms. "Tell me what you want to do, and we'll do it."

Slowly, she wrapped her arms around him too. "Maybe we can go to a movie," she said. "I'm feeling like some very buttery and very salty popcorn."

The buzzing nerves inside Ames settled, and he stepped back and threaded his fingers through hers. "A movie sounds amazing. Let's go see what's playing."

They did spend the day together, and things improved between them. Ames could still feel that something was off, and that evening, in the comfort of his own rental, he knelt beside his bed and poured his heart out to the Lord.

Please don't let me hurt her. Please guide me to the right piece of land, and the right training program, and the right place to be.

He'd spent hours making phone calls and taking notes. He'd printed forms from the Internet and researched training programs. He'd gotten names and numbers of people already training police dogs, and he wanted to schedule tours of their facilities and ask them questions.

None of that took place in Coral Canyon. He'd definitely have to leave town again at some point in the future. As far as he knew—because Sophia didn't talk all that much to him about her future plans either—she was still unwilling to relocate. So he honestly wasn't sure where they were, or what would happen, or how many more Wednesdays they had together.

"I should do the dog academy, right?" he asked out loud, and once again, Ames felt a very sure confirmation that yes, he should put his inheritance and his time and energy toward founding and establishing a police dog training academy.

Grateful, he finally collapsed into bed, the words, "Please let me know if I'm in love with Sophia Cooke," the last ones out of his mouth before he fell asleep.

CHAPTER 19

P atsy left the house with her purse and a smile, practically running toward Sophia's car. She hugged her best friend, who'd gotten out to greet her. They laughed together, and Patsy said, "Thanks for coming to get me. You didn't have to."

"I wanted to," Sophia said, stepping back and smiling at Patsy. She looked good—happier than she'd seen her in a while. Still, Patsy had lived in very small quarters with Sophia, and she saw something else in the woman's eyes.

"Why's that?" she asked, trying to keep her voice casual. She moved around the car, and Sophia waited until they'd both gotten in to even look at Patsy again.

"I need your help," Sophia said. She put the car in drive and started down the apple-tree-lined lane. She passed in front of Cy's motorcycle shop, where he was working today. Patsy had plenty to do in the orchard, but she'd decided that she couldn't sacrifice friends or family for work.

There would always be more work to do in the orchard. There wouldn't always be lunch with her friends, or a family dinner at Gray's house, or a boating trip after church on Sunday.

She wanted to be present for her own life, and that didn't happen under the shade of the apple trees.

"Help with what?" Patsy asked, trying not to sound too curious.

Sophia's fingers tightened on the wheel, and then she released them. "I need to call my mother, and I don't think I can do it alone."

Patsy didn't care if Sophia knew of her curiosity now. "Your mother? Sophia...what?" She didn't talk to her mother, at least that Patsy knew. She didn't know much, because they'd talked about her family very little. Sophia had said she didn't go home for holidays or to visit, because there was no family to go see, and no home to go back to. She'd grown up in the military, and her family had moved a lot.

"It's time," Sophia said, sniffling as she pulled in a breath. "I just keep thinking that if Ames and I get married, won't I want my mother at the wedding?" She glanced at Pasty, but what she'd said had rendered Pasty mute. "I mean, even your mother came, Pats."

"Yeah," she said, swallowing immediately afterward. "Yeah, she did."

"I want to call her," Sophia said. "I'm just not sure I'm brave enough to do it myself."

"Of course I'll help you." Patsy reached over and took Sophia's hand in both of hers. She looked out the windshield as Sophia reached the outskirts of town. They only had a few minutes before they'd meet the others, and Sophia would disappear right back into her shell. She usually let the other women dominate the conversation when they all got together, and though it had been a few years, Patsy didn't think Sophia had changed that much.

"You and Ames might get married?"

"What? No." Sophia wouldn't look at her.

"You just said that. If Ames and I get married."

"I'm just thinking too far ahead," Sophia said, but Patsy heard the lie.

"You told me once that you wouldn't be involved with one of *those Hammond brothers*," she teased.

"You said you wouldn't fall in love with Cy." Sophia cocked her eyebrows at Patsy, and they both giggled.

"What's Ames doing these days?" she asked, her voice a forced casual now.

"He's thinking of starting a police dog academy," Sophia said.

Patsy grinned, because if there was anyone who should be working with dogs, it was Ames Hammond. She'd seen him with the three dogs he had, because Ames and Cy were very close, and she often found the two men and the four dogs lounging in her living room when she got back from the orchard.

"That's great, Soph. He's perfect for that."

"Yeah," Sophia said, but she sounded absolutely miserable about it.

"What aren't you saying?"

"He has to get trained to do it," she said. "Find a place to house them. Get the puppies." She sighed as she pulled into a parking space at Devil's Tower. "There's a lot of moving pieces."

"I'm pretty sure there's no training academy here," Patsy said, reading between the lines.

"No, there is not," Sophia said. She looked at Patsy. "I feel like we're so close, and yet so far away."

"But you like him." Patsy wasn't asking, and she pushed against the giddiness building inside her.

Sophia gave another over-emphasized sigh. "Yes, okay? Yes, I like him. Probably too much. *Far* too much."

Patsy picked up her purse. "I know exactly how that feels. Every single woman we're meeting for lunch today knows how that feels." She started to get out of the car, but Sophia didn't move. Patsy twisted back to her, waiting.

"I don't want to go in," Sophia said. "You go without me."

"I'm not going to go without you," Patsy said. "Just come in, Sophia. You won't be so alone if you just come in."

Sophia finally turned her head toward Patsy, and she could see the glistening tears in her friend's eyes. "I know how to be alone. It's being with someone I don't know how to do."

"That is just not true," Patsy said. "We lived together for four years, and you were the best roommate I've ever had." She smiled and got out of the car. She went around it and opened Sophia's door too. "Come on, Soph. I can't go in there alone."

"Why not? You already belong to them."

"So do you," Patsy said, extending her hand for Sophia to take. Thankfully, she did, because Patsy didn't have another idea. She couldn't physically drag Sophia out of the car against her will.

Sophia slumped against Patsy, her footsteps heavy. "Listen," Patsy said. "Just ask Bree about the time Wes brought in that ladder to hang the art he'd bought. That'll help you feel like you fit right in." She smiled at Sophia, but the gesture didn't get returned. "Because you do, Soph."

She led the way inside, looking left and right to find their friends. Elise waved from a booth against the windows, and Patsy kept a firm grip on Sophia's hand as she turned right and started toward them.

They were the last two to arrive, which wasn't surprising, because Elise had picked them all up, and Elise was never late. She held her baby on her lap, but she still rose to hug Patsy and Sophia. Bree accepted a side-hug from Patsy, as did Annie, and the five of them settled down.

"Why does Sophia look like she swallowed a lemon?" Bree asked, unwrapping her silverware and laying her napkin on her lap. Everyone looked at Sophia, who sat on the end, and Patsy regretted sliding into the booth first.

She clamped her hand over Sophia's knee under the table, causing her to flinch. "She's fine," she said.

Elise switched Jane to her other side, pure concern in her eyes. "Sophia? What's wrong?"

"Nothing," Sophia said, but she literally couldn't infuse any more misery into her tone. "You tell them, Patsy."

"Okay." She drew in a deep breath to spill the beans, but the waitress arrived, and they all paused to put in their drink orders. Sophia ordered Coke—not diet—with lemon, and that once again drew everyone's attention to her.

"This is bad," Bree said.

"It's Ames, right?" Annie asked, reaching across the table to touch Sophia's hand. "Is he leaving, Sophia?"

She shook her head and said, "Not yet. But I don't see how he can stay here." She looked at Patsy. "I've done the stupidest thing. Why didn't I learn my lesson from last fall?"

"He just has to go away for the police dog training," Patsy said. "He'll come back here to open the academy."

Elise and Bree looked from Patsy to Sophia and back, both of them with wide eyes.

"Sophia doesn't want to talk about it," Patsy said, drawing her shoulders straight and pushing her hair out of her face. "We don't do this often enough, and we're not going to spend our lunch moping." She hoped Sophia would get the message too. After all, Patsy hardly ever left the orchard, and she didn't want to be more depressed when she went back than she'd been when she left.

"I just have to get something off my chest," she said. "I adore Cy, but the man seriously does not know how to load a dishwasher." She draped her napkin over her lap and looked at Bree, then Elise, and then Annie. "Tell me it's just him, because if none of those Hammond men can do it, I'm going to have to call his mother."

The three of them looked back at Patsy for a single heartbeat, and then everyone—except Sophia—burst out laughing.

"You should see Wes try to light a grill," Bree said with a giggle. "When I asked him if he'd ever done it before, he gave me the surliest look and said, 'Of course I have.'" She mimicked him in a really low voice. "But he hadn't, ladies. He dang near blew up our house." She let out another peal of laughter.

"Oh, I don't let Gray have matches." Elise shook her head as if Gray was her naughty two-year-old and not her husband. "He can bait a hook, and boy can he run. He can hang pictures—"

"Don't even get me started about hanging pictures," Bree said, her voice quite stern.

Patsy beamed around at all of them, almost afraid to look at Sophia. When she finally did, she found her hanging on every word the other women were saying.

"And you know what?" Annie asked, her face glowing with happiness. "I asked their mother about them once, and she said, 'Heaven knows I tried, Annie. I really tried.'" She laughed again, and Patsy joined in.

"But you do love them," Sophia said, looking around at everyone as they sobered.

"Of course," Annie said. "Colton is the best thing that's happened in my life."

"I'd be lost without Gray," Elise said, gazing down at their baby.

"I love Wes with everything I have," Bree said. "Doesn't mean I don't get annoyed when he drops his shoes by the back door and doesn't even seem to see them again."

"Yes," Patsy said. "They're not perfect, and they can be loud and obnoxious. But we love them."

Sophia nodded, a new look on her face. A thoughtful look.

"I have some news," Annie said as their drinks arrived. She waited for the five cups to be passed around and for everyone to start opening their straws. "Colton and I are going to adopt a little girl."

A breath of silence followed, and then the women at the table erupted.

"I MEAN, I'M JUST SO HAPPY FOR THEM," SOPHIA SAID. SHE was a completely different person than she'd been two hours ago, and Patsy felt like God had answered her prayers. "Can you imagine bringing an eight-year-old to live with you?"

"It won't be easy," Patsy said, already thinking about how she could help Colton and Annie. Bree and Elise were Colton's best friends, but Patsy had always felt welcome and comfortable with him and Annie. They'd go to movies together sometimes, and Patsy enjoyed that.

Sophia pulled up to the house in the orchard, and the two of them got out. Patsy groaned as she walked up the front sidewalk. "I should not have had that apple pie. It wasn't even that good."

"That's because you have apple juice running in your veins," Sophia said.

Patsy smiled at her, because it was good to see the real version of Sophia back. They went in the house, and Patsy put her purse on the kitchen table. "Okay," she said. "I don't think we should put it off. Let's call your mother."

Sophia's whole demeanor changed, and Patsy didn't want to pretend like she hadn't seen it. "Tell me what the real situation is," she said.

Sophia sat at the table, and Patsy took the seat next to her. "The real situation is that my mother did the best she could," Sophia said quietly. "In the end, she didn't want to keep working so hard, so she divorced my dad and left North Carolina. She doesn't talk to me much, but last time I spoke with her, she was living in California."

Patsy nodded, hating the way her friend deflated right in front of her. "Okay, give me your phone."

"You're going to call her right now?"

"Yes," Patsy said. "Right now." She held out her hand expectantly. "I'll dial while you go get a bottle of water out of the fridge. By the time you get back, you'll be ready."

Sophia looked like she was ready to throw up and nothing more. She dug her phone out of her shorts pocket and handed it to Patsy before going into the kitchen.

Patsy started to swipe to get to Sophia's contacts. She saw Dad at the top but scrolled down to the one labeled Mom.

She took a deep breath and closed her eyes, wishing she had the exact right words to use to pray for exactly what Sophia needed.

She didn't, so she let her finger drop onto the green phone button and watched as the call connected.

CHAPTER 20

"Sophia," her mother said, and Sophia nearly spit out the water she'd just taken into her mouth. "How are you, dear?"

She looked at Patsy, only to find her wide, blue eyes staring back. She looked shocked, though Sophia wasn't sure why she was. The surprise shooting through her bloodstream was definitely real, though.

How are you, dear?

Dear?

"Good," she said, clearing her throat. "I was just... thinking about you." She looked away from Patsy and closed her eyes. "Uh, how are you?"

"Good," her mom said, absolutely no tension or awkwardness in her voice at all. She acted like she'd just talked to Sophia that morning, and that they were all caught up on the details of one another's lives.

The truth was as far from that as it could get.

"Just puttering around the garden today."

"Oh, you have a garden?"

"Yes." Her mother sighed. "In this new place I'm in, it's mostly xeriscaping. I don't miss the lawn, that's for sure. The previous owner had a lot of rose bushes and succulents. I'm just trying to keep everything alive."

Sophia heard the tone of her mother's voice, but the words had jumbled together after "In this new place I'm in."

"You moved?" Sophia asked.

"Yes," her mom said. "Let's see, probably six or seven months ago now." That was it. No other explanation needed.

Sophia definitely needed one. Anger started to build in her chest, and she couldn't explain it.

"What are you up to?" her mom asked as if they could catch up on the last three or four years in a few sentences.

Patsy touched her forearm, and Sophia turned toward her. Patsy mimed taking in a deep breath and blowing it out, and Sophia copied her.

"I'm still working at Whiskey Mountain Lodge," she said, getting to her feet. Nervous energy ran through her, and she couldn't sit still. "And I'm nannying this summer for a professional bull rider. Well, he's retired now, but he was a pro bull rider. He's got three little boys, and I take care of them during the day."

Her voice grew stronger as she paced away from Patsy and toward the front windows. "I like the nannying more than I thought I would. It's pretty fun."

"That's wonderful, dear."

"Yeah," Sophia said. "I guess I just wanted to hear your voice." Emotion clogged her throat, and she pressed her eyes closed as she reached the window. She hadn't realized how much she missed her mother until that very moment.

She did need to slow down and breathe through the anger. She hardly knew her mom as an adult at all, and she couldn't judge her until she did.

"I'm seeing someone, Mom," she said, almost whispering to her faint reflection in the glass. She could see how wide her eyes were, though the color didn't come through. She'd once thought everything about her to be so plain, but Ames made her feel vibrant and colorful. He made her feel alive.

"What's his name?" her mom asked.

"Ames Hammond," Sophia said. "It's getting serious, and I...I guess I just wanted you to know."

A lengthy pause followed, and finally, her mother said, "I do want to know, Sophie. Thank you for telling me."

Sophia nearly broke down at the childhood nickname her mother had used. She'd been called Sophie so much, she'd wondered why her parents had named her Sophia instead.

She nodded, though that gesture didn't get communicated through phone lines. "Are you seeing anyone?" she asked.

"I'm still with Gabe," her mom said. "Same man as the last time we talked."

"We shouldn't let so much time go between this time and next time," Sophia said, using just one ounce of bravery. "I miss you, Mom."

"I miss you too, dear," she said. "And you're right. We should definitely not let so much time go by between this call and our next one."

"What else is the same in your life?" Sophia asked, glad when her mother gave her more than single-word answers. In fact, the conversation lasted almost thirty minutes before Sophia saw Cy and Ames pull up to the house on their motorcycles.

"Mom," she said. "I have to go, okay? Ames is here, and I want to tell him all about you."

"Oh, don't do that," her mom said with a light laugh. "I'm not very exciting."

"It was good talking to you, Mom."

"You too, Sophie. I love you, baby." Her Southern roots came out in those four words, and Sophia pressed her eyes closed as tears burned in them.

"I love you too, Mom," she managed to say through her very narrow throat. The call ended just as the back door opened and Cy and Ames entered the house.

"...is all I'm saying," Ames said.

"I know precisely what you're saying," Cy argued back. "And I'm telling you that it won't work."

"What won't work?" Patsy asked behind her, and Sophia turned around to observe the three of them in the kitchen. Cy started to explain about a motorcycle they were building at the shop, but Sophia didn't really hear him.

Ames had seen her, and he was coming her way, a playful smile on his mouth. "What are you doing here?"

He drew her into a hug, and Sophia should've giggled and clung to him in the same teasing way he'd spoken to her.

Instead, she clung to him like she needed him to survive, like he was the only thing preventing her from drowning. He realized instantly that something was wrong, and his grip along her waist tightened. "Sophia?" he asked quietly.

"I called my mom," she whispered, finally letting her first tears fall.

Ames said nothing, and Sophia was glad. She didn't need him to say anything. She just needed him to hold her, and he was very, very good at that.

———

"AMES, WILL YOU GRAB HARRISON, PLEASE? COME ON, Warren, we don't want to be late for your daddy."

"Daddy," Warren said, marching toward the front door. "Daddy, daddy, daddy."

Sophia tried to get Cole's second shoe on, but it seemed like his two-year-old foot had swollen two sizes. It probably had, because the child had gotten into the freezer that afternoon and eaten through half a carton of ice cream before Sophia had found him.

He was supposed to be down for a nap, and she'd been on the back deck with Warren, where the four-year-old splashed in a blow-up swimming pool. Instead of getting angry, Sophia had scooped the little boy into her arms and taken him out to the pool too. Sure, he'd made the water a little milky, but she'd been able to clean him up in under twenty seconds flat.

Ames had arrived soon after that, and he'd found the carton of ice cream still melting on the kitchen floor. Better him than Marcy, who'd come out of her office an hour later with a frown permanently etched in her face.

She'd said, "I have to go talk to Wyatt. Will you bring the boys to Crispers at six?"

Sophia had barely had time to say yes before the blonde powerhouse was gone. She knew just from being in the house with Marcy and Wyatt that Marcy wasn't super happy to be in Coral Canyon. She ran a crop-dusting business, and she spent most of the time while Sophia was there on the phone with someone in Texas or on the computer doing the books.

Wyatt sometimes took one or two boys with him to do whatever he was doing that day, and the man was a giant play-baby. He loved to go mountain biking, canoeing, hiking, four-wheeling, and any number of outdoor things. The problem was, he had a bad back, and after his most physical activities, he was laid up in bed for a day or two, with ice packs up and down his back and the baby balanced on his chest.

Today, he'd gone to a boarding stable to "help out," and Sophia had kept all three kids with her. She loved having the Walker kids around her, and she liked it even more when Ames showed up in the afternoons to help or hang out with her and the kids.

She got to see him interact with the children, and while he wasn't as bubbly and friendly as Colton was, and he didn't charm everyone from age two to eight with his charisma the way Cy did. He did laugh with the kids, and play Go Fish with Warren. He held Cole on his lap and cuddled him close when the boy wouldn't lay down for a nap, and coming up the steps to the loft to find Ames asleep on the couch there, with Cole snoring softly against his chest had been one of the sweetest things Sophia had ever seen.

She'd snapped a quick picture of the two of them, and while Ames was dark in every way, and Cole the complete opposite, they did love each other. Cole had a bit of a devilish streak in him, and that paired well with Ames's bad boy attitude.

"Let's put this on in the car," Sophia said, picking up Cole and tucking the shoe into her purse. "We're going to be late." She hurried into the garage, where she found Ames bent over into the SUV, buckling Harrison into his car seat. She could hear Warren singing at the top of his lungs, so she didn't have to wonder where he'd gone.

She went around to the other side, already sweating inside this hot garage. She put Cole in his seat and handed him the shoe. "See if you can get this on while we go down the canyon, okay bud?" She smiled at him and strapped him in, then got behind the wheel.

Ames had left the garage, and she stopped next to him as she backed out. "I'm dropping them off at six," she said. "Then I have to bring the SUV back here and get my sedan. Do you want to go to dinner? Go back to my cabin? I could come to your place." She didn't go to his rental house very often, but she'd been a time or two.

"Flo isn't feeling well," he said. "I want to keep her home tonight. My place?"

Sophia nodded and said, "See you in an hour or so."

"Sounds good." He backed away from the luxury SUV and lifted his hand in a wave. Sophia listened to the three boys babbling in the back seat, but her thoughts focused on Ames. It had been a couple of weeks since she'd called her mom after lunch with her friends. She'd told him about the conversation, and she'd called her mother two more times since then.

She sighed, because it was easier to do that than burst into tears. She couldn't deny that it hurt that her mother hadn't called her. Sophia wondered if she really could be the one to initiate contact for the rest of her life. At some point, she knew she'd feel like she was trying to push a relationship onto her mother that her mom simply didn't want.

The real problem was, she was completely powerless to change her mother.

She was powerless to make time stop moving forward.

She was powerless in her ability to persuade Ames to stay in Coral Canyon. With every day that passed, she felt one day closer to losing her heart—and she was completely powerless to keep it.

She'd already given it to Ames Hammond, and he got to decide what to do with it.

After she dropped off the boys, hugging Warren and Cole and passing them to their parents, Sophia started back to the Walker's mountain home. Her phone connected to the vehicle via BlueTooth, and she decided she didn't have to let Ames have all the power.

She tapped to call him, and his voice came over the speakers a moment later. "What's up, beautiful?"

"Ames," she said, her thoughts scattering. She looked straight out the windshield, her bravery building beneath her ribcage.

"Sophia?" he asked.

"I'd like to talk about what your plans are," she said. She wasn't going to give him her heart and let him decide what to do with it. She wasn't. She was going to be honest with him and give him all the facts.

As soon as she could figure out how to get the words out of her mouth.

CHAPTER 21

A mes could feel the turmoil in Sophia, and they weren't even in the same room. His heart beat strangely in his chest, but he gave her the silence and time she needed.

"I want to know your plans, because I'm falling—no, I've fallen in love with you—and I need to know if you're going to…well, I need to know what you're going to do."

Ames stood up, his pulse positively pouncing in his chest now. Had he heard her correctly? He pulled the phone from his ear and looked at it. Definitely still connected.

She said something, and he hurried to press the phone to his ear. "…still there?" she asked.

"Yes," he said, his voice rusty and croaky. "I'm here." He cleared his throat and looked around the house he'd been renting for a few months now. It didn't really feel like home, not the way Gray's house did, or Cy's.

He'd already talked to Gray about living in his house once his brother took his family back to Ivory Peaks. That piece was in place.

Ames had put in an offer on a parcel of land on the east side of town, where a lot of the flatter farmland was. A generational farmer had passed away, and the children had divided up the land to sell. He'd bought four of the pieces, which should be more than enough to construct the administration building he'd need to run the police dog academy.

He'd been on the phone with Josiah, the man who helped police departments get their dogs. He was willing to help Ames do the same thing.

All of those things had come together, seemingly falling into place as if God Himself was lining up the steps Ames needed to take to finally put his inheritance to good use.

"Well?" Sophia asked, her voice filled with challenge and desperation.

"Are you on your way here?" he asked, turning toward the kitchen.

"I'm going back to Marcy's."

"I have something to show you," he said. "I'll get it out and have it ready when you get here."

"Okay," she said, but she didn't hang up. "You heard what I said, right?"

I've fallen in love with you.

"Yes," he said, barely able to push the word out. His lips didn't move or anything. "I heard you." He couldn't get himself to say he loved her back. He wasn't entirely sure he did, and he would not say those words to a woman until he knew. One hundred percent, for sure, absolutely *knew* he was in love with her.

"Okay. See you in a minute." She hung up then, and Ames dropped his phone to the couch and strode into the kitchen. He didn't have to get anything out, because the foam board was right there, lying on the kitchen table. He gazed down at it, seeing his dream come to life right in front of his eyes.

He could practically taste the dust and smell the sunshine. He could hear the dogs barking, and he could see himself in the kennels with them. Sophia would— Ames cut the thought off at the knees.

Of course he'd dreamt of her at his academy. In his mind, everything worked out so well, and the little boys they took care of together in the afternoons would be theirs, not Marcy and Wyatt Walker's.

Ames sighed and pressed both palms into the table. He dropped his head and said, "Lord, she is a good woman. I do not want to hurt her." He looked up at the ceiling, noticing a stain in the corner where the roof had likely leaked at some point. He didn't care about that, because he wouldn't be living here much longer.

"Please," he begged. "Please help her open her mind to the possibility of leaving Coral Canyon."

He didn't know what else to pray for. He'd told her precious few details about the police dog academy since their argument a couple of weeks ago. She'd called her mother, and that was a huge step in the right direction for her. At the same time, Ames had noticed that she wasn't any happier. She called her mother, sure, but her mother didn't call her.

Ames had eyes, and he could read Sophia exceptionally well. He wondered—not for the first time—if he'd pushed her to do something he shouldn't have.

He just wanted to be able to make a decision without then having to riddle out if it had been the right one or not.

If she still had to get to Marcy's before heading his way, he likely had time to call his own mother. He retraced his steps to the couch and picked up his phone, quickly dialing his mom.

"Ames, my son," she said by way of hello.

Just the sound of her voice made Ames smile. "Hey, Mom."

"What's going on?" she asked.

"Uh, nothing much." He reached back and ran his fingers through his hair. "Actually, that was a lie, Mom. Sophia just called and said she loved me, and she wants to know my plans."

His mom sucked in a breath, and Ames knew enough to hold the phone away from his ear. She squealed just after that, and he'd barely saved his eardrum from certain rupture.

"Ames," she said. "That's great news. I'm so excited for you."

"Don't be excited, Mom," he said. "I didn't say it back, and I don't know what my plans are." His voice felt heavy in his own ears.

"Ames Bryce Hammond," she said, and he realized

calling his mother had been a mistake. "How much longer are you going to fight against God?"

"What?" he asked, glancing over as Cocoa jumped up onto the couch beside him. Florence hadn't moved from her dog bed in the kitchen, and that was unusual. Ames's worry for her was only overshadowed by the sting in his mother's question.

"You've had your answer for months, son," she said sternly. "You knew the moment you picked up those dogs."

"I've been working on the academy," he said, frowning. "It takes longer than you think to buy land. The guy hasn't even accepted my offer yet."

"Not that," she said.

"Then what?" he demanded, his defenses already up.

"You know you're supposed to be in Coral Canyon." She sighed, and Ames wanted to as well. Everything inside him was laced too tight though, and he couldn't. "I don't like it any more than you do, son, but it's the truth. Your dad and I will be fine here. Gray and Elise are here, and we actually like Matt Whettstein. He does a wonderful job with the farm, and his kids are polite and kind. They even made Grams a birthday cake, even though it's not her birthday."

"I wanted to talk to you about that too," he said. "I've been working on the plan for the big celebration. I haven't talked to the other brothers yet, but—"

"There's not going to be a celebration," his mom said.

Once again, Ames was left with only one reply: "What?"

"Grams hasn't been feeling well," Mom said. "Daddy and I—well, we think she's probably not going to last much longer."

Ames blinked, trying to make sense of the words. "We should all come home then," he said, already making a plan to do just that. "I want to say goodbye."

"You do what you think is right," Mom said. "I should let the others know."

"You definitely should," he said. "Colton will be upset if you don't. Wes too. Cy. Gray. We all love Grams, Mom."

"I'll call them all when I'm done here."

"I think we're done here," Ames said, reaching over to stroke Cocoa. She looked at him with such love in her eyes, and Ames didn't want to give her back to Ruff Rescue. He wanted to keep her. And Florence and Norman—and definitely Sophia.

"We are not done here," Mom said, adopting her hard tone again. "You belong in that town, Ames. I know you don't like it, but you better *learn* to like it. And you belong with Sophia. Stop fighting against yourself and what you know to be true and just admit it."

Ames looked out the front windows of the house, his mind moving like molasses. "Okay, Mom," he said.

"Okay," she repeated. "I love you, son. Maybe practice saying it a few times before she gets there."

Ames didn't confirm that he'd definitely do that, and the call ended. He couldn't admit anything to himself, and he wasn't sure how to say it out loud to Sophia either. He'd only told his mom that to get her off the phone.

He sat on the couch, feeling very much outside of his

own skin and bones. His awareness floated around somewhere above him, seeing everything and feeling everything. All he had to do was keep stroking Cocoa.

If he admitted to himself—and to Sophia—that he loved her, and she still wouldn't go with him…. Then what? What if love wasn't enough?

He pulled himself together when Norman gave a single bark and trotted toward the front door. "She's here," he said, and he hated how negative he sounded. He should be thrilled his girlfriend was coming over. Excited to show her the things he'd been working on. Happy he had someone to share his life with, even this tiny part of it.

Sophia knocked on the door, and Norman barked several times, as if Ames hadn't heard him the first time.

"Shush," he told the dog as he got off the couch. He swiped his cowboy hat from the end table and smashed it on his head. He'd likely need to hide behind it at some point in the next ten minutes. "Go to your bed." He pointed to the pillow next to Flo, and Norman obeyed. "Stay there." He held his hand out to Norman and edged toward the door.

Sophia stood on the other side, and her eyes were as wide as saucers. The nervous energy pouring from her made Ames jittery, but he stepped back to let her in. He closed the door behind her, the silence between them unbearable.

"Come see this," he said, and he took her hand in his. He loved the touch of this woman, and the way she made him want to be the strong, steady man she wanted in her life.

"What is it?" she asked.

He didn't answer as they crossed over to the table. "It's the dog academy," he said. "I started sketching it out. I put in an offer on the land last night, and I just have to wait to hear back from the seller." He put his finger on the length of fence that ran up the side of the rendition.

"Where is the land?" Sophia asked, her voice barely above a whisper.

"It's on the east side of town," he said. "It's the old Jacobsen farm."

"Oh, yes," she said. "Kenneth passed away."

"Yes." Ames couldn't look away from the drawing he'd been working on. "I think they'll accept my offer. Then I can get the construction crews out to start on the buildings." He reached for the edge of the blue folder, where he kept everything else. He pulled it out from underneath the foam board and flipped it open.

He looked at the top sheet of paper and handed it to her. "This is a contract I signed with Josiah Moon. He runs all the police dog puppies in the western United States. I've told him I only want German shepherds to start with, though it is quite a ways off."

She looked at the paper, but he didn't expect her to make sense of it.

The next thing in the folder was his estimated budget for the construction, and it included the price of the land. He gave her that, with a brief explanation. "I can get the facility, Sophia. I can get the dogs. What I can't do is then sell them without a certification."

He looked at the next piece of paper and scanned it,

though he had it memorized. Finally, he plucked it from the folder and handed it to her. "I was wrong. It doesn't take a year to train to be a dog trainer. For police dogs specifically, it only takes twelve weeks. I've been researching facilities all over the country, and this one's the best."

He took a breath and then a moment to swallow. "They have other courses I want to take too. On their website, it says I can bring two dogs, but I called, and they'll let me bring three because of my experience on the force in Littleton." He was aware of how fast he was talking, but he couldn't stop himself now.

"I want to take their detection program too, as well as their search and rescue program." He had, in fact, already registered for all three. His throat narrowed and dried right out, as if he'd just put a handful of cotton in his mouth. "They're each twelve weeks. The first one starts on September twenty-eighth."

He forced himself to stop talking. Sophia stared at the paper and then looked up at him. "It's in North Carolina."

"Yes," he said. "It's the best one, Sophia. I want to be the best. I know I can do it." He put the folder down. "It'll take at least nine months to build the facility, and I don't need to be here to do it."

She simply looked at him, and Ames could see everything in her face. Her hopes, her dreams, her fears.

He cleared his throat and pushed his cowboy hat back. He wasn't going to hide while he said this. "I want you to come with me," he said. "Because I'm in love with you too, and I *need* you with me."

Tears filled her eyes, but Ames wasn't sure if they were happy ones or sad. She looked down at the paper again, her voice high and squeaky when she said, "Why does it have to be in North Carolina?"

"Why does it matter?" he asked. He felt like his heart was hanging on by a string, and she was about to clip it free. Steal it right from his chest. "Did you hear what I said?"

"I heard you," she said, still weeping. "I *hate* North Carolina. I don't want to go back there. Ever." She looked up at him. "Maybe we can just press pause for nine months."

"I don't want to press pause," he said, frowning. "I want to be with you. I want to share this with you. I want you to come work at the facility with me."

"I can't train a dog."

"No, but you can run the facility while I train the dogs," he said. "And they'll need special diets, Sophia. You can be their cook." He actually smiled, as if he'd just cracked a funny joke. Sophia did not laugh or smile, and Ames saw everything he'd been fantasizing about wither before his eyes.

"I didn't go to culinary school to cook for dogs," she said.

"No, I know," he said. "That was a joke." He sighed, because this talk wasn't even going how he planned. Truth be told, he hadn't planned anything.

She looked at the rendition of the facility he'd made. Her eyes drifted over the papers he'd shown her. To Ames, it felt like an easy decision. Marcy and Wyatt would be gone by then, so she wouldn't be letting them down. She could give notice at the lodge now, six weeks in advance.

His phone rang, and he nearly jumped out of his boots. His realtor's name sat on the screen, and he said, "I have to take this. Sorry." He connected the call, turned away from Sophia, and said, "Hey, Alyssa."

"The seller has accepted your offer," she said, and she sounded like she'd just conquered the world. "You got the thirty acres, as well as the water rights. Congratulations, Ames!"

"Thanks," he said, a smile slowly working its way across his face. He wandered down the hall toward the three bedrooms in this house, a calm, peaceful feeling filling him. "That's great news."

You better learn to like it.

He'd better, because he now owned more land in Coral Canyon than any of his brothers.

"It sure is. I'll get you the signed forms in a bit when I get them from Xavier. We're not doing a loan, so things should be smooth sailing from here."

"I hope so," Ames said. He suddenly had so much more work to do, but he just thanked Alyssa again and hung up. His purchase of the land would surely convince Sophia that he was serious about staying here. He was serious about her.

He didn't want to press pause, and he'd spoken absolutely true. He wanted her with him, and if that meant they had to get married by September twenty-eighth, well, Ames wasn't opposed to that either.

He loved her.

Warmth filled him once, twice, three times over. He'd never been in love before, but this felt amazing. This felt precious. This felt right.

He turned around to share the good news with Sophia, but she wasn't standing where he'd left her. "Sophia?" He swept the kitchen and living room, and every cell in his body wailed when he saw the wide-open front door.

"Sophia," he said, almost running toward it. "No, no, no," he moaned.

Her car was gone.

She'd left.

And she'd taken his heart with her.

CHAPTER 22

"What do you mean you just ran out?" Patsy asked.

"I mean, he said he loved me, but he wants me to go to North Carolina with him," Sophia said, her voice almost a hiss for how quietly she was talking. "And I ran out."

"Sophia," Patsy said, and Sophia hated the condescension in it. At the same time, she deserved it. Who ran out on their boyfriend only a few minutes after he'd confessed his love for her?

The woman who simply can't go back to North Carolina, she thought as Patsy said, "Well, go back. Go back right now and tell him you'll think about it."

"I don't need to think about it," Sophia said. "You have no idea what it was like there. No one does. I'm not going to North Carolina."

"You're going to lose him," Patsy said, worry in her

voice. "Is that what you want? Is not going to North Carolina worth that price?"

Sophia opened her mouth to answer, but she closed it again. She glanced out the window, but no one drove down this stretch of deserted road. She was only around the corner from Ames, and she could get back to his house in under three minutes.

"Go back," Patsy said. "I'm begging you. Go back."

Before Sophia could answer, another call came in. She checked the screen, her breath catching right behind her tongue. "He's calling," she whispered.

"Good," Patsy said. "Answer it and tell him you just needed a minute to think. I'll get off this call." With that, she was gone, and Sophia had two choices: Let Ames go to voicemail or answer the phone.

"Hey," she said, her fingers having connected the call of their own volition.

"Where'd you go?" he asked. The wind swept across his receiver, sending an awful white noise into her ear.

"I just needed some time to think," she said. "I'm just driving for a minute."

"Are you coming back?"

Her hesitation screamed between them, but she said, "Yes," at the same time he said, "It's fine, Sophia."

"I'm coming back," she said.

"You don't have to."

"I'll be back in ten minutes," she said, and this time, she pulled a Patsy and ended the call before he could argue. But ten minutes was nowhere near long enough for her to figure out what to say to Ames.

How could she explain that she loved him so much she'd follow him to the moon and back? That she loved him so much she'd go with him anywhere...except North Carolina.

There was no explanation for that.

When she pulled into Ames's driveway, she found the man sitting on his front steps, hands between his knees, head down. He either didn't hear her sedan or he was ignoring her. When she opened her door and got out, he looked up.

He stayed seated, and Sophia was glad for that. He was so big, and he could intimidate her sometimes.

"I'm sorry," she said. "I just needed a minute."

"You took fifteen," he said, his eyes shrouded in darkness.

"Yeah." She sat down on the steps and gazed out over the lawn. "I don't know how to say this," she said. "So I guess I'll just say it. I can't go to North Carolina. Literally, any of the other forty-nine states, and I'm there. Just not that one."

"Why not?"

"My father lives there," she said. "That was the last place I lived before everything disintegrated, and I vowed I'd never go back." She hung her head too. "I guess I just never figured I'd have a reason to."

"It's that bad?" he asked.

"Yes," she said, her chest vibrating with the negative emotions piling up there. "I really think we could just push pause, and you could go do your dog thing, and then come back. I can keep an eye on your construction here, and there's email and texting and video chat...." She let her voice trail off, because she knew none of those things were even half as good as being in the presence of a real person —especially Ames.

She already missed him. Everything about him, from the warmth of his hands to the scent of his skin to the sound of his voice.

He reached over and gently took her hand. "I don't want to break-up."

"I don't want that either."

He looked at her then, but she couldn't carry his gaze, so she kept her attention on the front lawn and the road beyond it. She wished a couple of kids would ride by on their bicycles to remind them that the world would go on while they lived apart. This wasn't the end.

It was just a pause.

"I suppose I can push pause," he said. "If you're sure this is about North Carolina and not Coral Canyon."

That got her to look at him, her heartbeat thundering in her chest. "It's not about Coral Canyon. I just said any other state, and I'm there."

"What about Colorado, then?" he asked. "I could buy land there."

Sophia swallowed, Patsy's words ringing in her ears. She'd never thought of her desire and decision to stay in Coral Canyon as having a price, but it did. "Yes," she said. "I'd go with you to Colorado."

He studied her for another moment, and then he lifted her hand to his lips and kissed her wrist. He looked back out over the lawn and tucked her arm under his, their fingers still intertwined. He said nothing, and Sophia didn't want to ruin anything else between them, so she stayed silent too.

"That phone call was my realtor," he said. "I got the land here, Sophia. I'm not moving to Colorado."

"You'll be back here before you know it," she said, trying to infuse some false happiness into her voice. She failed, and they could both hear it.

"Right," he said. "Should I order some dinner? We can eat and cuddle with the dogs and help Flo feel better."

Sophia leaned her head against his arm and said, "Yes," but Ames didn't move. She didn't either, because she wanted this moment to freeze in time. She wanted to stay right here at his side for the rest of her life.

Tears filed her eyes, and she closed her eyes against them, managing to contain them. She breathed in deeply, and said, "I'm sorry, Ames."

"It's fine," he murmured. "It's not the end. It's just pause."

She hoped he was right, and they spent the evening just as he'd outlined. She'd tiptoed over to him close to midnight, leaned down, and pressed a kiss to his forehead. "I have to go, Ames."

"Okay," he said. It was more of a moan, but he managed to get the three dogs off his lap and legs and walk her out to her sedan. He kissed her under the August moon, and Sophia had never been kissed by a man who loved her.

She tried to hold onto the feel of his hands in her hair, and the taste of his lips against hers. But the moment she got behind the wheel and started back up the canyon, she'd forgotten all of it.

"How are you going to last nine months without him?" she asked herself, finally letting the tears come so quickly that she had no choice but to let them stream down her face.

———

"IT'S A MUFFIN BAR," A LITTLE BOY SAID, AND SOPHIA SMILED at his exuberance. She used a pair of tongs to put out more blueberry muffins, as they were the most popular variety she'd made that morning. She'd also baked up corn muffins, banana chocolate chip, raspberry vanilla, and lemon poppyseed. Those were her favorite, and she glanced down the line to see there were only a few left.

She'd kept one in the kitchen for herself, and after breakfast at the lodge, she took her muffin and walked back to the cabin.

It was a Wednesday, and on any other Wednesday this summer, she'd have found Ames sitting on her steps, her porch, or in her living room. He'd have his dogs with him, and Sophia's heart would expand with adoration for the man who carried his bad boy streak with him, but tempered it with kindness and attention to details.

He wasn't there that day, and Sophia sighed as she climbed the steps to her front door. He hadn't come last week either, and she'd called him just before lunch to find out if he'd like to eat with her. He'd said yes, and they'd gone out. She'd spent the rest of her day off with him.

All she needed to do was call. Heck, a text would work.

Instead, Sophia sat at the breakfast bar in the kitchen and ate her muffin, her mind moving through things one step at a time. She didn't want to be the one to initiate everything. She hadn't called her mom in a couple of weeks, because phone lines worked both ways. Her mother could dial out, Sophia was sure of it.

Ames could too, and he hadn't. He'd stopped inviting her to dinner. He'd stopped coming up to her cabin and suggesting dates he'd already planned.

"He's just busy with the construction manager before he leaves." Sophia was the master of making excuses—for herself or others, it didn't matter.

She finished her muffin and slipped into staring. She hated times like these. She wasn't good idle, and she hadn't had a lot of downtime this summer. But Marcy and Wyatt were loading up tomorrow, and they'd return to Three Rivers until next summer. She was going over to keep the boys out of the way while Wyatt and Marcy loaded their truck and trailer.

Then she'd have to say goodbye to them too. She sniffed, not even realizing that she'd started to weep.

Worse, Ames was leaving on Saturday. His grandmother would be one hundred years old in November, but his parents suspected she'd pass away before that milestone could be reached. So he'd been working for the past few weeks to put together the celebration now. All of the Hammonds were going, and Sophia put her head down and cried when she realized Ames hadn't even invited her to attend with him.

Everyone else was going, as Annie, Bree, Elise, and Patsy were Hammonds now.

"What do I do?" she asked, her voice so unlike her own. She'd been praying morning and night for an answer to that question. None had come. She'd think of something, and then the fantasy would derail, and nothing ever came out of her frenzied thoughts.

Today, she didn't want to be alone. She tugged her phone out of her back pocket and dialed Ames.

"Hey," he answered on the second ring. "I'm in line to order food, so I might have to do it while we're talking."

"Okay," she said, and she started crying again.

"Sophia," he said quietly. "Please don't cry."

"Will you come up to the cabin?" she asked. "Please?"

"Did you eat breakfast?"

"I had a muffin."

"I'll get you something," he said. "I'm at Good Crepes."

"Okay." Sophia could smile at his obsession with the new crepe store in town. Everyone seemed to be, and Sophia had never been by the place when there wasn't a line at least four cars deep.

"Banana and caramel?" he asked.

"Yes, please."

"See you in a few."

She ended the call and bent over her arms again. The tears slowed and dried up, but she didn't move. She just watched the trees sway in the gentle breeze on the other side of the kitchen window.

When Ames arrived, she'd managed to compose herself. She'd made no attempt to wash her face or make herself more presentable. She didn't turn toward him as he entered the kitchen, and he set down a bag beside her. "Here you go, sweetheart." He pulled out the barstool next to her and sat down. "I got the cookies and cream one. It's my new favorite."

Sophia smiled and lifted her head. Her shoulders ached from her bent position, but she managed to get her banana and caramel crepe out of the bag.

She loved the little triangular paper the crepes came in, and she did like the slightly yeasty smell of the batter, with the whipped cream and a drizzle of caramel peeking out the top. "Ames," she said. "I want to go to Colorado with you this weekend."

She looked at him, and he looked at her. "Okay," he said.

"Okay?"

"Yeah, okay. I'm going on to Havenville from there, but you can fly back with the others. Colt will have a car at the airport. I'm sure he'd bring you back up here." He didn't miss a beat, and he obviously didn't understand why she'd been weeping that morning.

"Why didn't you invite me to come?" she asked.

Ames took a big bite of his sugary breakfast and shrugged. That was going to be the only answer she got, and Sophia simply looked at her own crepe. Her mouth watered, and she took a bite of her breakfast too.

It didn't matter if he invited her or she invited herself. She was going to go to his grandmother's birthday celebration, and she allowed a bit of sunshine into her soul because of that.

Maybe she'd just have to learn how to ask for everything she wanted. He didn't seem to mind giving it to her, but it felt like another lead weight had been tied around her neck. She already carried one for her mother, one for her father, two for her two brothers, and now Ames.

Sophia wouldn't be able to carry them all for much longer, and she wondered what would break first—her neck or her desire to carry everything and everyone with her so she wouldn't ever have to truly be alone.

CHAPTER 23

"There she is," Ames said, infusing as much happiness into his voice as he was able. The truth was, he hadn't been happy in weeks, not since Sophia had asked him to push pause. The real trouble was, he hadn't been sure when to push the button. That very day? When he left? At some point in between?

He knew he didn't want to push Sophia into a place she didn't want to be, so he'd backed down quite a lot. He didn't show up at her cabin anymore. He rarely called her first, something he considered repenting of every day. He saw the pain she carried with her because her mother never called her first.

She'd stopped talking about her mother completely, and Ames hadn't asked any more questions. He shouldn't have asked any in the first place. He shouldn't care what her relationship was with her family. All that mattered was that she talked to *him*, told him what was on her mind, shared her life with him.

"Happy birthday, Grams," Colton said as he took her the cup of coffee.

"Pish posh," she said, taking the mug. "It's not my birthday. I may be old, but I'm not senile."

He just grinned at her while Cy tried explaining to Grams—again—that they knew it wasn't her real birthday, but they'd all come to celebrate with her early.

Ames couldn't wait to get old. No one seemed to mind Grams's surliness, and maybe he wouldn't have to work so hard to sound like everything in his life was hunky dory.

Of course it wasn't.

The front door opened, and Ames settled against the counter and listened as his brothers and their wives talked as they entered. They came into the back of the homestead, Wes leading the charge as he laughed loudly. He was followed by Bree, Patsy, and Cy, who carried Michael in his arms.

The little boy squealed when he saw Ames's mother, and wiggled to get down. Cy put him on the floor and he ran to his grandmother saying, "Nana, Nana, Nana!"

She laughed as she scooped him up into her arms, and Ames's heart started that screaming again. He wanted a little boy like that too.

Sophia came into the main living area of the house too, and Ames's heartbeat did a full stop. She wore a form-fitting pair of jeans and a blouse in his favorite color—red. He wondered if she'd done that on purpose, but he dismissed the thought. She'd worn red plenty of times, and it didn't mean anything.

He couldn't look away from her as she twisted to take Jane from Elise after Elise said something to her. The baby had clearly been crying, and Sophia bounced her on her hip and smiled at her, smoothing back her wispy, blonde hair.

Ames's desire for Sophia shot into the atmosphere, but so did his anger. He'd be forty-one by the time he returned from North Carolina, and while she was nearly a decade younger than him, he didn't want to be on pause. He wanted to be shopping for engagement rings and planning a proposal and then a wedding.

He wanted it all, and his impatience with himself and her rose to a new level that had his ears ringing with a wail that hurt.

He turned away from the scene, because everyone had arrived now, and he could slip away without being noticed. Ames went through the back door to the deck, taking a deep breath of the autumn morning air. It wasn't terribly cool yet, but fall would arrive in the Rocky Mountains soon enough now that September had arrived.

He went to the left to get out of view of those still in the house and leaned against the railing. It was quiet out here, and Ames needed the silence. He'd only been standing there for a few seconds before the door opened again, letting out the chatter and laughter from inside.

Ames didn't turn to see who'd come out. The clunking of boots crossed the deck and went down the steps. He probably hadn't been spotted, so he turned to see who it was. Hunter crossed the lawn, his intent the farm beyond.

Ames should go help him; that way, he'd have a reason to be out of the house. He sipped his coffee for another minute, trying to identify why he didn't want to attend his grandmother's birthday party with his girlfriend.

That wasn't right. He did want to be here with Sophia, but he wanted the status of their relationship to make sense to him and others. He wanted to greet her with a hug and a kiss and take her hand to introduce her to his parents. He wanted to sit next to Grams and say, *This is the gorgeous woman I'm in love with, Grams. Her name is Sophia, and she makes me so happy.*

He felt like he couldn't say any of that. He wasn't even sure if he could use the word *girlfriend*.

He left his coffee mug on the railing and followed Hunter into the barn. He heard his nephew's voice, and he paused before he saw him.

"It's fine," Hunter was saying. "Honest, Molly, it's fine."

To Ames's ear, whatever Hunter was saying was fine absolutely wasn't. For a moment, he wasn't sure if Molly was actually here at the farm or if Hunt was on the phone.

He heard the shuffling of his nephew's boots, and then Hunter said, "Sure, I want to be friends with other girls too," and Ames knew he was on the phone. Guilt pulled through him, because he didn't want to eavesdrop on his nephew. He was almost fifteen years old, and as far as Ames knew, he'd been Molly's boyfriend for a while now.

"Doesn't mean I want to kiss 'em," Hunter said. "That's only you, Mols."

Ames couldn't stand here for another second. He wouldn't want anyone to hear his private conversations. So he knocked loudly on the wooden doorframe of the barn and called, "Hunter? You need any help out here?" He took a couple of steps before his nephew came around the corner, his phone at his ear.

Ames held up his hand as if to say, *Oh, sorry. I'll wait.*

Hunter held up one finger, his dark eyes full of displeasure. "I said it was fine," he said. "Look, I have to go, okay? Can I call you later?" He nodded and turned away from Ames, but he didn't walk away. "Okay, sure," he said much quieter. "Yes, I said okay."

He lowered the phone and kept his head down for a couple of seconds. In that brief window of time, Ames connected to Hunter in a completely new way. He wanted to wrap the boy in a hug and tell him there would be plenty of other girls. Hunter was tall and broad and dark and good-looking. He probably had a dozen admirers right now, all of them just waiting for Molly to be out of the way.

Hunter turned toward him, and Ames asked, "Everything okay?"

The teen shoved his phone in his back pocket and shook his head. "We just need to make sure Lucy has fresh water."

He was so much like Gray that Ames could blink and see his brother standing there. He'd seen Gray do exactly what Hunter had done many times. Phone away. Head down. Work. It didn't matter what had just happened. He didn't want to talk about it.

He helped Hunter clean out a couple of horse stalls, though the boy hadn't said anything about doing that, and then they made sure the pregnant mare had what she needed. Thirty minutes later, Ames sat on a bale of straw with a cold bottle of water Hunter had given him from the mini-fridge.

"Can I ask you a question?" he asked.

"Sure," Hunter said.

"Say you have a girlfriend, but she doesn't want—no, that's not right." Ames sighed and looked at Hunter. "Sophia and I are dating, right?"

"Right," Hunter said.

"She doesn't want to come to North Carolina with me, but we don't want to break up. She said she wants to just pause, and when I get back, we'll pick back up." He couldn't believe he was telling a fourteen-year-old this. Somehow, it was so much easier than explaining anything to Colton or Cy. "What does that mean? How do I act in there?" He gestured in the general direction of the house.

"Is that why you're out here?"

"Yes," Ames said.

Hunter sat down too, his expression thoughtful. "I have no idea, Uncle Ames. Molly just called and said she wants to—I don't even know what. She said she didn't want to date anyone else, but that she wanted to be friends with other boys. And she feels like she can't because of me."

"I don't know what that means," Ames said.

"That makes two of us," Hunter said darkly.

"Maybe she wants to just pause too."

"I still don't know what that means."

"Me either." Ames took off his cowboy hat and ran his hands through his hair. "Well, we have to go in. Grandma is going to serve lunch in ten minutes, and she won't be happy if we're late."

"Or dirty," Hunter said, but he didn't get up.

A minute later, Ames did, and he extended his hand to pull Hunter to his feet too. He hugged his nephew and said, "You're a good boy, Hunter."

"Thanks, Uncle Ames." They started back to the house, and Hunter added, "You like Sophia, right?"

"Yeah," Ames said with a sigh. "I more than like her. I'm in love with her."

"Okay, well, then you should act like that." He looked at Ames, and he still had to look up a few inches. "That's what I think, at least. I mean, why not? You're not in North Carolina yet."

"Right," Ames said, his mind running in a new direction now. "I'm not in North Carolina yet."

Inside the house, he and Hunter went into the bathroom to wash up, because the kitchen was crowded with his mother, Annie, and Elise in there. Back in the living room, Ames went right to Sophia's side. "Hey, beautiful," he said, almost under his breath. He slipped his fingers down her arm and between hers.

She squeezed his hand, and when she met his gaze, she had tears in her eyes.

"I'm sorry," he said. "I left you in here alone."

LIZ ISAACSON

She swiped at her eyes, and said, "Introduce me to your grandmother."

He took her over to Grams and crouched down in front of her. "Grams, I wanted you to meet the woman I'm in love with. Her name is Sophia, and she makes me so happy."

Grams reached out one wrinkled, weathered hand and cupped his face in her palm. "You're a good man, Ames." She looked up at Sophia, and Ames tugged her down to his level.

"Sophia, this is Opal Walker, my grandmother."

"Nice to meet you," Sophia said, her voice strong and sweet.

"You're lovely," Grams said. "No wonder our Ames loves you."

Sophia pressed her shoulder to his and simply said, "Thank you."

"Okay," Ames's mother called. "Time to eat. Ames, bring Grams over here. Colt, put those dogs outside. Wes...." She continued to give all her sons something to do, and Ames was the last to complete his as Grams really didn't move very fast.

"I'll pray," his father said, and everyone swept their cowboy hats off their heads. Ames pressed his to his chest and kept his eyes open as others closed theirs and bowed their heads. He looked around at all of these people he could call his, and his heart swelled with love for each of them.

"Amen," everyone chorused, and Ames quickly stuffed his hat back on his head so he wouldn't have to admit he hadn't listened to the prayer. His spirit felt full already, but his stomach wanted the roast beef sandwiches and potato salad his mother made.

He bent down and asked Grams, "What do you want, Grams?"

"Oh, Patsy is getting mine," she said in her gravelly voice. "But get me some of that lemonade, Amesy."

"You got it," he said with a smile. He'd forgotten about the nickname, and he glanced at Sophia too. "Do you want some lemonade?"

"Sure," she said.

He moved to the end of the counter where the drinks were, avoiding the other end where everyone had lined up. He got the three of them drinks and staked out their spots at the table. "Might as well get in line," he said, taking Sophia by the hand again and taking her with him. They got in line behind Hunter and Gray, who were talking in low voices.

"…that's all she said," Hunter concluded.

"I don't know what to tell you," Gray said, glancing at Ames. He pretended to be reaching for a plate, like he didn't care about the conversation. And he didn't really. He handed the paper plate to Sophia as Gray added, "Sometimes girls don't get why they do things either, Hunt. Maybe just give her a little time?"

Hunter nodded, and the next thing he said was also classic Gray. "When we finish here, could you drive me to get new basketball shoes? The ones I have don't work for PE."

"Maybe," Gray said, and the conversation moved on.

Ames would happily take Hunter to get new shoes, because he didn't have all the responsibilities his brother did. Not here, anyway.

"When we finish here," he said to Sophia. "Would you like to come to my house in town and help me go through a few things?"

Sophia looked at him with pure surprise in her eyes. "Yes," she said. "What kind of things?"

"Basically everything I own," he said with a smile that should've been a frown. But the idea of getting to spend more time with Sophia made his heart happy. Perhaps he should've been doing what Hunter had suggested all along—acting like he was in love with her instead of like they'd already been paused. "I'm renting a trailer to take my stuff to North Carolina."

She glanced down then, but that could've been to pick up the tongs for the roast beef.

"And I have a limited amount of space. I'll have the dogs in the truck with me, so everything has to fit in the trailer."

"Have you found a place to live?" she asked.

"Yes," he said, realizing there was so much he hadn't shared with her. "I did. It's nice too, from the pictures anyway. The guy called and did a video walk through as well. Lots of land for the dogs."

"You mentioned being worried about the commute once," she said, her voice noticeably cooler.

He had mentioned it—once. "Yeah, it's not as far as some places, but I'll have to drive about thirty minutes to the training facility." He finished loading his plate with food and waited for her to pick a slice of chocolate cake. They went to the table together, and Ames ended up by Cy, thankfully.

Their eyes met, and whole conversations were had. Cy's eyebrows went up, and he looked at Sophia. Ames shook his head and sat down. "And the house in Three Rivers is up for sale now."

"It is?" Cy and Sophia said at the same time.

He looked back and forth between them. "Yep. Micah Walker finished all the remodeling, and he put me in touch with a realtor, and I signed all the papers to get up for sale, oh, I don't know. Tuesday or Wednesday."

"Wow, I hope it sells fast," Sophia said.

Ames didn't much care if it did or not. He felt foolish enough about the whole Three Rivers situation as it was.

Cy leaned closer to him and whispered, "You didn't tell her you put it up for sale?"

Ames suddenly wished he'd sat down by Wes. At least he'd be distracted by Michael, who was currently fussing over the noodles Bree put in front of him.

Ames just shook his head, glad when Patsy asked Grams how she'd met Grandpa. Grams loved talking about her late husband, and she entertained their end of the table until it was time for cake.

Ames sang along with everyone else. He laughed and hugged his grandmother, thinking that it might be the last time he did. He helped clean up the dishes, and he told Gray he'd take Hunter to get shoes if he didn't mind hanging out at his house afterward for a little while.

"Can I take Hutch?" Hunter asked. "I can play with the

dogs in the backyard. Maybe I can call Phil, and he can come to Uncle Ames's." He looked at Gray with such hope in his eyes, and Ames was transported back to when he was almost fifteen years old. He'd have done anything to be with friends, as they were astronomically more important than his family.

Now, he only wanted to spend time with his brothers, their wives, and kids, and his parents. It was funny how time changed things.

"Sure," Gray said. "Take Hutch. You'll have to talk to Uncle Ames about having Phil over. It's his house, and I think he wants you to help him work." Gray raised his eyebrows at Ames, who nodded at his brother.

He put his arm around Hunter and said, "I'm sure you can have a friend over. Get Hutch, and let's go."

Hunter bustled off to do that, and Ames turned to find Sophia. She sat on the floor in the living room, Jane on her lap and Michael threading a shoelace through a card with an extreme look of concentration on his face.

Sophia had her finger right on the next hole, and Michael got his chubby fingers to get the lace in the right spot. The world narrowed to the three of them like a spotlight from heaven had shone down right on her. Everything else faded away, and Ames was really glad he'd taken Hunter's advice.

He couldn't imagine what saying goodbye to her would feel like, and thankfully, he didn't have to do it until Monday.

"Hey," he said gently. "We're ready to go. Do you still want to come?"

"Yes." She lifted Jane up to him, and he took the little girl. She looked at Ames with wide eyes, and he smiled at her and gave her a quick kiss on the cheek while Sophia stood up.

Baby Jane smiled and reached for Ames's cowboy hat. He pressed it on his head and said, "You can't have that, baby," before turning to find Gray or Elise. He didn't see them, and Patsy said she'd take Jane, so Ames passed the girl to her.

"Have fun," Cy said as Ames walked behind the couch. "We're playing cornhole at seven. You should be back to defend your title, or you'll have to forfeit."

"Oh, jeez," Ames said, and he walked out the front door with Sophia, the two of them laughing about defending a cornhole title. Things between them almost felt normal, and Ames started to consider that perhaps he could go to North Carolina and pause his relationship with Sophia and things would be fine.

Perhaps.

CHAPTER 24

Sophia's heart pounded at the sight of the farmhouse. She'd loved her time in Colorado, and she regretted that she'd once said she wouldn't leave Coral Canyon for this place. She loved the Hammond family, despite her earlier vows to not let them take over her life.

It just goes to show how wrong first impressions can be, she told herself.

"Well," Ames said, bringing his truck to a stop behind a couple of others. "Here we are."

"Mm," she said, looking at the house. She was going back to Wyoming tomorrow. He wasn't. She'd go back to her real life at Whiskey Mountain Lodge, and he wouldn't be there.

He wasn't leaving for North Carolina for another week or so, but he had to go through his house and get packed before then. She'd helped a little bit this weekend, but not much. In the end, Ames had opened a few kitchen cupboards and said, "Maybe I can buy new dishes to use there," and Sophia had followed his lead.

They'd gone through his hall closet to pull out a few towels and sheets, and he'd half-heartedly put those in a box. Hunter's friend, Phil, came over, and then Ames and Sophia had sat in the swing on the back porch and watched the two teenagers play with the four dogs. Ames had been quite different this weekend than he'd been in the several weeks leading up to the trip. He'd held her hand and asked her to dinner. He'd kissed her with more passion, and he'd told her about the things he'd been doing to get ready to go, about the house in Three Rivers, and about the construction on the dog facility in Coral Canyon.

He'd spoken to her the most about that, because she was going to help him with it while he was gone.

"I don't want to say goodbye in a big group," he said. "Tomorrow, at the airport." He got out of the truck while Sophia was still trying to process his words and pull herself back to the present.

He opened her door while she did that, and he stepped into the space between the door and the truck. "I don't want to say goodbye at all, but especially then." He slid his hand along her leg, and then up the side of her hip.

She reached up and took off his cowboy hat. "I'm sorry, Ames."

"We don't need to talk about it anymore," he said, his eyes burning with an energy she'd rarely seen. They usually only blazed like this when he was angry. "Okay?

Can you just kiss me? This will be the last time for a while, so I'll try to make it good."

Sophia pushed her fingers through his hair, and he leaned into her. Because she was still in the truck and he wasn't, she sat higher than him. He pressed his cheek to her chest, and she held him. Her cells started to bubble, and her lungs seized.

This was goodbye. She had to say goodbye right now.

It wasn't September twenty-eighth, and somewhere in the back of her mind, that was the day she'd been preparing for to say goodbye to him. Not today.

She pulled in a breath and held it, the moment between them tender and sweet. He lifted his head, and she bent down, and he kissed her. He'd always made it good, but tonight, she noticed how slow he moved, and how deep he went.

He pulled away too soon and leaned his forehead against hers. "I do love you, Sophia."

She felt shaky as she said, "I love you, too, Ames."

He backed up and nodded, grabbing onto the door so she could get out. She wondered if her legs would be able to hold her, but when she slid from the truck and hit solid ground, she didn't fall.

He didn't actually say the word goodbye. He just threaded his fingers through hers as they went in the house together. She was staying with Gray and Elise in the main part of the house, and Ames had a blow-up air mattress in the generational house where his parents lived. So he paused at the end of the hallway leading back to the bedrooms and looked into the living room, where three of his brothers loitered with their wives. They'd put on a movie, but Sophia didn't want to join them.

"How was dinner?" Cy asked, looking over to them.

"Great," Ames said. He nudged Sophia down the hall and out of sight of everyone else. "I'm headed over to my parents'."

"Okay. I'm just going to go to bed."

"I'm sure you can sit with them."

She shook her head, feeling about five seconds away from crying. "I'm tired anyway, and I have to do dinner at the lodge tomorrow. I'll need all the sleep I can get." She looked up at him, expecting a smile. Sometimes he tucked her hair behind her ear. This time, he simply looked at her, really looked. He seemed to want to find something, and it was extremely urgent that he did.

She wasn't sure if he found it or not, but he did lean down and kiss her again. "See you in the morning," he whispered, and then he was gone.

Sophia leaned against the wall, telling herself not to slide down it and start sobbing. *Not yet*, she coached herself. *Not yet, not yet, not yet.*

She barely made it into the guest bedroom where she was sleeping before the tears fell, though, and she didn't slide down to the floor but buried herself in the blankets on the bed.

———

SEPTEMBER BECAME OCTOBER, AND AMES SENT A BUNCH OF pictures of himself on the first day of training. He sent pictures of him working with his dogs, and him working with a new dog named Rosco.

Sophia decorated her cabin and tried new recipes with the guests at the lodge. It snowed the third week of October, and she wasn't ready to face another winter, let alone another winter alone.

Halloween came, and Sophia walked around wearing a black dress and a pointed hat with Bree, Wes, and Michael. The almost-two-year-old was fascinated with everything, and it took forever to get from house to house. But Sophia didn't want to sit home by herself, in the lonely, cold cabin behind the lodge.

As she walked at a snail's pace, she couldn't help but think of the wassail she could make, and how much Ames would enjoy it. They could eat sloppy Joes and apple pie, and watch a scary movie while they cuddled in front of the fire.

Her fantasies were so out of control lately, and she didn't know how to rein them in. She'd texted Ames earlier that day to find out what he was doing for Halloween, and he hadn't answered.

She texted him a couple of weeks later to find out if he'd be flying to Coral Canyon for Thanksgiving. Their communication had fallen off in the past two or three weeks, and she told herself it was because his training had intensified. She was basically telling herself what he'd told her, because she didn't want to believe any differently.

She didn't want to believe he had time for a video chat but simply didn't do it. She didn't want to believe he read her texts and *chose* not to answer. She didn't want to even entertain the idea that their pause would become a break—or that it already had.

He answered with a quick, *No. I'll tell you more later*, and the text made everything in Sophia's life better.

But later never came. The next time she called, he didn't answer. He texted hours later to say he'd been in class, and he'd call now, but he was so tired, and he'd talk to her on the weekend.

Two went by, and she didn't hear from him.

She spent Thanksgiving Day with Julianne and Melinda, the two new hires to the lodge in the last year. They'd hosted it at the cabin where Bree and Elise used to live, and Sophia hadn't spent the day alone. That was something, but Sophia was beginning to wonder how much it really was.

Her mother hadn't called her. Her father didn't either. Neither of her brothers. As she walked back to her cabin, alone in the dreary, cold night, she considered calling all of them, just to see how they were doing. It was a day of gratitude, after all.

She looked up into the sky, but it was very, very dark. No moonlight shone down, and no stars winked at her from heaven. Clouds had rolled over the mountains that afternoon, and Sophia wouldn't be surprised if she woke in the morning to a foot of snow.

The world would be frozen, and it wouldn't thaw until March. She wished God would freeze her heart too, because it cracked a little bit more every day, and that hurt. It hurt so much, she didn't know how to go for a moment without thinking about the pain.

Once she'd made it back to her cabin and pushed up the thermostat a couple of degrees, she pulled out her phone. "Why does no one ever call me?" she wondered, her voice full of that agony that ran through her veins. She sat on the couch and leaned her head back, looking up to the ceiling. "Why hasn't Ames called?"

She felt like a call to him would be akin to her forcing their relationship to continue when he didn't want it to. *I do love you, Sophia.*

He'd said that to her. Right out loud. She hadn't doubted him for a moment. Maybe he really was just busy.

On Thanksgiving? her mind whispered, and there was no argument back. There were no classes today. He could find five minutes to make a phone call. He simply hadn't.

She tapped and tapped, and lifted the phone to her ear as the line rang.

"Sophia."

"Hey, Mom," Sophia said. "Happy Thanksgiving." Her voice cracked on the last syllable, and she pressed her eyes closed against the flood of emotion.

"To you too," her mother said quietly. "Is everything okay?"

"No, Mom," Sophia said, her eyes flying open again. "Everything is not okay. Why don't you ever call me? Am I just so horrible that you can't even call me?"

"No," she said. "That's not it at all."

"Then what is it?" Sophia demanded, her tears pouring down her face. "I feel like I'm trying to get to you, Mom. I'm trying to have a relationship with you, but you don't want it." No one wanted a relationship with Sophia.

She'd never felt so alone in her whole life, not even when everything in her family had fallen apart.

"It has nothing to do with you," her mom said, her voice low and gauged. "It's all me, Soph. I don't call, because when we talk, I end up feeling so guilty. I know I haven't done right by you, and it's honestly easier to ignore than it is to try to fix it."

Sophia looked straight ahead, her tears blurring the loveseat in front of the window. She had no idea what to make of that.

"I don't call, because my life is a mess," her mom said. "And I don't want you to know that. I don't want you to think I'm some…some loser who's lost everything. But the truth is, that is who I am." She sucked in a breath and lowered her voice again. "So I don't call. I'm sorry it hurts you. Of course it does. I just don't know how to…do anything different. I'm a failure. That's just the truth of the matter."

"Mom," Sophia said. "You're not a failure."

Her mom said nothing, but Sophia could hear a dog barking somewhere on the other end of the line, so she knew she hadn't hung up. She needed to go get another foster dog, and she determined she'd go in the morning. She needed to drive by Ames's construction site too, because she owed him an update, though he hadn't asked for one.

"Mom," she said, her mind flying through everything in her life now. Ames. Her father. North Carolina. Rescue dogs. Ames.

"Is Dad still in North Carolina?" she asked.

"No," her mom said with a long exhale. Her voice was pinched too. "No, he moved to West Virginia a few years ago."

Sophia closed her eyes, only one thought in her brain now. *Get to North Carolina.*

"Mom," she said again, her voice pitching up. "I need some help. I met this guy, and I fell in love with him, and he's stopped talking to me."

"I can't help with relationships," her mom said gently. "That's where I'm the worst."

"He's currently living in North Carolina and going to the dog training academy there. I didn't go with him, because…." She let her words trail off, because her reasons now were beyond stupid.

"You hate North Carolina," her mom said softly. "That's why you didn't go."

A sob came out of Sophia's throat as she nodded. It was answer enough for her mother, who said, "Oh, my sweet Sophie. I'm so sorry."

They cried together for a few minutes, and then Sophia drew in a long breath. She needed to get control of herself. "He's pulling away from me," she said. "My natural instinct is to let him go, just like I let you go."

"Don't," her mom said. "Hold onto him, Sophia." A few seconds passed, and her mother's voice was full of tears when she said, "And hold onto me, too, if you can. I love talking to you. Maybe one day I'll figure out how to forgive myself, and I'll be strong enough to call you first."

Sophia swallowed, refusing to let herself start crying again. "I love you, Mom."

"I love you too, Soph."

The call ended, and Sophia listened to her mom's words repeat through her head. *Hold onto him, Sophia.*

But how could she hold onto something that she couldn't grasp? She was trying to hold water with her bare hands.

She needed a plan. She needed to confront him and find out what *his* plan was. The last time she'd done that, they'd taken a huge step forward in their relationship. Could it work again?

She quickly typed out a text and sent it. To give herself a break, she left her phone on the couch and went into the kitchen to make coffee. She forced herself to wait while it brewed, and she only went back to her phone once she had a cup of fresh coffee, all creamy and sugary, in her hand.

Several minutes ago, Patsy had texted back, *Yes, all the Hammonds will be in Coral Canyon for Christmas. We're hosting at our house, and you're invited. Ames didn't tell you?*

Sophia burst into tears again, because no, Ames had not told her.

He'd be done with his first program by then. She knew the calendar, and she knew the police dog training ended before Christmas. They'd spoken little about their holiday plans, because well, they'd hardly spoken about anything over the course of the last six weeks.

She tapped to connect a call to Patsy, and her best friend answered with, "Sophia, Cy is on the line with Ames, and he is not happy."

"Which one?" Sophia asked, not caring that Patsy would know instantly that she was crying. "Cy or Ames?"

"Either one of them," Patsy said. "Ames didn't tell you about Christmas here, so Cy is mad about that. Ames is mad that he has to answer to Cy about his relationship with you." Her voice got softer and softer as she spoke. "I'm sorry," she whispered. "We didn't know you two had broken up."

"Is that what he said?" Sophia asked, an inferno of rage moving through her.

"Not exactly," Patsy said. "He said he hadn't told you, because he wasn't sure he wanted to spend Christmas... here."

Sophia's tears felt useless now. She heard what Patsy was really saying. Ames hadn't told her about the family Christmas party at Cy and Patsy's, because he didn't want her there. It was *her* he didn't want to spend Christmas with, not them.

She needed to talk to him, but at the same time, she didn't want to. If he wanted to break up, he should call her and say so. He could be a big enough man to do that.

"You can have Cy tell him I won't be there, so it's not a big deal."

"Oh, I am not telling him that," Patsy said. "You're coming. The end. You're my best friend, and I want you here."

"Patsy," Sophia said with a sigh. "I'm not part of the Hammond family."

"Yes, you are," Patsy said with enough force to make Sophia wonder if she was wrong. "Ames is a big boy. He can deal with it." She wasn't speaking quietly anymore either, and Sophia loved the fire inside her friend.

"Okay," Sophia said, her mind whirring again. She'd made a mess of things with Ames, but she wasn't going to be like her mother. She wasn't going to wallow in that mess.

She was going to fix it.

"I have to go," she said to Patsy.

"Sophia—"

"I'm fine," she said. "Honestly, I am. Okay? I just have to talk to Graham."

She hung up with Patsy, and she immediately called Graham Whittaker.

"Sophia," he said, surprise in his voice. "Everything okay?"

"Yes," she said. "Well, at the lodge, yes. I have a personal problem though, and I'm afraid I have to leave Whiskey Mountain Lodge."

"Oh," Graham said. "That is bad news." He sighed. "When? Like, right away?"

"I can stay on until Christmas," she said, a plan forming in her mind as she spoke. "I'm sorry, Graham. I've loved it here. I really have. I'd like to come back, actually. I just need about six months off."

"Can I ask why?" he asked.

"Sure," she said. "I fell in love with Ames Hammond, and he's currently taking some dog training courses in North Carolina. I can't stand being away from him, and I'm going to move there to be with him. He'll be done at the end of June, and then we'll be back in Coral Canyon. I'd love to return to the lodge then."

Graham chuckled, and he said, "I've never heard anyone say falling in love was a personal problem."

Sophia blinked, and a moment later, she laughed too. "Well, in this case, it kind of is." Especially if she couldn't get Ames back. She hadn't even realized she'd lost him. He'd just slipped away—and she'd let him go.

But she wasn't going to do that anymore. She was going to figure out how to hold tightly to water, no matter what it took.

"I'll talk to Julianne about hiring a temporary chef," he said. "Until July."

"Thank you, Graham," Sophia said. Her third phone call for the day ended, and Sophia sank back onto the couch, wondering if she had enough energy to make a fourth.

She needed an answer from Ames, and she felt like if she called him now—right after his argument with his brother—and he answered, she'd tell him she'd be moving to North Carolina with him after the holidays.

If he didn't...well, that was as good as him saying he wanted to break up.

She dialed his number. Her heart pounded as the call connected. She stared straight ahead as the line rang and rang and rang....

CHAPTER 25

Ames was still fuming when his phone rang for the second time that night. He'd paced away from it, and as he went back to see if Cy had called back to chew him out some more, he saw Sophia's name on the screen.

His heart seized in his chest. Patsy had told her about the family Christmas celebration they were hosting in the apple orchard that December. Ames was supposed to tell her and invite her, and he hadn't.

He wiped his hand down his face and stared at the screen.

The call finally went to voicemail, and he sank onto the couch. "I'll call her back later," he said, but he knew he wouldn't. He'd told himself the same types of things when she'd texted him over the last couple of months, and he always found something else to do instead of responding to her text.

Foolishness and guilt had become his constant companions. A dog whined, and Rosco pushed his nose into Ames's knee.

"Yeah," he said, reaching over to pat the dog. "I screwed up." Rosco was a gorgeous German shepherd, with so much intelligence, Ames could see it in the dog's eyes. He looked at the animal and asked, "Why did I do that? Why didn't I text her back?"

He wished he had someone giving him cues. Someone to whistle when he should go, and someone to yell when he should come back. Someone to hold him back when he wanted to charge forward, and someone to release him when it was time to take down the bad guy.

The problem was, Ames had become the bad guy out of him and Sophia. At first, he had been extremely busy. He still was. He couldn't afford to take a day off in Rosco's training, because the dog only had three more weeks to pass his training. And if he didn't.... Well, dogs only got one shot at becoming K9 officer partners.

Ames was desperate for the dog to pass, and he worked with Rosco every single day, both in class and out.

He sighed and leaned back against the couch, wishing it was actually comfortable to sit on. "Seven more months," he said to himself. "I can do this for seven more months."

He knew that in seven months, he wouldn't have Sophia in his life. She wouldn't stick around with the way he'd been treating her. The problem was, he didn't know how to act. He didn't know what a pause was. Constant phone calls and texts and video chats felt like a lot of work. Way more than simply pausing things where they were.

His phone buzzed, and he reached for it, knowing it would be Sophia. She'd said, *If you want to break up, just say so. I just need to know what your plan with us is.*

"I don't have a plan," Ames said. "Isn't that what a pause *is*, Sophia?" He hated that he was annoyed with her, but the truth was, he was.

He wanted her here with him. That was his plan, and she'd rejected it.

Before he could pick up his phone to tell her that, it rang. He dang near dropped it, but he managed to catch it before it hit the table, and he marveled at his ninja moves. Colton's name sat on the screen, and Ames wasn't sure he could handle another brother-to-brother talk.

He considered the consequences if he didn't, and Colton wasn't as kind as Sophia. He'd just call again. Right when the call was about to go to voicemail, Ames tapped the phone button and gave it a second to connect.

"Hey," he said. "Happy Thanksgiving, Colt." He thought he sounded pretty upbeat, and maybe Colton would just ask him where he'd eaten his turkey dinner. Cy hadn't even asked that. He'd called upset, and he'd led with, *You didn't even invite her for Christmas? What is wrong with you?*

Ames hadn't appreciated that, especially coming from Cy. He'd come to stay with his brother after he'd had a panic attack and near mental break-down. And he was asking Ames what was wrong with him?

And he got help, Ames told himself as Colton wished him a happy Thanksgiving. "Just wondering what your plans are for Christmas," Colton said. "Cy said he wasn't sure, and we're getting Kate by then. We'd love for her to meet the whole family."

Ames relaxed, because this wasn't about his failure to make holiday plans with his maybe-girlfriend. This was about his brother and the daughter he and Annie were adopting.

"I'm coming to Coral Canyon," he said. That part had never been up in the air, and Ames rolled his eyes to the two dogs on the couch beside him. Cy. He was just trying to get all the brothers after Ames to guilt him into coming.

"Great," Colton said, his voice falsely bright.

"You don't sound like it's great," Ames said.

"I'm scared," Colton admitted, and Ames liked that he was real. Maybe he could be real with Colton too. He swallowed, his throat so sticky. "I mean, I don't know very many eight-year-olds, and I have no idea what to do with one."

"I think you'll figure it out," Ames said.

"And we don't know what she'll need," Colton continued as if Ames hadn't even spoken. "Annie's worried about doctor's appointments and therapy, and I'm feeling like I did something wrong." With every word he spoke, his voice got quieter and quieter, almost like he wasn't in private but still wanted to talk.

"You didn't do anything wrong," Ames said.

Colton sighed. "Annie says that too. I feel good about it one moment, and like I might throw up in the next," he said. "And I don't know what that means."

Ames could relate. Boy, could he relate. He opened his

mouth to give his brother advice, and instead said, "I feel the same way, except about Sophia."

Colton paused for a moment. "You do?"

"Yes," Ames said. "I've messed up. She wanted to pause, and I thought that meant pause. But she thinks it means we just live apart. I don't know what that means. I don't know how to have one foot in Coral Canyon and one foot here. I don't know how to be a long-distance boyfriend. I'm scared out of my mind." He sighed. "This isn't about me. Sorry."

"Don't be sorry," Colton said softly.

They sat on the line together, and it was nice. It was almost like they were in the same room, and Ames appreciated Colton. Ames finally drew in a deep breath and said, "Cy knows a lot about therapy, Colt. He'll help you with that. And you'll have a case worker, right? She'll help you too. You've wanted to be a father for a long time, and you're getting what you want."

"Yeah," Colton said. "You're right. I know you're right."

"God would not have allowed that little girl to come into your life if it wasn't right," Ames said.

"Thank you," Colton said, his voice filled with gratitude. "I knew I'd feel better if I called you."

Ames wasn't sure why. He'd hijacked Colton's freak-out session with one of his own. "Where did you eat today?"

"Annie cooked," he said. "She's amazing. Her daughters and their husbands came. Em is doing great. Three months left in the pregnancy."

"That's great," Ames said, reaching over to stroke Florence.

"Where did you eat today?"

"The school had a big dinner for anyone not going anywhere," he said. "It was in the cafeteria, and I think there were more dogs there than people." He smiled just thinking about it. "It was really good, actually. They have a real chef here and everything. I bought a meal plan, so I can eat in the cafeteria every day."

"Sounds amazing," Colton said.

Ames's phone buzzed, and he realized he was getting another call. He pulled the phone from his ear and looked at it. "Colt," he said. "Gray's calling."

"I'll let you go," Colton said, and Ames said goodbye. He switched the call to Gray, wondering if all of his brothers would call.

"Hey," he said.

"Happy Thanksgiving," Gray said.

"You too."

"Listen, I know you're busy," he said. "I'm just wondering if you could talk to Hunter for a minute? He's been having some problems with Molly, and he said he's talked to you already?"

Ames wasn't sure if that was a question or not, but he said, "Yeah, a little."

"He said you'd understand, and he didn't want to talk to me about it." Scuffling came through the line, and Gray said almost under his breath, "He wouldn't even tell Elise about it, and that's got her red flags all over the situation. I told her I'd call you and find out what you knew. I don't think Hunter will call. But I think if you reach out to him, he'll spill his guts."

"Gray," Ames said. "Breathe."

Gray exhaled, and audibly drew in another breath. Ames had no idea what it was like to be the father of a fourteen-year-old, so he couldn't judge Gray's concern.

"I'll talk to him," Ames said.

"I don't want you to, like, betray his confidence," Gray said. "But Elise and I are concerned about him."

"I'll talk to him," Ames said again. "And I'll judge what I think you should know and weigh that with what he wants to tell you." He cocked his head to the side like his dogs did so often. "In fact, I'll encourage him to tell you himself."

"He used to," Gray said. "But he's changed."

"No," Ames said. "He's changing. He's almost fifteen, Gray. Think about when you were fifteen. What did you want to do more than anything else?"

"Hunt," Gray said. "Fish. And...."

"Kiss girls," Ames said. "It's not a crime. He's not abnormal."

"He's not like that," Gray said. "He actually started therapy a while ago, because he wasn't sure he liked kissing Molly."

Ames's eyes widened. "I'm pretty sure he likes it now."

Gray sighed. "Yeah, I know. You're right."

"He likes that girl," Ames said. "Have you met her? Do you know what she's like?"

"Yeah," Gray said. "You know her too. She's the pastor's daughter."

"Pastor Benson?"

"Yes," Gray said.

Ames whistled. "No wonder Hunt is upset she told him she wanted to be friends with other boys. Those Benson girls *are* cute."

"Wait. She told him she wanted to be friends with other boys. What does that mean?"

"Heck if I know," Ames said. "Hunter didn't either. This was months ago, Gray. At Grams's birthday party." He hadn't talked to Hunter since, and guilt threaded through him. "I'll text him tonight."

"Yeah, sure," Gray said, his voice suddenly twice as loud. "Bring her out tomorrow. I'm sure Elise would love to have a play date for Jane. She's just not feeling well tonight."

Ames suspected Hunter had just walked in. "Talk to you later, Gray."

"Sure, call her in the morning."

Ames chuckled as he hung up, and he'd literally been off the phone for two minutes before Wes called.

Ames felt more loved clear across the country than he had while with his family. None of them had forgotten about him. None of them made him call them first, though he would and not even think twice about it.

By the time he got off the phone with Wes, a headache had started behind his eyes. He told himself he'd take some painkiller. Work with Rosco for twenty minutes. And then—then—he'd text Sophia back.

CHAPTER 26

"I still think this is the stupidest thing in the world." Cy glared at Ames, who sat beside him in the kitchen. Patsy was cutting his hair—into the exact same style as Ames's.

He wanted to pretend they were sixteen years old again and do a switcheroo with Sophia.

"You're going to ruin this," Cy said.

"Cy," Patsy said. "Leave him alone."

"She's going to see right through it," Cy said, folding his arms under the drape. "I can't believe I'm cutting my hair for this. He's got this woman he's in love with, but he can't face her? I don't get it."

"We don't have to get it."

Ames said nothing, and that only made the fire in Cy's stomach bubble with more intensity. "Tell me again what your goal is," Cy said.

"I'm just nervous," Ames said. "And this way, I can

observe her for a few minutes. You're not going to have to talk to her or anything. You're not going to pretend to be me." Ames glared at him, but Cy gave it right back.

"You've been talking to her this month, right?" Cy asked.

"Yes," Ames said. "I didn't ghost her again."

"How much have you talked to her?"

"Enough," Ames said. "Enough that she's coming, and enough that I'm nervous, and enough to think she might break up with me the moment she sees me."

"Then that's not enough," Cy said. "She might break up with you? Why? Why haven't you cleared the air between you?" He really didn't understand. He wanted to understand.

His wife ran her fingers along his scalp, and Cy looked up at her. "Tell me I'm not bald."

"Your hair grows back," she said with a smile. She stepped back and looked at him and then Ames. "You look good, Cy. Very sexy."

"Does that mean I'm sexy too?" Ames asked. He laughed in the next moment, and Patsy did too.

Cy rolled his eyes. How she could be so casual about this, he didn't know. Sophia was her best friend, and she was willing to make her do a double-take so Ames could play this little game?

"Am I done?" Cy asked.

"Yep." Patsy stepped back to him and unsnapped the drape. He stood up and brushed his hands through his hair.

He wasn't bald, but he threw Ames a dirty look as he

headed for the bathroom. "Oh, wow," he said. "It's so short."

"It's sexy," Ames called from the kitchen, and Cy dang near punched the glass. He didn't, because he didn't want to celebrate Christmas with stitches. They were attending the tree lighting ceremony tomorrow night, Christmas Eve, up at the lodge with the Whittaker family. Patsy was still very much part of them, and Cy could admit he enjoyed the celebration there. He actually loved the lodge, as that was where he'd asked Patsy out and proposed to her.

On Christmas Day, everyone would gather here, and Patsy had coordinated with Annie and Bree to make a holiday feast.

Cy went back into the kitchen and faced his twin. "I think this is a mistake, and I think you should just call her and ask her to please forgive you, and if she can, that you'd love to be her husband, and maybe she'll say yes to that."

"You're insane," Ames said.

"And then you can go back to North Carolina engaged," Cy continued, because he'd seen Ames and Sophia together, and it was obvious they loved one another. "And maybe that'll be easier to do than just being her boyfriend-on-pause."

Ames shook his head. "I have a plan, Cy. It's going to work." He looked at Patsy, who simply kept sweeping up the hair. Cy sensed something there, but he didn't ask his wife.

He did later, once they'd gone to bed, and she said, "Just trust him, Cy. And pray. In fact, let's pray right now that they'll be able to work everything out." She took his hand and drew in a deep breath. She said nothing out loud, and Cy kept his prayer silent too.

His was easy: *Please, please, please help Ames. Please, please, please....*

———

CHRISTMAS DAY CAME, AND WITH IT, SO DID ALL OF CY'S brothers. His parents had been in a conundrum, because Grams was too weak to travel. Cy honestly hadn't thought she'd live until Christmas. In the end, his father stayed in Ivory Peaks with his mother, and Cy's mother had come to Coral Canyon with Gray's family.

He noticed that Ames never got too far from him, and that only drove annoyance through him over and over again.

Finally, Sophia walked in dressed in a black winter coat, a pair of jeans, and furry boots that went all the way to her knees.

She wasn't Cy's type, but she had Ames written all over her. She shrugged out of her coat and gave it to Patsy, who hugged her tightly for a long time. Patsy tossed the coat into the office they shared, and the two women faced the dining room table, where Ames sat right next to Cy.

"This is so stupid," he said. Without a word, Ames stood up and made a beeline for Patsy and Sophia. He kept his back to Cy and said a few things, and then to Cy's great surprise, he and Patsy went into the living room together and sat down next to Elise.

In that moment, Cy's mind cleared. Ames had just told Sophia how to tell them apart, and Cy had been brooding and glaring—exactly what bad boy Ames usually did.

He got up too, because he was done with this charade, but before he could take two steps, Sophia stepped in front of him. "Hey," she said, clearly nervous. "Can I talk to you for a minute? Alone?"

"No," he said, because he couldn't do this to her. She deserved the truth, and the truth was, he wasn't Ames.

Sophia nodded at him and said, "Yes, I can. Come with me." She put her hand in his and towed him through the kitchen and down the hall toward the bedrooms. Cy really needed to get out of this situation, and fast. He couldn't believe this woman who stood six inches shorter than him and weighed at least a hundred pounds less could command him so easily.

In the hall, she dropped his hand and faced him. He opened his mouth, but she said, "I know you're Cy," and folded her arms. "Listen, I need your help with Ames."

"My help?" he asked, so confused.

"Yes," she said.

"How did you know I was Cy?" he asked. "We look exactly the same, and he went off with Patsy."

"The same way Patsy knows when it's you and not Ames," Sophia said. "I just know, because I know Ames."

That made no sense to Cy, but he let it go. "What do you need help with?"

"Pushing play," she said, a smile on her face.

The day had just gotten a whole lot better, and Cy only had one question: "Is there anything I can do to make him feel *really* stupid? Because he made me cut my hair and I've been mad at him for a month." He looked at Sophia. "I know he loves you, Sophia. I know that. He's just really bad at showing it."

"I know," she said.

"I was so mad when I found out he hadn't even asked you about Christmas."

"I know."

"I've been telling him for weeks to make it right."

"I know, Cy," she said. "It's fine. I'm fine. He has his issues, but the reason he's been acting like this is my fault. And I'm going to fix it. I just need you to…."

Cy listened to her plan, and boy was it better than anything Ames had come up with. Of course, Cy didn't know the extent of Ames's full plan. But what he did know was that yes, Ames was going to feel really stupid…and then really grateful…and then really happy.

"I'm in," Cy said. "You need him in front of the sliding glass door? I can make that happen."

CHAPTER 27

S ophia looked at Cy, and while she knew he wasn't Ames, he sure did look like him. "You go now, and then I'll come out."

"Okay." Cy didn't wait for further instructions. He ducked out of the hallway where they'd been standing, and a raucous round of laughing came from the living area. She had full faith in Patsy and Cy, and her best friend's text from ten minutes had made her laugh.

We're going to show him, Patsy had said. She'd spent a long time on the phone with Sophia while she worked in the heated office in the shed. She's promised that she hadn't told Cy anything, and while Sophia had had her doubts, Patsy had delivered.

Cy would too, and Sophia took a big breath and stepped out into the main area of the the house.

She'd been here before, because it was the dead of winter, and while Patsy worked full-time, she had a lot more time off when there was snow on the ground. Sophia had astronomically more free time since Marcy and Wyatt had returned to Three Rivers, and she'd spent some lunch hours with Patsy in this kitchen.

Those had tapered with the decline of her relationship with Ames, because Sophia didn't want to explain anything to her. It was really hard to explain what she didn't understand, besides.

But she'd gotten the inside scoop from two Hammond brothers now, and she wasn't going to stand idly by while Ames disappeared to North Carolina. Colton had said that Ames would be in town for the holidays, and Cy had confirmed the itinerary and that Ames was pretty miserable.

Not only that, but Patsy had texted a very vague, *He has plans, Sophia*, and those four words had really buoyed her hopes.

Part of her wanted to wait and see what his plans were, and the other part couldn't wait to tell him that she'd just worked her last day at Whiskey Mountain Lodge—at least until next July.

A dog barked, and she jerked toward the Akita, who she'd literally never heard make a sound. Ames stood in front of him, a huge grin on his face. "See? He speaks."

Her heart warmed at the sight of him working with his dogs. He loved them so much. His gaze lifted from the canine, and it landed right on her, as if drawn by a magnet.

He wore the same look on his face when he met her eyes that he did when he watched the dog.

"Go on," Ames said to Norman. *Titch.*

That made more than one dog perk up, and the next thing she knew, all four of his dogs lined up in front of him.

To her surprise, Flo wasn't in the front. The retired police dog had led the pack at Ames's house, but now, the most beautiful German shepherd hunkered down only a couple of inches from the tips of Ames's cowboy boots. Rosco waited for Ames's next command, her giant tongue lagging out of her mouth.

Florence had taken up a spot on the shepherd's left flank, with Norman on the right and Cocoa in the back. She wasn't really a service dog, and Ames wasn't training her to be one. She'd obviously learned some things though, because Ames held out a single hand to control all four dogs, and none of them moved a muscle.

"Find," he said next, and the dogs leapt into action, even Cocoa.

Rosco gave a bark from deep in her throat, and she started trotting toward Sophia. Her nose worked and Colton said something. So did Wes.

Sophia stood very still while she watched Ames's animals come straight toward her.

Rosco barked again, this time louder and sat down right in front of Sophia.

Norman came right up to her and nosed her thigh, then barked, looked over his shoulder to Ames, and sat.

Cocoa just sat, but Florence circled her once, and then twice, her eyes keen and bright. She barked, barked, barked, and that got Rosco going too.

Florence finally sat down beside Rosco, and they looked up at her and barked.

"They're so loud," someone said, and they were. But Sophia loved them with her whole heart.

Their master approached and he stepped between Norman and Cocoa and behind Flo and Rosco.

"Quiet," he said, and the dogs stopped barking.

She lifted her eyes to his, everything inside her storming. The breath she drew in shook in her lungs, but she steadily blew it out.

"Present," he said, almost like he was commanding a group of soldiers about to present the American flag.

Rosco barked, and Ames said, "Quietly."

Rosco whined, but she didn't bark again. She turned toward Ames, and he pointed to Patsy.

Rosco clicked her way over to the blonde, and she bent down and handed the dog something.

Rosco returned to Sophia, something in her mouth. Sophia looked around, noticing that everyone in the family had simply settled in for the show. Most of them wore some level of smile on their face, even Cy, who had looked like a hurricane when Sophia had walked in.

Rosco invaded her personal space and put her nose right against the side of Sophia's leg, which brought her attention back to the dog.

A collective gasp went up, and Sophia glanced up to find that Ames had dropped to both knees in the middle of his pack of dogs. "Sophia," he said. "I can teach these dogs to do pretty much whatever I want. They listen to me, and they love me when I'm grouchy, and they're willing to work hard for me."

He took a deep breath. "I love them with everything I have, and I'm still the most miserable man in the world. Because I don't have you."

Sophia blinked, because this wasn't how today was supposed to go. *She* was the one with a surprise for him, not the other way around.

"I love you more than these dogs. I love you more than the training program in North Carolina. I think I've proven that I'm a terrible boyfriend when I can't see you every day. I might be terrible anyway, but you seemed to put up with me over the summer. I'm hoping—I'm *begging*—that you can forgive me and find some sort of Christmas spirit to let me try one more time to show you that I'll do better. I'll *be* better. I'll—"

"Stop talking now," Colton said, and several people twittered.

Annoyance crossed Ames's face, and his eyes switched to someone beyond Sophia, coming quickly back to hers.

"Drop it, Rosco," he said.

The dog, who had not so much as moved an inch during his speech, dropped whatever she'd been holding in her mouth.

Sophia bent to pick it up, giving Rosco a friendly pat on the head. She didn't know this dog very well, but she was hoping to.

Her fingers met the hard case of a box, and when she lifted it, she found it to be black, and small, and exactly the kind that held diamonds.

She sucked in a breath and looked at Ames. "Ames," she said.

""Will you marry me?" he asked. "I'll quit the program. I don't care. I just want to be with you."

"No," Sophia said, shaking her head. A murmur moved through the crowd, and she realized what she'd said. "I mean, no, this isn't supposed to go like this." She surveyed the people gathered in the living and dining rooms. "He wasn't supposed to—I mean—I have a surprise you were supposed to open at dinnertime."

"It's past dinnertime," Gray said dryly, and Elise threw him a dirty look.

"Cy?" she asked, and Ames's twin brother stepped out from behind Colton and Annie.

"We're good, Sophia," he said.

"Let's eat then."

"The man is down on both knees," Wes said. "And I know he can't get up, or he would've by now."

"I can get up," Ames said, but he had to take Wes's hand to do it. He looked at Sophia, his eyes dark and hooded now. "No?"

Her heartbeat thrashed in her chest. She cracked open the box and looked at the diamond, and it was huge. Sparkling and merry, and exactly what she'd dreamed about receiving from Ames.

"It's not a no," Colton said. "Look."

"Colt," Cy said, his voice full of scolding. "That's not yours."

"I want to eat in this century," Colton said. He walked toward Sophia and Ames. "This was under your place at the table." He handed Ames the envelope, and Sophia had nowhere to hide.

She reminded herself she didn't *want* to hide. If she'd wanted to approach Ames in private, she could have. No, she'd wanted his family here, because she wanted them to be her family too.

"Is this diamond ring my Christmas present?" she asked.

"Yes," he said, ripping open the flap on the envelope. He lifted his gaze to hers. "Is this mine?"

"Yes." The gift suddenly wasn't enough, and Sophia almost lunged forward and ripped it from his hands. She thought his canines might attack if she did, though, so she held very still while he pulled out the papers she'd printed and put inside.

Ames frowned as he read, his expression changing every second. His eyes widened, and he held up the paper. "Is this real?"

"One hundred percent," she said, raising her chin.

"What is it?" Gray practically growled.

Sophia stepped next to Ames and faced most of the Hammond family. "I quit my job at Whiskey Mountain Lodge, and I've rented a house in North Carolina. See, I love him, too, and I hate being apart from him, and I want to be with you." She turned toward him at the end, the shock on his face almost sending her into a fit of giggles.

"I was going to apologize to—"

"Don't you dare," he said. "You haven't done anything wrong."

"He's right," Colton said, clapping his hand on Ames's

shoulder. "And he's already apologized, and there's a very important question on the table."

"Yeah," Wes said, stepping next to Ames as well. "Ames has always been a little slower than the rest of us."

"Will you marry him?" Gray asked, joining the Hammond brothers.

"You'd make him the happiest man in the world, even if he only smiles for five seconds before complaining about the consistency of the gravy." Cy grinned at Sophia, and she looked at the five of them standing there.

She looked down at the ring and back at Ames. "Yes."

Everyone except Ames burst into cheers and applause, and Rosco and Flo joined their barks to the noise.

Sophia smiled, and Ames did too. It lasted longer than five seconds though, and then he took her into his arms and kissed her.

This reunion was much more the type she'd envisioned in her fantasies, and while it hadn't gone exactly the way she'd thought it would, the outcome was far more than she could've hoped for.

She kissed him back—her fiancé—while his brothers catcalled, and when the cheering started to fade, Ames pulled away.

"I love you," he said. "I'm so sorry."

"I am too."

"No,' he said. "Don't apologize to me. *I'm* the one who's messed up almost from the moment I met you. But I'm not going to do that again, okay? I'm not." He set his jaw and shook his head.

"We're going to pray," Cy said loudly, and Ames

tucked her into his side as they faced the dining room table. Sophia basked in the warm family feeling the Hammonds brought with them, and she realized that it wasn't Whiskey Mountain Lodge that had healed her heart and provided a safe place for her. It was the people she'd chosen to surround herself with.

She could have this feeling anywhere—if she was with Ames.

The prayer ended, and Sophia turned quickly to Ames. "Can we talk in private for two minutes, do you think?"

He glanced at the surge of people lining up along the island in the kitchen. "I think we have five at least."

"The master bedroom is just down the hall," Patsy said with a smile. "Don't hurry back."

CHAPTER 28

Ames pulled away from kissing Sophia, because he was pretty sure she hadn't asked him to do only that when she'd asked him to "talk."

"I can't believe you quit your job," he whispered.

"I can't believe you showed up with a diamond ring—*and* trained the dogs to stage the proposal."

He grinned at her, warmth moving through him. "We worked on that for a long time."

"I bet you did. Rosco didn't move a muscle for the whole speech." She giggled, and Ames sure had missed the sound of it.

"Did you really rent that house?" he asked. For some reason, he couldn't believe it.

"Yes," she said. "Tell me you didn't quit your program."

"I may have an email drafted," he said. "I wasn't sure if you'd say yes or no."

"And yet, you asked me in front of everyone."

"They're all mad at me," he said. "Especially Cy and my mother."

"Why?"

Ames shrugged and stepped away from her. He had a hard time thinking with her so close. "They think I've been fighting against myself, and well, they're not wrong. My mother has been lecturing me for weeks to stop fighting against what's right, and let God direct me."

Sophia said nothing, and Ames turned back to her. "Soph, it's you. Every road leads back to you, and I really am really sorry for acting like such an idiot."

"You just don't know how to pause," she said.

"Not even a little bit," he said. "I guess I'm a little obsessive. What's in front of me, I focus on. And it's way too hard to do the dog programs and maintain a relationship with you all the way across the country."

"Well, according to my research," Sophia said. "I'll be a seven-minute drive from your house."

Ames loved the smile on her face. He loved the sound of her voice. He loved her forgiving heart. "Is that right?"

"That's right." She tiptoed her fingertips up the front of his shirt. "Now, come on, let's go eat Christmas dinner with your family."

Ames followed her back into the dining room, where his annoying brothers led another round of applause. Still, he chuckled as he held up one hand—the one not holding Sophia's—and said, "All right, all right. Settle down."

He got his ham and potatoes and took the empty seat

next to Cy. As he picked up his fork, he looked at his twin. "Are we okay?"

Cy reached up and touched his short hair. "Ask me in a couple of months." But he wore a smile, and the glint in his eyes said that he'd forgiven Ames too.

"I had a plan," Ames said.

"You could've done that without making her think I was you."

"I needed to gauge the situation."

Sophia sat next to him, and she'd certainly given him the right cues. He'd probably have proposed even in she hadn't, because he was that in love with her.

"Patsy's going to oversee the construction," Sophia said. "By the way."

"I'm helping her," Cy said. "So I guess we're okay."

Ames put his arm around his brother and said, "Thanks, Cy. Love you, brother."

"As much as I hate to admit it, I love you too." Then he cut his roll in half and started slathering it with butter and jam.

Ames stayed silent while the others talked and laughed around him, basking in the spirit of family and the presence of Sophia at his side.

He really was the most blessed man in the world in that moment.

SIX MONTHS LATER

Ames gripped the wheel and looked at Sophia. "Almost there."

"Are you nervous?"

"Yes," he said.

They'd managed to fit all of her stuff in the trailer with his, and the three dogs rode in the back.

Cy and Patsy had been great to send pictures of the progress of the dog training academy, and Cy had been calling every other day for the past two weeks.

Ames had a good idea of what he'd find on the thirty acre plot of land he'd bought, but he was still nervous to get there. Once there, his life wouldn't be on hold anymore. Once there, he'd have to make the attempt to spend his inheritance wisely and make a name for himself in the world.

Sophia had called Graham Whittaker a few months ago, and she'd said she wouldn't be back at the lodge at all. They'd talked about it, and she'd decided to work at the dog academy with him.

In the last three months, she'd taken the police dog training he'd taken last fall, and while she probably wouldn't work directly with the dogs, she understood the program now.

"After we go by here," he said. "We can go to the house."

"Patsy said it's ready," Sophia said. "She and Cy left my car there."

"You'll only have to be at their place for two nights," he said.

"Yeah." She looked out the passenger window, and Ames watched her for a moment before returning his attention to the road in front of him.

"You still want to marry me, right?"

"Yes, of course," she said. "I'm just thinking about my mom. She'll be here tomorrow night."

"Are you nervous about it?"

"Yes," she said, leaning her head back. Florence inched forward and sniffed Sophia, and she giggled at the dog.

"I'm nervous about it, too," he said. "But it's our wedding, and I think it'll go okay."

"I think so too," she said. "I'm just nervous about seeing her for the first time in years. Once that happens, I think things will be fine."

Ames knew she was trying to convince herself, and Ames didn't try to do the same. It was okay to be nervous about the reunion.

"Here we are," he said, slowing as the three story building came into view. "Oh, wow. It's amazing."

"Look at it, Ames," Sophia said, her voice filled with wonder.

The brown-brick building stood tall and proud, and the sign declaring the facility the Hammond Police Dog Training & Rehabilitation Academy was the most beautiful thing he'd ever seen.

He'd consulted with his father to name the business, and his dad had told him to remember who he was. And while Ames had hated the Hammond name in Colorado, it definitely meant something.

He *was* a Hammond, and he wasn't ashamed of it. He had a woman who loved him for him and not the name— or the bank account.

He pulled into the parking lot and went around the back of the building. The asphalt back here gave way to grass and fields, and Ames marveled at the fences, the individual training areas, and the smaller buildings that would house the dogs in the extreme months when it was either too cold or too hot for them to live outside.

Perhaps Wyoming wasn't the smartest place for a dog training facility, but Ames didn't care. It was the absolute right place for him and Sophia to build their life together, and he couldn't wait to start that chapter.

He pulled over and got out of the truck. "C'mon," he said to the dogs, and when he opened the back door, they jumped down in an orderly fashion.

Rosco stayed low to the ground as she started assessing the situation, and Ames experienced a flash of affection for the canine. He'd had to buy her out of the program, which he'd happily done. He needed her to be his pack leader and his example for all the other dogs he was going to train and sell.

He hoped he could actually sell them. Every dog he'd worked with in the past year, he hadn't been able to part with, and he'd had some very stern talks with himself over the past couple of months.

He'd have to sell the dogs he trained, plain and simple. They'd be happier in a police program than in his facility, though as he looked around, this place was pretty dang perfect.

"This is phenomenal," Sophia said, sliding her hand along his waist and leaning into his side.

He draped his arm around her shoulder and looked out over the facility. "I love it."

"It's wonderful." She pointed at Florence and Rosco. "They're going to get in trouble."

"Let 'em," he said, taking her fully into her arms. "I love you, Sophia. Thanks for being by my side through this."

"There's nowhere else I'd rather be." She gazed up at him. "I love you, Ames Hammond."

"I can't wait until Sunday," he whispered, leaning down.

"Two more days," she said, and then she kissed him. Ames now knew what heaven was like, because he felt more joy when he kissed Sophia than he ever had in his life. When the dogs started barking, Ames chuckled and pulled away.

"We better practice the ring ceremony one more time," Sophia said. "I don't want those dogs messing up my wedding."

"They'll be perfect," Ames promised. "But I'll go over it with them several more times before the ceremony." He looked at her, so, so happy. "After all, it's my wedding too."

She just giggled and tipped up to kiss him again.

HAMMOND BROTHERS
EPILOGUE

C olton Hammond adjusted the bow tie around his neck, already ready to be out of the monkey suit. But it was Ames's wedding—the last one for the family for a while—and he could wear the suit for a couple of hours.

He reached for the hat Wes had bought for him, and put it on. He couldn't even look at himself for one second before he burst out laughing.

"This thing is ridiculous," he said, swiping it from his head. "How did he wear this?"

Wes looked at him from down the counter. "I can't even bring myself to put mine on."

"You should return these," Gray said, tossing the hat in front of Colton. "I'm not wearing that."

"Even for five minutes?" Cy asked. "Can you imagine us walking down the aisle with them on? It's going to be hilarious." He headed for the door, adding, "Let me go see how close we are."

"We have to do this to show him what a fool he looked like at my wedding," Colton said. He'd never forgotten how stupid Ames had looked in that top hat at his wedding.

"Five minutes," Gray said. "And I'm setting a timer. And I'm going to have Hunt hand me my cowboy hat as soon as the clock is up."

"Good idea," Colton said. "I'll ask Kate to hold mine for me." He loved his daughter with his entire soul, and he and Annie were almost finished with the process of adopting her.

Colton had never been more grateful for his wife's good heart. Not only had she allowed Colton to push the issue of fatherhood on her, but she'd fallen completely in love with Kate the moment they'd brought her home.

Colton had too, and they'd both gone to the salon to have Teresa show them how to take care of Kate's hair.

Annie had gotten quite good at the braids, and Colton helped put in the oils and brush out the braids after Kate had been wearing them for a while. He loved her afro more than the braids, though both were adorable.

He drove her to school every morning and picked her up every afternoon. Annie still ran her cleaning business with her youngest daughter, and her eldest had just returned to Coral Canyon with her husband and new baby daughter.

Colton loved that little girl too, as he loved all the babies his brothers had started having. Thankfully, the Lord had taken his jealousy after much prayer and faith, and Colton felt like himself again.

"How much longer until Ames wants us out there?" Wes asked.

"Cy said he'd come get us." Colton picked up his cowboy hat—one of Wyatt Walker's, who'd recently come out with a new line of cowboy hats for men who liked a smaller brim. That was Colton for sure, and he liked the cowboy hat much better than the top hat.

Behind him, someone knocked, and he turned as Cy entered the room. He wore the top hat, as well as a very serious expression, and Wes burst out laughing. Gray scoffed like he couldn't believe he had to be there, and Colton laughed too.

"He's ready," Cy said. "We're lining up. Patsy is getting the girls."

"He gets five minutes," Gray said, smashing the top hat on his head.

"Not yet," Ames said as he ducked into the room. He looked at Cy and paused. Then he laughed too.

He held up his arms, and the five of them gathered into a huddle.

"Where's Dad?" Gray asked.

"He's sitting with Sophia's parents," Ames said. "He really is the most diplomatic person on the planet, because wow, her dad is *hard* to be around."

He took a breath and blew it out. "I love you guys," he said, his voice tight and slightly lower than normal. "Thank you for being good examples to me. Thank you for not being perfect but trying anyway. Thank you for being real."

They bent their heads together, and Colton had never felt such a strong brotherly bond between them.

"Love you guys," he said too, and everyone repeated some rendition of the sentiment.

"All right," Ames said, stepping back. "Me and the dogs are now officially late, and I don't want Gray to go nuclear." He grinned at Gray, who stared steadily back.

"You sure don't," he said, and Ames hurried out of the room.

Colton picked up his top hat and put it on, then tucked his cowboy hat under his arm.

"Start the clock," Gray said, straightening his ridiculous hat and facing the door. "Lead us out, Wes."

––––––––

WES HAMMOND HAD ALWAYS HAD TO LEAD OUT. HE WAS THE oldest, and as such, he went first. He'd been the first to inherit his money, and the first in his line to run the family company, and the first to have a baby—kind of. He sometimes forgot about Hunter, but Gray's son was definitely first.

He hadn't been first married, despite his attempts to find a wife. As he approached Bree, who waited at the front of the line of women, he experienced pure joy.

He loved her so much, especially after watching her carry two of his children to full term and deliver them happy and healthy to his arms.

He'd worried for several weeks that he wouldn't love their second child as much as Michael. The boy was his pride and joy, and Wes adored everything the two-and-a-half-year-old did. He saw the world with eyes Wes hadn't had in a long, long time, and it was as if everything was new again.

She'd given him another son eight months ago, and Wes had learned that the human heart could love unconditionally and without limits.

They'd named him Easton, and he definitely had more of a wild streak than Michael, and Bree spent a lot of time trying to keep the boy from killing himself.

He loved to climb, and he'd been getting out of his crib for a month now.

Bree linked her arm through Wes's with a dark sparkle in her eyes. "You look ridiculous," she said with a giggle.

"Don't let Gray hear you say that," Wes said with a smile. "And you look fantastic, love." He bent down and kissed her quickly, because she wouldn't want him to ruin her makeup.

He faced the altar, glad Ames and Sophia had chosen an indoor venue to get married. Then there was no worry about heat or fans or misters or wind.

The Secret Garden had just opened up a few months ago, and Sophia had been able to book the venue by a stroke of luck—and a miracle. Wes liked the hand-painted walls, which sported vines and trees, rocks and waterfalls, and rabbit holes and secret gates.

The grand hall in front of them had white chairs on both sides of the aisle, and plenty of light spilling down through the skylights above.

He'd attended the rehearsal dinner, so he knew exactly

when to start walking, and his heartbeat pulsed as he waited. Though Ames and Wes weren't as close as he was with some of his other brothers, he wanted everything to be perfect for his wedding. It was such a special day, and Wes wanted only the best for his brothers.

He spent many minutes praying for them, and he'd somehow taken on some responsibility for their happiness here in Coral Canyon.

He spotted his mother and father down at the far end of the aisle, and they were looking back toward the line.

Their sons.

Wes suddenly felt so lucky to be their son, and he needed to tell them that—and that he loved them—more often.

He'd always been close to his father, and that hadn't changed even though he'd moved to Coral Canyon. He still spoke to him several times a week, and he'd been helping Laura at HMC a lot this year as the company transitioned further into the digital age.

The music paused, and Wes tensed. Behind him, Gray said, "Three minutes. If they want us to wear these down the aisle, we better get moving."

Someone behind him laughed quietly, and Wes timed his first step to land with the beat of the music.

He put a smile on his face, and it was easy and natural. The crowd stood up and faced the wedding procession, and several people twittered and giggled at the line of tall, dark, Hammond brothers and their ridiculous top hats.

Ames laughed too, shaking his head, and Wes beamed at his boys, who were sitting with Bree's parents. They'd made the trip from Vermont, and they were staying in Coral Canyon for a few weeks to visit.

Wes loved them, because they'd given him Bree, and Bree loved having them here, because she didn't get to see them very often. Michael had taken immediately to them, because that was simply his nature. Wes could see the boy at the helm of HMC in thirty years—and he hoped he'd still be alive to see it.

He made it to the end of the aisle, and he took a moment to hug his mom and dad. "Love you," he said to each of them. He shook Ames's hand and then drew him into a hug before escorting Bree to her spot behind the altar and taking his.

Gray had just barely stepped next to him when his watch went off, and Wes glanced at him. "Really?"

"Five minutes are up," Gray grumbled, and Wes almost laughed at his brother's surliness. It was just a top hat. Ridiculous, sure. But he could manage to be ridiculous for ten minutes if it made his brother's wedding magical.

———

GRAY TOOK HIS TOP HAT OFF THE MOMENT THE LAST groomsman was in line—who happened to be his son. He'd walked with Molly Benson down the aisle, and Gray was *not* happy about it.

Elise had been flitting around the girl for days now, and Gray had never been in a worse mood. Fine, he probably had been, because he'd once run the entire law division at

HMC, and there had been some really unpleasant situations in the office.

Hunter and Molly had gotten back together sometime near Valentine's Day, and Gray hadn't really known that they'd broken up. Ames had told him precious little about the situation, because as he'd said, "there's nothing to tell. Your son likes a girl, and the girl likes him too, but she's worried about having a boyfriend in high school."

Gray was worried about Hunter too. He'd tried talking to him about dating a lot of different girls, but Hunter seemed stuck on this one. He'd either end up with a broken heart, or he'd break one. In Gray's opinion, a relationship this serious wasn't smart at Hunter's age, but he didn't want to alienate his son.

So when he'd asked if Molly could come to Coral Canyon for a "week or two," Gray hadn't been able to say no. He had over the summer, because Hunter was *fourteen*. He didn't need to bring his girlfriend to Coral Canyon for anything long-term.

But Molly was here for the wedding, and she was staying with Colton and Annie, which only made Gray annoyed with them too.

He knew his feelings were unwarranted and had created some tension between him and everyone else—even Elise. He took a big breath and released it, because he couldn't be mad about this forever.

Molly was here, and she was a nice girl. She was polite, and she said please and thank you to everything Elise and Gray did for her.

Ames glowed as he gazed down the aisle, and Gray's

mother couldn't stop crying. His dad held her hand, and Gray couldn't help missing the spot where Grams should've been.

She'd passed peacefully in her sleep a couple of days before the New Year, and while she'd been old and ready to go, she'd still left a hole in all of their lives that Gray personally was still struggling to fill.

He looked across from him and met Elise's eyes. She lifted her eyebrows, her way of telling him to stop frowning.

More of his tension bled out, and he managed to put a smile on his face. She grinned back at him, and she was so beautiful in the pale yellow bridesmaid dress that all the women wore. She wore flowers in her hair too, and just the right amount of pink lip gloss to make Gray want to be alone with her.

Finally, he pushed away all of the anger and annoyance and was able to enjoy the wedding.

Just in time too, because Ames's dogs started down the aisle, completely unassisted.

Rosco led the way, completely decked out in a tuxedo coat and a matching bow tie. She seemed to know exactly when to step to be in time to the music, and she never tried to run to Ames.

He held out his palm, and the dog sat. Florence came next, and Gray wanted to give Hutch to him to get the dog trained up right. Elise loved the silver doodle, and Gray did too. Hutch just needed a firmer hand, and Gray worked the farm a lot while she was home with Jane.

She spent a lot of time with his mother and father too,

and Gray tried to keep his finger on the pulse of how Elise was doing with regards to that, because he didn't want her to feel like she *had* to entertain his parents.

They'd started talking about having another baby, though Jane wasn't even two yet. Honestly, Gray wasn't sure he could handle another baby right now. His fifteen-year-old was going to be the death of him.

He looked at Hunter, and his son looked so...happy. Gray wished Hunter would look at him so Gray could somehow telepathically apologize for how he'd been acting.

He'd tell him afterward.

In that moment, Hunter looked at him, and Gray reached up and touched his palm to his heart. It said everything he needed to say, and Hunter did the same.

Relief filled Gray, and he was so grateful for his son. He'd been blessed beyond measure when that boy had come into his life, and Gray clapped with everyone else as the last dog joined the wedding party at the altar.

He looked to the end of the aisle, and Sophia stood there, on the arm of Cy, and Gray's gaze flew to her father. He was facing away from Gray, so he couldn't judge how the man felt.

No matter what, Gray didn't want to miss out on a single moment of his children's lives, and while he knew family relationships could be complicated, he silently vowed right then and there to forgive—himself and others —so that he could have the family unit that shared everything.

———

Cy Hammond felt a bit foolish walking down the aisle for a second time, but both Sophia and Ames had asked him to be her escort, and he hadn't known how to say no.

He'd been so angry with Ames, but things changed at Christmastime. His brother had done his best. He'd apologized. He'd made things right.

Cy was still working on that, and he hated with everything inside him that Patsy had apologized to him. They'd talked about it several times since, and Cy was still talking to his therapist about it too.

He wished he'd been stronger—the way Ames had been when Sophia had tried to apologize to him—so that Patsy hadn't felt like anything that had happened between them was her fault.

She'd told him to stop obsessing over it. They'd been married for a year now, and he needed to let it go.

He was trying, but sometimes things took a long time to let go of.

He walked steadily toward Ames and the four dogs, smiling for all he was worth. He finally reached the altar and passed Sophia to his twin, then retook his spot between Hunter and Colton.

Ames had said something to Sophia, and he straightened so they could face the pastor together.

Cy couldn't help watching Patsy, who'd already started crying. She was doing that a lot more lately, because her hormones were all out of whack. She was due with their first baby in February, and they hadn't told anyone yet.

Not his parents. Not hers. No one.

Cy loved the little secret between them, and he couldn't wait to see what a child of theirs would look like. She was blonde and blue-eyed, and he was as far from that as someone could get.

"We gather here today," Pastor Michaels said. "To celebrate the love and lives of Sophia Dawn Cooke and Ames Bryce Hammond."

Cy listened to the ceremony, thrilled he'd been able to play some small part of it.

He was glad he'd landed in Coral Canyon, and thrilled Ames had finally accepted it as where he was supposed to be too.

God is good, Cy thought, and that idea had helped him through some of the darkest times of his life in the past couple of years.

———

AMES HAMMOND HEARD THE WORDS COMING FROM THE preacher's mouth, but they honestly blended all together.

He finally said, "You can kiss your bride, Ames."

He turned to Sophia, who was laughing and smiling. He drew her into his arms and held her tight before leaning down to kiss her.

"Speak," Hunter said, and the dogs started barking.

The crowd cheered and clapped, and Ames couldn't help laughing too. Sophia held onto his shoulders, and he loved the way she made him feel strong and powerful. She made him feel necessary, and he craved that more than anything else.

He turned toward the crowd that had gathered in Coral Canyon that day—mostly people she knew from the lodge and his family—and raised their joined hands.

"We're having dinner and dancing in the ballroom," he called above the scattered applause still moving through the room. "Thank you all for coming."

He was instantly surrounded by his brothers. He hugged them all while Sophia stepped over to her mother to embrace her. Patsy brought the women over, and they hugged and congratulated Sophia.

Ames hugged his mother and said, "I love you." He embraced his father, and said the same thing to him. He was grateful they made the trip to Coral Canyon as often as they did, and he couldn't wait to start building his family with Sophia.

Wyatt and Marcy Walker came forward to congratulate them, and Ames really liked the two of them. They'd been back in town for at least a month, and they'd found a different nanny for that summer.

Sometimes, Ames felt guilty for all that Sophia had given up to be with him. When he'd asked her about it, she'd said, "I didn't give up anything but my pride."

He loved her beyond comprehension, and he hoped he could be the kind of man she deserved—and wanted.

He couldn't wait to be done with the celebration. Done with the tuxedo. Done with the people. Then he'd get to be alone with his wife, and there was nothing more enticing to him than that.

He went through all of the motions—the dinner, the cake-cutting, and the first dance. As he swayed with her in his arms, he gazed down at her and said, "I'm the luckiest man in the world. I love you so much."

"I love you too, Ames," she said, closing her eyes. He leaned down and pressed a kiss to her lips, his love and gratitude for her rivaling that which he held for God.

He knew without a shadow of a doubt that God had led Sophia to that drugstore in Three Rivers, over a year ago.

They were simply meant to be, and he kissed her again, beyond grateful that she was now his wife.

————

Read on for a sneak peek of the Ivory Peaks series, which starts 10 years after this book ends with your favorite Hammond child…Hunter!

That's right! You can see Hunter and Molly's forever romance in **HIS FIRST LOVE, now available in paperback.**

THEN, keep reading on for a sneak peek of **THE MECHANICS OF MISTLETOE**, which begins my next family saga romance series of cowboys - which takes place back in beloved Three Rivers at Shiloh Ridge Ranch. **This book is also available in paperback.**

SNEAK PEEK! HIS FIRST LOVE
CHAPTER TWO

Hunter Hammond sat down on the bench, the beautiful organ music filling the chapel, and rested his forearms on his knees. His head bowed, he tried to clear his mind and push all the achy-ness from his muscles.

He closed his eyes and prayed, letting his thoughts move wherever they were wont to go.

"You okay, Hunt?" his dad whispered from down the pew, and Hunter just nodded. He just wanted to sit for a minute. Ponder, and try to rejuvenate before he started full-time at Hammond Manufacturing Company in the morning.

Am I in the right place, Lord? he asked, and the answer came instantly.

Tingles ran down his shoulders and into his fingers, sliding down his spine and all the way to his toes.

Yes, he was in the right place.

Exhaling the last of the tension out of his back, he raised his head and looked up to the pulpit. He'd missed coming to church here for the past seven years as he'd been off at MIT, learning and working and trying anything he thought he wanted to try.

He'd earned his master's degree in Bioinformatics, which blended computer science with genetics, molecular biology, math, database creation, and operating systems. He loved computers almost as much as he loved crossword puzzles, and as he'd progressed through high school, he'd realized how very good at math and science he was.

The horses and goats on the family farm where he'd grown up and worked until he'd left for college hadn't cared about his skills with numbers and formulas, but MIT had. He'd earned a full scholarship there that he only came close to losing once.

He glanced down the row, over the tops of three children's heads. His half-siblings. Really, they felt like his full siblings, and he grinned at the youngest of them, Deacon, a cute five-year-old that finally looked like a Hammond.

"Hunt, look," the little boy said, and Hunter pulled the dark-haired child onto his lap to look at what he'd been writing.

"It's your name," he whispered. "Remember, we have to talk quiet at church."

"Shh," Deacon whispered back. "How do you spell your name, Hunter?"

Hunter started to spell it for him, pleased when Deacon knew all the letters and got them all about lined up in a row. "Good job, buddy," he whispered, pressing a kiss to the boy's head.

"Good morning, friends," a man said, and Hunter looked up to the pulpit again, where Pastor Benson stood. He'd definitely aged since Hunter had attended church here for the last time, and he had plenty of gray hair now, with wrinkled laugh lines around his eyes.

Hunter loved Pastor Benson—and not just as a pastor. He'd spent a lot of time at the Benson's house, as he'd dated their oldest daughter for years.

His father hadn't been pleased with Hunter and Molly's relationship. Looking back, Hunter could see his dad's point of view, and he knew that twelve was way too young to start dating.

At the same time, he'd been devastated when Molly had finally ended things between them completely the week before his sophomore year started. Hunter had disappeared for a while that year, and he'd discovered his tenacity and talent for science and math while he hunkered down and tried to figure out who he was.

"We have a lot of visitors today," Pastor Benson said. "It's nice to see all the young people home from college." He beamed out at the congregation, and added, "Let's stand and sing hymn forty-two."

Hunter set Deacon on his feet and picked up a hymn book as he stood too. He didn't count himself as one of the "young people home from college." He was twenty-five years old and had been living in Massachusetts for years now. He'd graduated a year ago but stayed back East to finish a project he'd founded during his collegiate career.

He'd gotten his two billion dollars on his twenty-first birthday, and he'd done something with it already. Now, he was set to start at HMC in the biometric lab, and his voice scratched on the first note. He recognized the nerves, though his dad had been telling him not to worry. Everyone at HMC knew him; he'd be fine.

Hunter sang the hymn, using the music and the message to once again relieve his rising anxiety. He'd been seeing a therapist for over a decade, and he was glad to be back in the Denver area so he could see Lucy in person. She'd been amazing over the past several years, and he'd been able to do video counseling with her to keep himself mentally strong.

He glanced down as Deacon stepped on his foot, and found his next oldest sibling trying to wrench the pen away from the five-year-old. "Tucker," Hunter said quietly, and the seven-year-old looked up at him. Hunter shook his head and nodded his cowboy hat toward the front.

Tucker was the middle child of Dad and Elise, and he looked like it. He was half dark and half light, with blonde hair that came from Elise and brown eyes that came from Dad. Beside him stood Jane, a ten-year-old that looked like Dad hadn't had any part in her creation. She had Elise's blue eyes and blonde hair, though if Hunter looked further than surface colors, he'd find the Hammond chin and nose on Jane's face.

She looked at him and smiled, and Hunt smiled back. He'd loved these kids as he'd grown up. He'd left for MIT only a week after Tucker had been born, and he'd come home to hold Deacon for a whole weekend before he had to return to Massachusetts.

The song ended, and Hunter sat down. He reached over and took the pen from Tucker and gave it back to Deacon. Tucker glared at him, and Hunt reached into his breast pocket and pulled out another pen.

He lifted his eyebrows at Tucker, who softened and nodded. Hunter looked at Deacon, his message clear. Tucker leaned over and said, "Sorry, Deac," and Hunter handed Tucker the pen.

When he looked up, he met his father's eyes, and Hunter saw so much of himself in his dad. Gray Hammond had grayed too, but he still radiated power from his broad shoulders and strength from his eyes. Dad had been a corporate lawyer for the first twelve years of Hunter's life, and he'd been his absolute best friend forever.

Hunter hated disappointing him, and he'd worked as hard as he knew how to make sure he upheld the Hammond legacy and made something of the money his father had given him. Extreme gratitude flowed through him as he continued to hold his father's gaze, and finally Dad grinned and whispered, "We need to go fishing."

Hunter nodded, his chest tight. He missed fishing with his father terribly. He missed hugging Elise. He missed laying on the floor while the littles crawled all over him, trying-but-not-really-trying to get away from him as he tickled them.

He'd missed Ivory Peaks and his life here with a force he hadn't even recognized until now.

You're back, he told himself as Pastor Benson got behind the mic again and began his sermon.

Hunter refused to look around and find the rest of the Benson family. He and Molly had managed to stay friends through the rest of high school, but Hunter hadn't kept in touch with her over the past several years. She'd earned some money to a university in Denver, and as far as he knew, she'd gone, graduated, gotten married, moved on.

Hunter had tried to do that too. He'd taken his uncles' advice and kissed a lot of girls. Uncle Colton had said there was nothing wrong with kissing, and after a rocky start, Hunter found he sure did like it.

His senior year, he took a different girl to every available school dance, and he'd kissed them all. In college, he asked out anyone who caught his eye, and he kissed all of those women too. He'd met a girl named Abby, and he'd started to fall for her. They'd dated for a year before he finally had to accept that they were on two different paths.

His had always been coming back to Colorado and Ivory Peaks. Always. He loved the farm with every cell in his body, and he loved his grandparents more than that. He knew he'd use his degree at the family company, and he'd known Abby had her own family obligations.

When she'd finished her bachelor's degree at MIT, she'd returned to New York to work in that family business, and they'd broken up.

Hunter could still hear her voice sometimes, if he held very still and blocked out all other noise. He missed her too, but it had been a couple of years since that relationship had ended, and he'd once again taken some time to find himself before he asked anyone else out.

For the past year, he'd dated only casually, and that had been enough for him.

Looking down the row of children to his dad, he thought he might like to get started on a family earlier than Dad had. He'd just turned fifty-five, and he had a five-year-old. Elise was much younger than Dad, but they'd stopped with three kids, because Dad didn't want to be eighty when they graduated from high school.

The sermon ended, and Hunter started helping Deacon and Tucker to pack up their notebooks, books, and pens. "Come on, guys," he said. "You can ride with me if you don't dawdle."

"Can I, Dad?" Tucker asked, spinning to their father. "Hunt says we can ride with him."

"Are you going back to the farm?" Dad asked, handing Jane something she'd dropped. "I thought you might stay for the luncheon."

Hunter shook his head, unable to come up with a reason why he'd do that. Why did Dad think he would?

Deacon slipped his hand into Hunter's. "I'm ready, Hunt. No dawdling."

"Good boy," Hunter said, smiling down at a carbon copy of himself. In that moment, he realized that Deacon could be his son. If he'd met someone and fallen in love and they'd had a baby when he was just twenty years old....

Hunter looked up and away from the thought. "I'll take

the boys," he said. "Maybe I'll stop by the store and get ice cream on the way out."

"We have plenty of ice cream," Elise said with a smile as she leaned around Dad. Hunter loved her too, because she'd first loved him when he was an awkward and unsure teenager. She'd loved his father through everything imaginable, and that made her a saint in Hunter's eyes.

"Grandma made a cake last night," Dad said. "Trust me, we have everything you could want."

Hunter paused as others moved up the aisle in front of him. "Is it for me, Dad?"

"Of course," Dad said with a healthy grin. "Grandma and Grandpa can't wait to see you again."

Hunter hadn't stayed at the farm last night, because he hadn't quite been in town yet. He'd driven in that morning, just in time for church. Everything he owned was either in the back of his truck or on its way from Massachusetts.

"I don't need a big welcome home party," he said, his mood darkening. He didn't really like having the spotlight on him, and he gave his father a glare.

"It's Grandma," Dad said. "What am I supposed to tell her? That she can't make a cake for her favorite grandson?"

Hunter softened then. "Where are they?" He eased into the flow of people moving toward the doors at the back, his hand still gripping Deacon's.

Dad moved into the aisle with him, and they stood at the exact same height, shoulder to shoulder. "They don't get to church much anymore," he said. "Not since Grand-pa's fall."

Hunter nodded, his teeth automatically clenching together. He hadn't been here for that; he hadn't had avail-ability to come visit. Regret laced through him as he moved slowly toward the door.

In the foyer, the crowd dispersed a little, and Hunter had more breathing room. "I'm over this way," he said to Deacon, tugging on the boy's hand to get him to go left. "You comin', Tucker?"

"Yeah." Tucker hurried over to Hunter while Dad and Elise and Jane went right. He dropped his bag, and Hunter paused to wait for him to pick it up.

"I still think we should get ice cream," he said to Deacon. "Do you think Grandma got butter pecan?"

"She got vanilla," Deacon said, looking up at him. "And cookies and cream, and that gross bubble gum kind that Jane loves."

"Hmm." Hunter looked up, thinking the definitely needed more ice cream, and everything around him fell away.

Molly stood fifteen feet in front of him, next to her mother. She still had that gorgeous smile framing white teeth. Her reddish-brownish-blonde hair had always struck Hunter right behind the heart, as had her bright green eyes.

Hers met his dark ones, and he saw the moment she recognized him. Those eyes widened, and she lifted one hand to cover her mouth, which had opened slightly.

Her mother said something to her, but Molly didn't

react. Hunter knew exactly what was going on, because everything around him was muted too. Just gone, because there was Molly, and she was all he'd ever wanted or need.

Hunter realized in that moment that he'd never gotten over her. He may have kissed other girls, but he'd only ever wanted to kiss her.

She blinked, leaned toward her mother, and said something to her.

Her mother's eyes flew to Hunter, and he managed to lift one hand in a half-hearted wave.

"Hunt," Deacon said, and all kinds of chatter and noise met his ears as his senses returned.

"Yeah?" Hunter glanced down at the boy for a fraction of a second. "What?" He looked back to where Molly had been, but she'd moved.

No! his heart cried out. He had to find her and talk to her. He had to know if she was seeing someone or if she might be available to be his again.

"Tucker's gone," Deacon said, and that got Hunter to focus.

"What?" He turned around, expecting Tucker to still be collecting his bag from the floor. He wasn't there. He wasn't anywhere behind Hunter. "Where did he go?" He scanned the front doors, but bright sunlight poured into the building, blinding him.

"Hello, Hunter," Molly said, and Hunter felt like he was being whiplashed all over the place. He swung around again, and she stood in front of him now, definitely older than the girl he'd first crushed on, but still just as beautiful. She smiled and tucked her hair, just as she'd done in the past. He remembered when *he'd* tucked it for her, and then kissed her. He'd done that many times, and he wished he could think of something else. Anything else.

"Hey, Molly," he said. "I, uh, sort of have a problem."

Her smile faltered, and she glanced at Deacon. "You do?"

"Yeah," Deacon said. "He lost our brother."

SNEAK PEEK! HIS FIRST LOVE
CHAPTER TWO

Molly Benson had felt an incredible energy when she'd arrived at church that morning. She hadn't known what it was, and her father's sermon, while great, hadn't been the source of Molly's excitement that day the way she'd expected it to be.

Now, she stood face-to-face with Hunter Hammond, having been drawn across the foyer toward him by some unseen magnetic force. *He* was the reason for the renewed energy at church today, and Molly wished the Lord had given her some hint that the boy she'd shared her first kiss with would be standing in front of her that morning.

He wasn't a boy anymore, that was for sure.

In fact, he'd bulked up and grown another two inches during the last three years of high school, and Molly had regretted breaking up with him more than anything else in her life.

At least until she met and married Tyrone Hensen.

Trepidation moved through her, and she told herself it was because Hunter's brother was lost, not because she'd already been divorced before she'd turned twenty-five.

"What's his name?" she asked, glancing around for another miniature of Hunter Hammond.

"Tucker," Hunter said, and he raised his voice and called the name again. He looked at Deacon. "Did you see if he went outside?"

There were three entrances to the foyer, one on each slanted side of the front of the church. Molly's mother and father stood next to the one on the right, as that one led to the parking lot most patrons used. The crowd had thinned enough now that Molly could look over her shoulder and meet her mother's eye.

She managed to convey that she needed help, and her mother started toward her. "We can split up," she said. "My mother will have seen him if he'd used the east door."

Mama arrived, and she said, "Hunter Hammond. How are you?" in the most pleasant voice. She stretched up and hugged Hunter, and Molly was jealous of her mother. Ridiculous, but oh, so true.

Hunter smiled, and such a gesture should be illegal because of what it did to Molly's pulse. "Real good, ma'am."

"He's lost Tucker," Molly said as they parted. "Did you see him go out the west door?"

"No." Molly's mother sobered and looked from Molly to Hunter to his little brother. "Let's check out front."

"I'll take Deacon out the east door." Hunter moved that way, and Molly couldn't seem to get her feet to work.

"Mols," Mama said, and Molly jolted back to attention. She didn't have time to stare after the handsome man Hunter had become. As she followed her mom out the front doors, she wondered if Hunter had felt any of the electricity she had. Had he simply moved on? Was he married? What was he doing now? Where was he living?

He might not even be back in town for good, Molly told herself. *Don't go getting your hopes up.*

There were a hundred different things that could keep Molly from reconnecting with Hunter, and her mind started to list all of them as a defense mechanism.

She heard Hunter calling for Tucker around the corner, and her mother did the same thing. A little boy came around the corner to their left, and Mama said, "There you are, Tucker Hammond." She moved down the steps, holding tightly to the handrail, Molly noticed. Her mother was getting older, and while she still possessed every ounce of charm and sophistication she always had, her last round of fighting off her uterine cancer had taken a lot from her. Molly's divorce hadn't helped anything, and pure regret moved through her as she followed Mama.

"Your brother is looking for you, baby," Mama said, scooping the child into her arms.

"I'll get Hunter," Molly said as she looked at Tucker. He definitely had the same brown eyes as his brother and father, and coupled with that light hair, Molly thought he'd break more hearts than Hunter had.

After she'd broken up with him, he'd dated plenty of other girls. A different one every weekend. Once, he'd taken Laurel Phillips to a football game on Friday night and Teri Childs to a movie on Saturday night.

He didn't stay with any one girl at all, and Molly had told herself over and over that he was doing what she'd said they should. Meet and go out with a lot of different people. Then they'd know who they really liked.

Hunter had told her for about a year that he liked her, and that he didn't need to take anyone else to dinner to know it. And yet, when she'd finally ended their four-year relationship, that was exactly what he'd done.

She pushed the high school memories out of her mind as she went around the corner. "Hunter," she called to the tall man on the edge of the cement, looking out over the cemetery and the woods behind that.

He turned toward her, his anxiety plain to see. She gestured for him to come to her, saying, "Mama found him. He's okay."

Relief painted over his handsome features, and he strode toward Molly, his youngest brother in his arms. Time slowed for Molly. All sound disappeared. All she could see was Hunter Hammond in that cowboy hat, a boy who looked just like him on his hip, and her entire future with him right in front of her. Just out of reach.

"Thanks, Molly," he said as he passed, not slowing down for even a moment. Time sped again, and Molly spun around as the scent of Hunter's cologne lingered in her nose. My, he knew how to put together an arsenal against a girl, didn't he?

The dark slacks, white shirt, and trendy tie. The cowboy hat. The good looks—superior looks. Molly had never met a man as handsome as Hunter. No woman had. He was just that gorgeous.

And the cologne too?

It was almost like he knew he wasn't playing fair.

She ducked around the corner too, just in time to see him take Tucker from Mama, now carrying both boys in his arms. He pressed his forehead to Tucker's, his mouth moving. Molly was too far away to hear what they were saying, but the soft, adoring look on Mama's face said enough.

She loved Hunter too.

She always had; it had been the Pastor who'd warned Molly about getting too serious with a boy too young. To her knowledge, Hunter's father hadn't been very keen on their relationship either.

Molly approached slowly, smiling at her mother. Mama linked her arm through Molly's and said, "I have to go check on Dad. We'll see you at the house for lunch?"

"Yes," Molly said, glancing at her quickly. She couldn't keep her eyes off Hunter, and she really wanted to invite him to lunch too.

Mama left, and Hunter set both boys on the ground beside him. He adjusted his hands in theirs and looked at her. With the crisis over, he seemed calm, confident, and perfectly collected.

"Thanks for your help," he said, that smile appearing again.

Neither of them moved. Molly finally reached up and tucked her hair behind her ear, her voice stuck somewhere down inside her chest.

"Do you live with your parents?" Hunter asked.

Molly raised her eyes to his. "No, I have my own place."

"So you live here." This time, it wasn't a question.

"Yes," she said. "You? Just visiting?" He'd gone to college at MIT. Like, the actual MIT, where only geniuses and future Nobel Peace Prize winners went to get educated.

"I'm starting at HMC tomorrow," he said, the smile faltering. "I'm literally moving back today."

"To the farm?"

"For now," he said. "I'll probably get a place in the city. It's too far to commute for long."

She nodded, every cell in her body buzzing with the words *Hunter Hammond is back in Ivory Peaks. Hunter Hammond is back!*

"Do you want to come to lunch at my house?" she blurted out before she could think too hard about it.

His eyes widened a little bit, and he looked down at his two brothers. "Hey, you guys," he said, dropping into a crouch. "Will you go wait for me on the steps? I just need to talk to Molly alone for one second."

"All right," Deacon said, and he took Tucker's hand. The two of them walked away while Hunter straightened. He kept his eyes on them until they'd sat on the bottom step, and then for another few seconds.

When he finally looked at her, a storm rolled across his face. Molly wanted to recall the invitation, but it was too late. She wasn't sure what was going through his mind, because Hunter had never said a whole lot. He'd felt deeply, but he'd gone to therapy to learn how to do that. For a long time, he'd told her he'd simply existed behind a barrier made of frosted glass.

He softened and lifted one hand toward her, sliding his fingertips along the side of her face and tucking her hair behind her ear again. It took all of Molly's will power to stay still and not lean into those hands she'd known so well.

"I want to, Molly," he said as his hand dropped back to his side. "But I literally rolled into town ten minutes before church started. I haven't seen my grandparents yet, or really talked to my parents. So I really shouldn't."

"Okay," she said, her voice a bit ragged. She cleared her throat. "It's okay. You go have fun with your family."

He nodded, and Molly wished with every birthday candle on the planet that he'd ask her out for another time. She'd clear any schedule she had to in order to be there.

He didn't though. Instead, he just nodded, ducked his head so his cowboy hat concealed most of his face, and said, "Deacon, Tuck, let's go."

The little boys came toward them, and Hunter looked up at her as they took his hands. "See you around, Molly." He started toward the parking lot where most people parked, and Molly turned as he went by and watched him take the boys to a large, gray truck that had a white trailer attached to it.

It was exactly the kind of vehicle someone as masculine and male as Hunter would drive, and he lifted Deacon into the backseat while the child laughed. Molly smiled too, because wow. Hunter Hammond interacting with children was another low blow to her feelings for him. She'd seen him hold his sister when she was a baby, and she'd suspected then that he'd be a caring and attentive father. To actually *see* his concern for his brothers only cemented that.

He closed the door and turned back to her. Embarrassment leapt to Molly's face, and she ducked away from him, hurrying toward the steps that led back inside. She'd made her feelings for him known. She didn't need to add further humiliation to her already burning life.

Inside, she met her mother as she came down the hallway that led to Dad's office. "He's going to be a few minutes," she said. "That means at least an hour. Can I ride with you? Or were you planning to go home and then come to the house for lunch?"

"I can take you," Molly said. They went out the east doors and around to the back of the church, where Dad always parked. Only a few spots were available, and usually the family took them.

Ingrid's car was gone already, which meant all of Molly's younger siblings had already left. She clicked the button on her fob to unlock her car, and the vehicle beeped. Molly's neck felt so tense, and after she got behind the wheel, she pushed out her breath and rolled her shoulders.

"Is Hunter coming for lunch?" Mama asked.

"No," Molly said miserably. Too miserably. Her mother's gaze on the side of her face felt too heavy to bear, and Molly quickly started the car and put it in reverse.

"You invited him, though, didn't you?"

"Yes, Mama," Molly said. Her mom didn't ask another question, and that drove Molly crazy. She knew this tactic, because she'd grown up with it. She'd seen her mother fall silent when talking to Ingrid about her prom date, and when asking Lyra if her boyfriend was going to propose soon. Eventually, they all broke and spilled way more than necessary, and definitely more than they would've said if their mother had simply kept questioning them.

Molly wasn't going to give in this time. They only lived eight minutes away from the church, and she flexed her fingers on the steering wheel as she approached the first red light. The blocks passed, and Molly started to congratulate herself on staying silent as she made the final turn onto the street where she'd grown up.

"Molly," her mother said as she pulled into the driveway beside Ingrid's sporty red hatchback. "Did you at least get his number?"

"No, Mama," Molly said, putting her plain white sedan in park. "He doesn't want me anymore." She looked at her mother then, her eyes wide and all of her hurt feelings streaming from her.

"You don't know that." Mama reached over and brushed Molly's hair off her shoulder.

"He didn't ask me out," Molly said. "He didn't even say if he was seeing someone."

"He wasn't wearing a wedding ring," Mama said. "There's still time, Mols."

"No." Molly shook her head. "He won't want me once he finds out I've been married."

"Molly," her mother started, but Molly opened her

door and got out of the car. She didn't want to hear how she was good enough for another man, and that a divorce was not the end of the world.

It felt like the end of the world, like the biggest failure of Molly's life, and she didn't want to hear anything her mom might say.

Thankfully, inside the house, all three of her sisters stood in the kitchen, all of them seemingly trying to talk over each other.

The youngest, Kara, had just graduated from high school. In just a few months, she'd go off to school in the city. Ingrid would return to college for her last year, and Lyra would go back to Utah, where she went to school in Salt Lake City.

Mama and Dad would be empty nesters for the first time, and Molly would keep getting up and going to school every day, teaching the second graders in her class how to read and how to be kind to one another.

She just needed to make it through this summer. Somehow.

Without much to do to fill her time, Molly had been working around the church, helping her father with some of the annual cleaning he did.

She needed more to do. Another job. Something worthwhile where she could donate her time. A hobby. A class to learn something new.

"Molly," Ingrid said, smiling as she caught sight of her. "Get in here and tell Lyra that there is *no way* Harry Styles is as cute as Niall Horan." She grabbed onto Molly's hand, blissfully unaware of Molly's encounter with Hunter, and dragged her into the kitchen.

Molly said, "Okay, I can entertain some arguments on both sides." She put a smile on her face, and it wasn't long before her blues got eradicated by the laughter and loud voices of her sisters. She'd always been able to rely on them to cheer her up and take her side, and Molly loved them powerfully.

At the same time, she couldn't spend the rest of her life with her sisters, and when her father came home and they all sat down to dinner, Molly could see an empty spot at their table specifically for Hunter.

She looked away and closed her eyes for the prayer. Once her father finished that, he looked at Lyra and said, "I hear Rick is coming by tonight."

Molly's hand froze as she reached for her fork. In fact, only her father continued to move at all. All the females in the room had frozen.

"Daddy?" Lyra asked.

Her father put a bite of meatloaf in his mouth, his bright eyes dancing. As he swallowed, a smile lifted the corners of his mouth. "He came to see me after church, Lyra."

"Quinn," Mama said, almost breathless herself. "Did he ask you for your blessing?"

Dad shrugged one shoulder and said, "maybe."

Chaos erupted at the table, with Lyra bursting into tears and Mama praising the Lord that the proposal was finally going to happen. Ingrid talked about how she could record the whole thing, and Kara kept agreeing with everyone else.

Molly was happy for her sister. Of course she was. Her parents and sisters had acted with the same level of excitement when she'd gotten engaged too. She didn't want to ruin anything for Lyra, and no one knew about Hunter's return to Ivory Peaks except her mother.

So she painted a smile on her face, and said, "I'll help you with your hair, Lyra. Doesn't Rick like it when you curl it?"

———

Oh, boy, I'm so excited about this new love story! Hunter and Molly have a ways to go before they can be together, and you'll get to see it all in **HIS FIRST LOVE. You can read it in paperback right now!**

SNEAK PEEK! THE MECHANICS OF MISTLETOE
CHAPTER ONE

B ear Glover stood in the equipment warehouse, his mood growing darker by the moment. Bishop and Ranger both lay on the ground, and Bear could only just see the tips of Bishop's boots. Ranger wasn't underneath the tractor nearly as far, but if it suddenly started, he'd lose plenty of skin.

Bear felt himself transforming into the grizzly some of his friends and family members often told him he could become. He worked against the instinct, but he honestly didn't have time for a downed tractor. They had field prep to do, and it it didn't get done on time, crops didn't get put in on time, and then the ranch was behind for an entire year.

He really didn't want to wear the grizzly skin for a year, though he'd done it in the past. He finally entered the warehouse, trying to tamp down the temper he'd been graced with. As the oldest of the Glover family, he'd been running the ranch since his daddy had fallen ill, almost fourteen years ago.

Truth be told, he'd probably been too young to take over, but sometimes a man had to do what needed to be done, and Daddy couldn't be out in the fields, with the cattle, or on the horses anymore.

Several dogs entered the warehouse with Bear, most of them never getting too far from him. Bishop liked to tease him about that too, claiming Bear even let one canine sleep in the house with him every night. That he'd made a rotating schedule for their cattle dogs.

None of it was true. The last thing Bear wanted was another heat source in the bed with him. He blew a fan all night as it was, even in the winter.

"Ranger," he said, and his cousin pulled himself out from underneath the tractor. "Where we at?" Bear tried to act like he didn't care. No one in the family would buy it, but Bear had managed to keep several cowboy employed for years now by acting like he didn't care. His falsely calm demeanor in the face of trouble had also kept Samantha Branton coming to fix his equipment when it broke down.

Except she couldn't come for another couple of days, which was why Ranger and Bishop had grease all over their hands.

Bear's pulse kicked out an extra beat at the simple thought of Sammy. He'd wanted her to move onto the ranch and work for him full-time, but she wouldn't. She had good reasons, he supposed, but that didn't make Bear any less of a well, bear about having to wait for her services.

Truth be told, he'd harbored a crush on the woman for three solid years now, and he should just ask her out. She seemed settled with her new responsibilities as a single mom, and her shop hummed along without her there twenty-four-seven.

"You're not even listening to me," Ranger said, and Bear blinked out of his own mind. He could sometimes get caught in there, especially once he started thinking about Sammy and all that dark hair she had, with a reddish-purple tint.

"I am," Bear said. "You said you can't get it to start."

"I said," Ranger said with a growl in his voice. "It won't start, and Bishop thinks it needs new fuel pump. So we went to town and got some. He's puttin' it in now, and then we'll see." Ranger wiped his hands on a dirty towel and turned back to the tractor. "Sammy can't come till when?"

"Friday," Bear said, another dose of darkness filling his soul. He should just replace all the equipment when it broke down. He had plenty of money. But that wasn't the Glover way, and Bear had been raised to repair rather than replace.

"Start 'er up," Bishop said, sliding out from under the tractor.

"Moment of truth," Ranger said. He came from Bear's uncle Bull, but he had the same brown hair as all the Glovers did. Before Bear's grandmother had passed away, she'd called it "earthy." The color of good, rich soil that had just been overturned. Bear just used the word "brown."

Ranger climbed up into the cockpit of the tractor and yelled, "Clear."

Bear and Bishop backed up a couple more feet, because who knew what could come spewing out of an engine once it started. The tractor grumbled, then growled, finally roaring to life and chugging along in an irregular pattern.

"That's not right," Bishop said over the noise. He waved both hands over his head to get Ranger to shut the tractor off. "I know we need this fixed," he said to Bear. "Don't worry, Boss. I'll get it." He grinned at Bear and dove under the tractor again.

Oh, to be in his thirties again. Bear wished he had half the energy his brother did, but as the oldest, and comparing himself to the youngest, he didn't.

He also didn't want to stand there, growing ever more impatient while Ranger and Bishop fiddled with settings and trims and all kinds of belts known to mankind. Everyone on the ranch knew the fields had to be ready by next weekend, and they'd get it done. He himself had worked through the night once to make sure the crops got put in on time.

He left the equipment shed in favor of the corral, where his team led over the horses had let all the equines out today as he worked to get the stables cleaned. Bear's family was a traditional ranching family, doing everything from horseback, with dogs and men. None of the fancy ATVs and helicopters some ranches used. He was never as comfortable as he was in the saddle, with a few dogs streaking along beside him as they moved cattle.

Therefore, the horse care at Shiloh Ridge Ranch was

crucial, and Bear kept his finger on the pulse of all of it. He stroked the nose of one horse, stealing some of the calm energy, and saying, "You don't think I'm a grizzly, do ya?"

The horse didn't answer, and Bear wasn't sure he'd have wanted to hear the animal disagree anyway. His phone rang, and Bear didn't even want to look at it. Tuesdays weren't usually this rough.

Evelyn Walker's name sat on the screen, and Bear's mood changed instantly. He connected the call with his rough rancher's fingers, nearly knocking the phone out of his own hand. "Hey," he said easily, actually smiling while he did it.

"Bear," Evelyn said. "Sammy is at Micah's, fixing Simone's kiln."

His heart started dancing in his chest. "How long will she be there?"

"She just arrived," Evelyn said. "It's impossible to know, but Simone said the kiln has been acting up for a few weeks now. Could be a while."

"Thanks, Evelyn." Bear normally didn't waste words, especially when he didn't have much time. A sliver of humiliation went with him as he turned from the horses in the corral and strode toward his truck.

He could get to Seven Sons Ranch, where Micah lived and his wife did her antiques restoration, in fifteen minutes. Fine, the drive was usually twenty, but Bear was unusually motivated today.

He hadn't been able to figure out how to ask Sammy out on a date. He'd been the nicest to her out of anyone who set foot on Shiloh Ridge property, that was for sure. And he wasn't the only one who'd noticed.

His brothers—and he had plenty of them—had been teasing him for months and months, but he didn't see any of them dating anyone.

He drove down the dirt road as fast as he dared. He didn't need anyone asking questions later, and if he didn't kick up too much dust, no one would even know he'd left the ranch.

Several months ago, he'd had the thought that he just needed the right situation to present itself for him to ask Sammy to dinner. Nothing ever had. No amount of prayer had produced a different result than Bear giving her tasks around the ranch, Sammy completing them, and him paying her for a job well done.

He needed a matchmaker. And that was when he remembered a small town scandal from several years ago, when Evelyn had married Rhett Walker to prove her worth as a matchmaker.

It had taken Bear four more months to get up the nerve to call her, and he never would've done that had Micah not encouraged him. He said Rhett and Evelyn were real happy in their marriage, even if it had started out fake.

Micah was a good man, and his wife was Evelyn's sister. So Bear had made the call.

Evelyn had said it would take some serious planning to get Sammy in a situation where Bear would just happen to show up. She'd said they'd have to be patient and wait. She'd never called before.

Bear's mind blanked as he turned onto the asphalt and

started down out of the foothills. Sammy was working on a kiln. He was just stopping by to see Micah's...something.

Bear frowned at himself. This was going to fail spectacularly.

And yet, he kept driving.

He turned onto the main highway and really got his truck going now, arriving at Seven Sons only a few minutes later. Sure enough, Sammy's rickety, old red and brown truck sat in Micah's driveway.

Bear parked right behind it, his heart thumping out a strange rhythm in his chest. He sat in the cab of his truck—much nicer and newer than Sammy's—for a few minutes, trying to convince himself to get out.

He didn't want to be made the fool. At forty-five years old, he didn't need to feel like such a spectacular failure.

Micah came out onto the front porch, and Bear couldn't just leave now. So he got out of his truck too, trying to remember the scenarios Evelyn had created for him.

"Bear," Micah said with a big grin. And why shouldn't he be smiling? He had a beautiful wife now too. A baby boy born last month. In fact, Simone came outside too, that little infant in her arms with a shock of dark hair.

"He wants you," she said, passing the baby to Micah. She gazed at her son for a moment, and Bear thought he was made of all head. Though he supposed all newborns were. "Afternoon, Bear."

"Ma'am." He touched the brim of his cowboy hat. "Micah, I was wondering if you'd show me that wall of bookcases." He met Simone's eye, and she grinned widely at him. Micah simply looked confused.

"In Simone's she-shed?"

"Yeah," Bear said. "I want to get some pictures of them for my brother. He's going to be doing some remodeling, and he's got it in his head that his house needs a library."

"All right," Micah said. Of course the man wouldn't suspect anything about Bear's story was off. He did have a brother that definitely leaned toward the eccentric side. Simone certainly knew though, and Micah had been the one to suggest Evelyn's services in the first place. Maybe he'd just forgotten, because it had been months since Bear had talked to Evelyn, and longer since Micah had mentioned the possibility of having Evelyn create a situation for Bear and Sammy that would get them out of the friend zone.

But Bear followed Micah through his house silently, grateful he'd hired the man to design and build his new homestead too. Yes, it had been outdated. No one could argue with that. No one in the family had protested when Bear had torn down the old homestead and put up another one. He lived there with two of his brothers now, and his place was as amazing as this one.

Micah went out the back door and down the steps to an expansive patio. "It's just over here," he said, as if Bear couldn't see the huge shed to the left. The baby in Micah's arms fussed, and Micah bounced the little boy, shushing him.

"What did you name him again?" Bear asked.

"Travis," Micah said. "We call him Trap, though."

"You'd fit right in my family," Bear said with a chuckle. His real name wasn't Bear, of course, but

Bartholomew, after his father. Bear had never been called anything but Bear, at least in his memory. Once or twice, his momma had called him Teddy, but that went with Bear.

Just like Grizzly does, he thought as Micah stepped to the door. Bear's heart throbbed against the back of his throat, filling his mouth and rendering him mute.

Trap continued to fuss, breaking into a wail that said he wasn't more than a few weeks old, as Micah went into the she-shed. "I don't know why she said he wanted me," Micah said. "He's clearly hungry."

Bear just followed Micah inside, automatically looking around for Sammy. He didn't see her immediately, and then she poked her head up from where she knelt next to the kiln in the far corner.

His heart thrashed now, part of it telling him to do something. Ask her something. The other half warned him against doing anything, saying anything, just in case they got broken again.

"I have to take him inside," Micah said over his baby's wails. "I'll be back in a minute." He looked at Sammy and back to Bear, and Bear saw all the dots connect in Micah's mind. A slow smile crossed the man's face, and Bear almost growled at him to get him to leave.

But he didn't want Sammy to see him act like that, especially toward a friend. And if there was someone outside of Bear's family he considered a friend, it was Micah Walker. All the Walkers really, as he knew Jeremiah quite well from their ranch owners meetings too.

"Take your time," Bear said, and Micah's grin only

grew. He thankfully ducked out of the she-shed a moment later, leaving Bear alone with Sammy.

Finally.

Alone with Sammy, away from his own ranch. Outside of anything that had to do with their professional, working relationship.

In Bear's fantasies, he wanted a completely different kind of relationship with the woman, and he managed to smile at her as she stood up. She wore a dark blue tank top and jeans, both of which had plenty of dirt and grime on them.

Bear absolutely loved that about her. She was strong and sexy and not afraid to get dirty. She shook her hair over her shoulders and smiled back. "Hey, Bear," she said easily, like she didn't think about him in her quiet moments.

Panic reared inside Bear, and he couldn't say anything back.

She looked down at her tools, which she'd spread over a nearby counter, flicking her gaze back to his a moment later. "What are you doing here?"

Ah, it was a great question. And Bear had no idea how to answer it.

SNEAK PEEK! THE MECHANICS OF MISTLETOE CHAPTER TWO

Samantha Benton picked up another wrench, though it was the wrong size. Bear Glover had been touched by God Himself when he was created—at least in Sammy's opinion. He exuded power, and he was easily the most handsome man Sammy had ever laid eyes on. With hair the color of fresh motor oil and those bright, bright blue eyes.

Yes, the Lord had definitely carved Bear out of a special piece of cloth. Very special indeed.

Sammy could feel those eyes on her, though the man said nothing. She put down the wrong wrench and picked up the flat-head screwdriver. She was of the opinion that almost any problem could be fixed with a wrench and a flat-head screwdriver, and while she'd only spent twenty minutes with the kiln, she knew the exhaust fan just needed to be cleaned or replaced.

She'd try to clean it first, and if that didn't work, she'd

order a new fan for the unit. Things with moving parts spoke to her, and Sammy could diagnose almost any machine within the first hour of meeting it.

If only Bear Glover had cogs and wheels and screws inside him. Then maybe she'd be able to figure him out too.

"Sammy," he said, and she nearly fell to her knees when he said her name. Down she went, all the same, and he didn't need to know it was because of the care he put into the two syllables of her name.

"Yeah?" She got right back into the side panel of the kiln. The man had serious pull over her, and everything would be easier if she just focused on her work. That was what had gotten her through going out to Shiloh Ridge for the past three years. That, and the excellent money he paid for the work she did. And yes, he was easy to look at and made her feel like the young woman she'd once been.

The woman she'd been before she'd had to become a mother overnight, grieve the loss of her sister and brother-in-law, and hold the remaining members of her family together.

Sammy's dating life had dried up when she'd gotten custody of Lincoln. It was already on the decline, because she'd opened her mechanic shop six months before the terrible accident that had claimed her sister's life.

She kept telling herself that she'd go on a date when Lincoln started school. Then it was when he could read by himself. Then when he could tie his shoes without help. Then when he knew how to ride a bike.

The truth was, no one was asking, and Sammy didn't

have time to find someone herself. She felt perpetually surrounded by men—at the shop, at the ranch—but none of them interested her half as much as Bear.

She looked up again to find he'd moved closer. He ran his fingertips along some of her tools, and she said, "Did you say something? Sorry, I got lost inside this thing for a second."

He looked at her, those eyes overpowering her in less than a breath. "I was just going to ask you—" He pulled his hand back from her tools. She kept them in a bag she'd bought online that was made for chefs to carry their knives.

And it went with Bear's hand, her tools clattering all over the cement floor in the she-shed. The noise was absolutely astronomical, and she clapped both hands over her ears as the metal bounced on the cement.

"I'm sorry," Bear said while her ears were still ringing. He got down on the ground and started picking up the pliers, the wrenches, the screwdrivers.

"It's fine," Sammy said, finally getting her senses back. She reached for a ratchet at the same time Bear did, and they froze, their hands touching.

"Listen," Bear said, maybe a little roughly. He turned his hand, and slipped his fingers between hers. "Would you go to dinner with me?"

Sammy's world turned white for a moment. "What?" she asked, out of instinct and nothing else. A light giggle followed, one she'd never made before and would likely never make again.

Bear released her hand and stood, seemingly in one

motion. For a big, tall cowboy, he could move really well. He laid her bag out on the countertop and said, "Forget it."

Forget what? her mind asked, and Sammy looked down at her hand. Her skin tingled for some reason, and she could still feel Bear's fingers between hers.

Dinner, her brain whispered. *He asked you to dinner!*

But Bear had already started walking away.

Wait, she called to him in her mind.

He opened the door and walked out, leaving Sammy mute and alone on the floor. Everything that had happened in the last thirty seconds rushed at her, and Sammy groaned as she realized she'd laughed when Bear had asked her out.

Legit *laughed* at him. At the idea of going out with him.

"Why did I do that?" she asked, looking up at the ceiling. "Dear Lord, can't anything go right for me? Would it have been so hard to make me loquacious for that one moment?" She felt like crying, but the door opened again, and Sammy spun onto her hip and hid her face from whoever came into the shop.

"Hey," Simone said. "How's it going? Did Bear get his pictures?"

"Pictures?" Sammy asked, glancing over her shoulder. "I have no idea."

Simone frowned as she bounced her baby in her arms. "What do you think?"

"I think you need a new exhaust fan," Sammy said, deciding on the spot not to try to clean the one inside the kiln. "I'm just getting the serial number and make and model so I can get one ordered for you."

"Oh, that sounds easy," Simone said.

"It should be," Sammy said, standing up. Her tools were an absolute mess, but she needed to get out of this shop and away from this ranch. She folded them up to deal with later and practically ran from the she-shed with, "I'll call you when it comes in, okay?"

"Oh, okay," Simone said behind her, and Sammy knew she'd have to answer the woman's questions later.

Right now, that didn't matter. Right now, she needed to get back to the shop, because Clayton would be there with Lincoln in less than thirty minutes. She didn't like leaving Lincoln alone for any amount of time, though he'd turned eight last fall and could certainly go inside and get a snack by himself.

She lived next door to the bus driver who brought the kids home from the elementary school, and Clayton had agreed to bring Lincoln to her mechanic shop every afternoon after the regular run. The system had been working for three years now, and Sammy always made sure she was in the shop at three-forty-five.

Sure, Lincoln could stay with the other mechanics there, and he'd probably prefer it. But Sammy carried a great burden to care for her nephew according to her sister's wishes, and she was going to do that the best way she knew how.

Sammy practically flew through the garage, only to find Bear's big, black truck parked behind hers, blocking her escape. He sat behind the wheel, looking down at something in his hand. Probably his phone.

He'll move, Sammy told herself as she opened the

passenger door and tossed in her tools. She walked around the back of her truck so he'd see her, but she didn't look directly at him. Looking directly at a man like Bear Glover was like looking into the sun, and she'd already made a big enough fool of herself for one day. For a whole month, in fact.

"Sammy," Bear said, getting out of the truck.

"Hmm?" She didn't turn fully toward him as she put her hand on the door handle of her beat-up pickup. It had been her brother-in-law's, and it was familiar to Lincoln, so Sami kept fixing it when it broke down, and she kept driving it to keep something of Lincoln's father's in their lives.

Bear said nothing, forcing Sammy to look at him. He commanded every room he stepped into, and she wondered what it was like to hold that much power in the palm of one's hand.

"Look," he finally said. "I'm a real idiot, and I've gone about this all wrong." He held up his phone. "I've got a whole script, and I can't say it." He sighed like his ranch had been infested with tens of thousands of grasshoppers, as it had been in the past.

"I like you," he said, sort of yelling the words at her. "I like, you know, *like* you, and I wondered if maybe you'd go to dinner with me, so we can get to know each other on a personal level, not just a ranch level."

Sammy's brain threatened to shut down again, but she steadfastly refused to let it. "I'd have to get a babysitter," she said.

"And...you don't want to?" He looked absolutely

miserable, but he was still standing there. Still looking at her, even as a flush colored his neck and stained his cheeks. Oh, that wasn't fair. Seeing him in a vulnerable state only made him more attractive than he already was.

"I can ask around," she said.

"We'll take Lincoln," Simone called from the porch, and Sammy spun that way. She didn't know they'd had an audience.

"We've got older nieces and nephews," Micah added. "He'll love it out here."

They both beamed like this was the solution to world peace or something equally as great. Sammy looked at Bear; Bear looked back at Sammy.

Together, they burst out laughing, and he took another step closer to her. "Just one dinner," he murmured so Simone and Micah couldn't overhear. "If it doesn't go well, at least it'll be free."

"Why wouldn't it go well?" she asked.

"Well, I mean, I've already thrown your tools all around and stomped out of the room like a grizzly. So dinner can't be as bad as that, right?" He grinned, one side of his mouth pulling up higher than the other. So adorable, and she never thought she'd use that word to describe a man like Bear Glover.

Of course, she'd never seen him smile much around the ranch either.

"All right," she said. "I'll go to dinner with you."

"Yeehaw!" Micah yelled from the porch, and Sammy's face heated with embarrassment too.

She looked at Bear, who had glared Micah into silence.

"And I'm expecting to hear about this script at dinner. Tonight?" She looked back to the porch. "Does tonight work for you guys?"

"Tonight is fine," Simone said, completely unashamed to be standing there, intruding on this private conversation. Or what Sammy wished was a private conversation.

"I'll pick you up at seven," Bear said. "Does that work? We can bring Lincoln out here together, and then go grab something to eat."

"Sounds like a date," Sammy said. She finally opened the door and got in her truck, glad when Bear waved to the porch and did the same. He backed out first, and she expected him to trundle on down the lane. He didn't, but waited for her to leave.

She did, watching in her rear-view mirror as he pulled back into Micah and Simone's driveway and got back out of his truck. She finally had to look away as the road curved toward the highway, but she acknowledged the jittery feeling in her stomach as she came to a stop and looked both ways.

She wasn't sure if it was because of what Micah, Simone, and Bear might be saying about her, or because she'd finally accepted a date and would be leaving Lincoln with someone besides his teacher.

"Or because the best-looking man in the state asked you out," Sammy said as she turned onto the highway and pressed on the gas pedal to get the truck going. It shuddered in protest, its acceleration not very good.

"And you said yes." A smile curved Sammy's mouth, and she enjoyed the excitement until she pulled up to the mechanic shop on the south side of town. Then she realized she'd need to pick out something to wear and put on makeup without her sister's help.

————

That's right! There's more ranch romance and another amazing family — the Glovers of Shiloh Ridge Ranch — to meet in beloved Three Rivers, Texas! Get ready for heartwarming Christmas traditions, true-to-life family drama, Christian cowboy romance, and strong women in unconventional occupations in the Shiloh Ridge Ranch in Three Rivers Romance series.

THE MECHANICS OF MISTLETOE is available now in paperback!

Keep scrolling to view series starters from three of my other series!

CORAL CANYON COWBOYS ROMANCE SERIES

Visit stunning Wyoming for another family of cowboys... The Youngs! The series includes second chance romance, friends to lovers, family saga, Christian values, clean and sweet romance, single dads, equine therapy themes, police dog training, brotherly relationships, return to hometown, fish out of water, and country music stars!

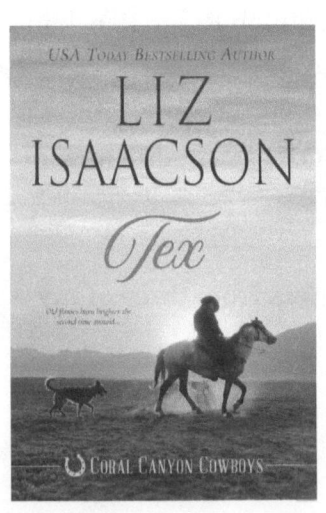

Tex (Book 1): He's back in town after a successful country music career. She owns a bordering farm to the family land he wants to buy...and she outbids him at the auction. **Can Tex and Abigail rekindle their old flame, or will the issue of land ownership come between them?**

GRAPE SEED FALLS ROMANCE SERIES

Journey to the beautiful Texas Hill Country for heartwarming, clean cowboy romance with that hint of faith you'll love. This series includes an Army cowboy, a cowboy billionaire, seasoned romance between older characters, Christmas romance, and three brothers looking for a ranch and a the woman of their dreams!

Choosing the Cowboy (Book 1): With financial trouble and personal issues around every corner, can Maggie Duffin and Chase Carver rely on their faith to find their happily-ever-after?

This is an introductory novelette to the Grape Seed Falls Romance series, with full-length books starting with **CRAVING THE COWBOY**.

A spinoff from the #1 bestselling Three Rivers Ranch Romance novels, also by USA Today bestselling author Liz Isaacson.

SEVEN SONS RANCH IN THREE RIVERS ROMANCE SERIES

Meet the cowboy billionaire brothers at Seven Sons Ranch. The Walkers are new in Three Rivers, and they've got the women circling. Every contemporary romance in this series features a fake marriage that turns to more, family holiday traditions, and the family saga that will create a space for you in the Walker family too!

Rhett's Make-Believe Marriage (Book 1): To save her business, she'll have to risk her heart. She needs a husband to be credible as a matchmaker. He wants to help a neighbor. **Will their fake marriage take them out of the friend zone?**

ABOUT LIZ

Liz Isaacson writes inspirational romance, usually set in Texas, or Wyoming, or anywhere else horses and cowboys exist. She lives in Utah, where she writes full-time, takes her two dogs to the park everyday, and eats a lot of veggies while writing. Find her on her website, along with all of her pen names, at <u>feelgoodfictionbooks.com</u>